DARWIN'S

SWORD

By D.L. Whitehead

PUBLISHER   PRINTER   BOOKSELLER
Reno, NV
www.lrpnv.com

A LeRue Press (LRP) Book/January, 2014

www.lrpnv.com

First Edition

Cover Art: Travis Szudajski

Library of Congress Cataloging-in-Publication Data
Whitehead, D.L.
Darwin's Sword/D.L. Whitehead

p. cm

ISBN   978-1-938814-02-0

I. Title

2013954056
CIP

First Edition, January, 2014
10 9 8 7 6 5 4 3 2 1

Printed on acid-free, FSC paper, responsibly sourced

DEDICATION

For Aubrey Whitehead,
Patsy Whitehead
and most of all, Beth.

Hopefully, the first of many!

D.L. Whitehead

PROLOGUE

February 1995
Bellevue, Washington

R ain glistened on the wet roadways, dripped from Douglas firs, rolled off shingled roofs, into gutters, through drainpipes and into saturated soil that could hardly contain more water. Drainage ditches filled to capacity, overflowed into the streets creating rivers of floating debris that clogged storm drains and turned intersections into vast lakes.

Seven straight days of hard rains created more than a few problems in the ranchlands in western Washington. Rivers, normally high during early spring from snowmelt as warmer air masses settled over the area, now flowed freely over their banks, flooding small farms and ranches and, in a few cases, drowning stranded livestock. Several deaths from drowning were blamed on the continuing lines of storms coming in off the Pacific Ocean.

Dr. Jonathan Masters, noted geneticist and physician, drove through this deluge as if it weren't there, on his way to his office building in Bellevue, a suburb just two floating bridges across Lake Washington from Seattle. Masters drove the BMW on autopilot, deeply steeped in thought about his new project.

Genetisource had been the love of Master's life since he started the company ten years ago. Although much of the research the company initiated was widely reported and lauded in their own industry, they were virtually unknown to the general public. Masters knew that this new project would soon change that.

He would never have admitted this to anyone, but Genetisource was his only true love. Never married, he saw no point to having a family. A family for him would merely be window dressing. Good for parties and for his own fascinations, but not really a part of his life. Working long hours in his lab, he rarely went home.

Genetisource sat on a prime piece of real estate in the small neighborhood called Eastgate in south Bellevue. Masters had designed the building with the assistance of a local architect whom he had chosen because his designs looked more like artwork than buildings. Pentagonal shaped, with blue and gold glass covering most of the exterior except for the first floor, which had a stone facade broken only by one entrance on the south side of the building. An underground parking garage could be entered at the rear of the building. The blue and gold glass often reflected sunlight that could blind drivers on a sunny day.

Using a remote control built into the BMW's dashboard, he opened the rolling gate covering the entry to the parking garage, and drove the car inside. Parking in his assigned space, he turned the ignition off and closed his eyes. Sighing deeply, he leaned his head against the headrest and closed his eyes. His head was killing him, but he was ready to move forward. If he needed a break later, he could lock himself in his office. But he was impatient to get started on his new project and the other researchers he employed would be looking to him for guidance. He must be ready to push them beyond their own self-imposed limitations.

Several months ago, Masters was contacted by DARPA, a research think tank that developed new technologies for the United States government. The development group was responsible for the Internet and other top-secret research projects. DARPA requested his opinion on the possibility of creating human tissue that would regenerate when damaged. Masters initially thought the committee had lost their collective minds, but after contemplating the issue for several weeks, Masters drew up a research proposal and submitted it along with a request for substantial funding. Yesterday, his request was approved and the funding made available to begin the project.

DARPA contracted him to perform experiments in the past. His lab had produced several-drought resistant strains of corn and other grains and vegetables, then a cloned calf that produced twice the lean beef of an ordinary bovine. Now, he was shooting for the apex of his research life. He would clone a human being outside the womb. With the government funding he had just secured, Genetisource would be in the forefront of the cloning race.

Of course, his benefactors supplied the billions of dollars for his research, with no hope for success. They assumed he would spend the money then come up with no real way of accomplishing the task without a surrogate. They assumed he would make every effort, but come up short of their ultimate goal. They failed to understand that he only knew success. Failure, for him, was not only *not* an option, but not even in his vocabulary. Determination and a lot of ego had driven him this far in his life and now it would propel him even further. He didn't believe in failure, only minor setbacks.

Leaving his car, he took the elevator to the fifth floor of the building where his office sat behind large glass doors. The opulence with which he decorated his building served his ego as much as the research that placed his company at the top of its field. His secretary had the latest in modern furniture and his office was decorated in the best in early American hardwood furniture. His desk alone weighed hundreds of pounds, adorned with hand-carved features only the finest craftsmen could build. Masters felt he deserved it.

Placing his briefcase on his desk, he grabbed his lab coat and took the elevator down one floor to the laboratory complex. Before leaving the offices last night, Masters had given instructions to two of his researchers, Mario Alonga and Jack Monroe, on how he wanted the lab arranged for the new project. They were hard at it when Masters entered the lab. Monroe was one of the world's leading immunologists and Alonga played an important role in previous cloning procedures for other firms. Masters hired him away with the offer of fame and fortune and Alonga had proven invaluable in his research. Of course, the only person within Masters' organization who would benefit publicly from their research was Masters himself. Alonga would forever be in his shadow and that was just the way Masters wanted it.

Genetic research was a very competitive field with no room for morality issues. Masters chose his people with special regard for their moral ambiguities. He didn't have time to argue the merits of what they were about to embark upon. He just wanted them to do what they were told without regard to how it might affect the universe. He would let no one stand in the way of their goal. Create human life from pure DNA and proteins.

Alonga was moving a heavy piece of equipment when Masters came striding through the doors. Placing the analyzer on the table with a thump, Alonga faced Masters.

"Good morning, Doctor Masters," Alonga huffed, breathing hard. "We're just finishing up here."

"Good, good. Please assemble everyone in the conference room," Masters said absently, walking through the lab surveying their progress. He stopped at a machine used for gene sequencing, inspected the surface and made a clucking sound with his tongue. "Please clean this mess up when we finish our meeting."

Alonga glared at his back, but Masters failed to notice. He just continued out the opposite doors toward the conference room.

Alonga and Monroe looked at each other and rolled their eyes, then placed their dirty coats in the laundry bin for pickup later. Washing their hands, they each grabbed a clean lab coat and walked towards the conference room. As they entered the hallway outside the lab, Mario bumped into Marie, who was coming from another part of the complex.

Marie was a genetic engineer from Barcelona and from the moment Mario first saw her, he was smitten. With an IQ of one-hundred-eighty and a body that belonged to a runway model, Marie was the epitome of an egghead's dream. Smiling, she balanced herself easily then proceeded past Alonga and Monroe.

Once they were all seated around the large table in the conference room, Masters stood up and walked to a dry-erase board at the far end. Picking up a marker, he pulled the cap off and spoke with his back turned to the group, writing notes on the board.

"Today, we begin a new chapter in Genetisource's history. A chapter that will cement us all at the top of our fields and make Genetisource a household name. This project will place everyone in this room in the history books."

Masters turned toward them clearing their view of the board behind him. They could see the sentence and the attribution included with it. Alonga rolled his eyes at Monroe, who smiled, shaking his head. They were all thinking the same thing. This guy is nuts.

PROJECT: DARWIN
*"One is only the best when he is remembered forever.
Immortality is what we must strive for and achieve."*

"Now let's begin," Masters said, smiling at his protégés. He turned and began writing assignments on the board as everyone took notes behind him.

§

PART ONE

Some Things Should Be Left Alone

☉NE

February 2009

"**W**hat the hell was that?" Jake whispered as he made his way through the bow of the ship. There were two men following him into the lower areas of the front of the supposed cargo vessel. SEAL Team Ten, assigned to the USS Anchorage patrolled the Mediterranean Sea in international waters off the Libyan coast when they received a distress call from a vessel five nautical miles to their east. Jake received orders to intercept the boat and find out what was happening.

Jake and his team found the boat stopped dead in the water, directly in the Anchorage's path of travel. The vessel was a small ship, hardly more than a boat, but it sat low in the water, indicating it was heavily weighted with cargo. The ship was totally dark as they approached. The lack of running lights gave the vessel a deserted feel that made Jake's hair stand on end. This was the worst kind of mission because there was no way to gain intelligence without boarding the boat, leaving a greater danger of getting attacked.

Boarding the boat, they secured the main deck and checked the bridge for a pilot, but found no one. The main deck was deserted as well, so he alerted his commander aboard the Anchorage that he was splitting his team for a bow-to-stern search. Splitting his team up seemed like a bad idea under the circumstances.

His second-in-command, Ensign James Trower, led the aft team while Jake took the remaining SEALs into the bow with the thought that should one of the teams get attacked, the other could provide support from the other end of the boat.

Descending into the first level below decks, Jake thought he heard a furtive movement near the backside of the metal stairs. He could see the areas lit like daylight in green glow within his night vision goggles, but nothing moved. His internal protection voice was screaming something was wrong, but he continued on. Once his team secured the hallway, he asked Trower for their SIT-REP, or situation report, and was told the aft was secure and they were working their way amidships.

After a quick sweep of the area where he heard the noise, Jake began to think he was hearing echoes from within the bowels of the ship. Noises could carry strangely on ships when hatches were left open. The noise could have come from anywhere, which didn't ease his concern that they weren't alone.

After completing their search of the forward hold and finding no one inside, they met in the center aisle between the crates. A quick inspection of the crates gave them no further clues about what they contained. They were unmarked and couldn't be searched until the ship was secured. Looking down the aisle at the hatches at both ends, Jake once again got a bad feeling. On instinct he went to the hatch at the aft end of the hold, shut it and secured it with a crowbar he found leaning against the wall nearby. Locking the hatch meant cutting off their only means of escape, should they come under fire, but they were no longer vulnerable to an attack from behind.

Moving towards the forecastle, he wondered what new, fresh hell awaited them beyond the hatch at that end of the hold. He had noted the fact that the hatch was the only secured door at that end of the boat, when they first descended into the hold. Closed hatches were bothersome when they were at your back, but having to open one was even more dangerous.

Moving toward the hatch, he thought he heard a clunking sound coming from beyond the hatch in front of them, like someone tapping on metal. Turning to the two men behind him, one of them pointed at his ear, then at the hatch and Jake nodded.

The noise could have been a creak of the ship, but he didn't think so. Surrounding the hatch, Jake motioned for Chief Roberts, the man to his left, to open the hatch. Jake and the other two men with them covered the door as Roberts let his MP-5 assault rifle drop on its sling and turned the wheel, unlocking the forward hatch.

Backing slowly away from the hatch as he swung it open, Jake saw movement and heard the metallic rattle of something hitting the metal deck. Jake saw the grenade hit the deck in slow motion in front of him. Leaping to the side, he knocked the two men nearest him halfway behind a crate as the explosion ripped through the hold, splintering several crates and twisting the hatch door.

Jake felt himself thrown into the air by the force of the explosion, landing on top of one of the men he had collided with earlier. Jake felt something heavy and very hot slam into his back and his legs went numb. Hearing movement, he rolled over in time to see several armed men coming toward him through the blasted hatch. Rolling on to his back, he depressed the trigger on his MP-5, spraying the open hatchway with bullets. He could only grip the weapon in one hand because his other hand was incapable of movement. His chances of hitting any shooters seemed pretty bad, but his bullets ripped through the first four men advancing through the hatchway, blasting them backward. Through the loud humming in his ears, he heard another assault rifle firing.

Rolling to his left, Jake stopped firing. He tried in vain to drag himself into a sitting position then began to feel sick, as darkness clouded his vision. He could hear sporadic gunfire and someone screaming, but couldn't make out who it was. Sinking through the darkness, the ringing in his head intensified.

Opening his eyes, Jake found himself lying in a dark room. The only light came from the red numerals of a digital alarm clock, flashing 2:12. Jake realized that the ringing he heard was not from the battle that occurred in his dreams, but the insistent ringing of his cellular phone on his nightstand. Within seconds he realized the year was 2009, not 2002 and he wasn't in the Middle East, but in his own house in Renton, Washington, U.S.A. Shaking his head to clear the cobwebs, he sat up and grabbed the phone, hitting the send button just before it went to voicemail.

"Boss, this is Cedric. Sorry to wake you, but we have a problem at Genetisource. We saw some movement in the garage about half an hour ago and I sent Don Allen and Jim Washburn to check it out. They found a body in one of the dumpsters."

Jake swung his feet to the floor, elbows resting on his knees. "Terrific. Any idea who it is?"

"It's quite a mess, boss. Lots of blood, but we haven't taken a close look yet. If you like, I can go down and have a look while I have you on the phone."

"No. Leave everything as it is," Jake said shaking his head. Glancing at the clock he saw that he had only been in bed for three hours. He attended a charity event the night before. "Have you notified local law enforcement?"

"No. I called in an extra team to secure the building then called you."

Cedric was one of the best SEAL team soldiers that Jake knew. His battle hardened instincts were comparable if not superior to his own. Nothing fazed the big man, but in these early morning hours he sounded rattled.

"Don't call in the LEOs. Secure the area and I'll be right there," Jake said, a headache already beginning to form in his left temple. "After we figure out what we have, I'll call in the NSA. They have jurisdiction over this project and Genetisource. They'll debrief everyone in the building then clean up the mess."

"Do you think it's wise to leave the locals out?"

"We have no choice. This is about national security, at least that's how DARPA and the NSA see it. We have to dance to their tune. Just secure everything so we can find a way out in case they try to make us the scapegoats."

"Already done, Boss. Sorry for waking you."

Punching the end button with his finger, Jake sighed heavily. Getting to his feet, he went to the bathroom, turned on the faucet and stuck his head under the frigid water to bring himself fully awake. Taking the bottle of mouthwash from under the sink, he swished some in his mouth, spat it out and ran a comb though his short brown hair. Dressing quickly, he inspected his appearance in the mirror, judging he looked as neat as possible considering the circumstances. Retrieving his Glock .40-caliber handgun from his nightstand and clipping the holster to his belt, he left the house for the damper confines of his garage.

Jake owned two cars. In one section of his three-car garage, a Mercedes E-430 sat silently. In the center a 1968 Ford Mustang Mach I was parked. The third bay contained a workout bench with free weights sitting on the floor, which he tiled with black and white checkerboard vinyl. He restored the Mach 1 after the event on the ship sidelined him. He found it parked outside a junkyard in Norfolk, Virginia. Opening the center door and taking the keys from a pegboard just inside the door from the house, the Mustang's engine growled low when he turned the key.

Entering the 405 from Renton Highlands, he could see the lights of Boeing Field past the southbound lanes. Rain fell lightly, coating his windshield in a dirty spray out of the cold darkness. Jake thought back to the dream that plagued his sleep. He relived that nightmare, usually during times of stress. They killed every terrorist on the hijacked ship, but four of his team members died, two in the hold where he had been injured, the others from the aft team. There were ambush teams waiting for them in several areas of the small freighter. Trower was one of the dead. Jake felt he had failed as their commander that day. They took him from the hold on a stretcher and flew him to Germany, then back to the United States after he was stabilized.

Six surgeries and two months in the hospital, then six more in therapy, he'd finally recovered from three fractured vertebrae in his spinal column and a severe contusion to the precious cord contained within. After the surgeries and a week for the swelling to subside, he regained some of the feeling in his legs and, after ten days, he began to feel everything. His entire body hurt for months from the injuries he had sustained when the chunk of hatch smashed him in the back. Surgeons removed several pieces of shrapnel from the grenade and shattered hatch from his back and legs. His doctors told him he was lucky he wasn't paraplegic. Eight months after the incident, recovering in Norfolk with his fiancée, Lisa, he returned to active duty. His attempt at returning to full duty as a SEAL was denied, so he resigned his commission and was recruited to join the Central Intelligence Agency.

Long after he began his new life, the dreams remained a constant bother, but eventually were relegated to resurfacing during periods of intense emotional stress. Lisa eventually left him, claiming he was unable to commit to her. His work with the CIA had been unfulfilling. The hours were long and often grinding so, after four years, he pulled the plug and entered private service.

Just before retiring from the Agency, he was assigned to protect a defecting Russian Foreign Services agent, a CIA asset who had been compromised by an Agency internal investigation. She was to testify at a hearing in Congress about intelligence activities by both the Russians and Americans in her country. After receiving intelligence stating that the location of their safe house was compromised, his team moved her to a hotel outside Vienna, Virginia. During the night, they were attacked and while the assassins were killed, the woman had been shot, dying as Jake tried to save her life.

Getting off the freeway, Jake came out of his thoughts of his past and back to the subject at hand. Who would dump a body in the dumpsters at Genetisource? Who was the unfortunate person who got dumped?

Rain pelted the windshield in a continuous flow as he parked in front of the building. Cedric met him as he reached the front door escorting him out of the rain. Cedric was a huge black man with a bald head and thick black mustache and goatee. His shoulders were so wide that he sometimes had to turn sideways to get through doorways.

Shaking the rain off his jacket, Jake looked over the group of people standing in the lobby. He recognized only a few of the researchers, but one man stepped to the front of the group. Jake knew Jonathan Masters by sight.

"Mr. Storm, I must speak with you immediately," Masters said as he stepped toward Jake. Masters seemed uncharacteristically out of sorts. His salt and pepper colored hair was sticking out at odd angles and his eyes darted about as if he expected a monster to jump out at him and gobble him up. Master's voice reminded Jake of Vincent Price.

Jake put his hand in the air to signal the scientist that now was not the time and turned away. Masters had been rattling off something about the image of Genetisource when Jake interrupted him. The doctor stalked away like a semi-truck lumbering up a steep grade. Masters was an odd man, but this behavior seemed strange at best. He didn't seem concerned about the corpse down in the garage.

"The building is sealed up tight, Boss," Cedric said.

"Nobody comes in or out until I call the NSA. I want to speak to Washburn and Allen then we'll take a look around before calling in the team. Get Mike downstairs to take photographs of everything."

"Yes, Sir." Cedric radioed Mike in the control room and told him to meet them in the garage, then led Jake down the hallway to a bank of elevators. When the doors closed, Jake turned to Cedric as the elevator began its decent into the parking garage.

"You guys didn't see anyone on the monitors?" Jake kept his voice lowered because he knew there were microphones in the elevators as well as cameras.

"Nobody, just shadows, but it's kind of dark in that area of the garage. I usually keep a close watch on that part of the building. I can tell you one thing for sure. She wasn't brought in from the outside."

"Have you seen the body?"

"Not yet. Washburn and Allen are guarding the area, along with several more guarding the exterior entrances to the garage."

"Outstanding," Jake said sarcastically. Cedric hadn't made any mistakes. Jake was just feeling pissy. "At least you were here when this happened and not one of our newer agents. They might miss things you wouldn't."

When the elevator stopped, a bell rang once and a voice told them they had arrived at the garage level. When the doors opened, they stepped out and Jake noted that the large steel grates had been lowered on all of the entrances to the garage. A cool breeze swept through the cavernous structure, making the chill in the air even more penetrating. Fifty feet from where they stood Washburn and Allen stood on either side of a large steel garbage container. Jake and Cedric walked toward them.

Clearing his mind, Jake observed the scene, locking as much detail into his mind as he could. He noted that the lighting in the area surrounding the dumpster and for twenty feet in either direction was dimmer than the rest of the garage. About ten feet from the dumpster he saw several pieces of glass littering the concrete floor and looked up to see that the fluorescent light fixture had been shattered. Someone wanted to conceal themselves from the cameras, so they had bashed the only light source in the area.

Stepping carefully around the broken glass, not wanting any stuck to the bottom of his shoes, Jake looked around the area and saw a stack of red cones that were used by the crew who was resurfacing the parking lot asphalt. Taking three of the plastic cones, he placed them around the shards of broken glass. This would note the location of the glass for Mike and the investigators who would soon descend on Genetisource.

"Now we know why you didn't see anything," Jake said, pointing to the glass. Cedric grunted and shook his head. Cedric led Jake to the dumpster and spoke to the two men guarding the container.

"Gentlemen, tell me everything," Jake said.

Washburn and Allen recounted the tale with little interruption from Jake. When they finished, Jake put on a pair of latex gloves Cedric handed to him and opened the heavy iron lid covering the trash bin.

Jake saw the body immediately, in spite of the fact that someone had gone to great pains to conceal it within heaps of trash. Someone had beaten this person so badly that several compound fractures and dislocated joints were visible. Pulling a few scraps of debris away from the face, being careful not to move anything that might prove essential to identifying the killer, Jake identified the woman immediately, in spite of the swelling that distorted her facial features. Dr. Wilma Braeden would no longer need her assigned parking spot in the garage. Jake saw she wasn't dressed in a coat, which meant she was probably killed inside the building and not in the garage.

"Was the lid open or closed when you found it?"

"It was closed. Why?" Washburn asked.

Jake didn't answer, but grabbed the lid and closed it. "You guys go upstairs and wait for me in the security offices. You'll be relieved of duty until you're debriefed." Washburn and Allen headed for the elevators and Jake looked at Cedric gravely.

"This is a fucking mess, Cedric. The NSA will crucify us if we were negligent in any way. We have to make sure that we find out how this happened. The NSA will have orders to make this go away. The investigation team will arrive and cleaners will come in right behind them and make all evidence disappear. Anyone who gets in their way will be dealt with."

Cedric nodded and continued to stare at the dumpster.

"What do we do?"

"Keep our heads down and hope that they find nothing wrong with how we handled the situation," Jake said, glancing up from the floor where he had held his eyes. "We also need to find out how this woman died and who did it. If for no other reason than to give her justice."

Leaving the dumpster, they walked up toward the elevators, passing Mike Harper who hurried toward them with a digital camera held in his hands. Mike had also been a member of Jake's SEAL team and one of the survivors from the night on the boat.

"Mike, I want pictures of all of the cars parked in here, including the license plates. Also, photograph the glass on the floor by the red cones and the light fixture above. Then photograph the body as well as you can without disturbing anything, then leave everything as you found it."

Mike nodded and went about shooting pictures, the flash firing again and again, reviving Jake's headache.

"Cedric, when he downloads the photos, run the license numbers through our database to make sure they all belong here."

"Right away, Boss." Cedric turned and ran back to where Mike stood, photographing the two vehicles nearest the elevators. Cedric said something to Mike. The other man nodded then Cedric held up his thumb in Jake's direction.

Jake pressed the call button that brought the elevator to the garage level. When it arrived he stepped inside and pressed the button for the first floor. Arriving on the first floor, he walked directly to the security room, where he spent ten minutes grilling Washburn and Allen for more information. When he finished, he told the agents to step outside and picked up the secure phone, dialed the NSA field office in D.C. and after a few seconds, a voice responded. He relayed the situation to the duty officer on the other end.

"I will dispatch a team right now. Expect them within the hour. Shut everything down and don't let anyone leave the building until they have been debriefed," the voice said then hung up. Jake replaced the receiver and called the agents back inside. Jake headed for the lobby.

As he entered the lobby, he sighed deeply, preparing himself to deal with the unhappy employees standing before him.

§

TWO

As first light encroached on the rain soaked darkness, Jake stood just inside the main doors of Genetisource, awaiting the investigative team's descent on the building. Standard procedure called for an investigation and debriefing of everyone in the building at the time of the murder. After calling the NSA, he herded all of the employees into the commissary to await their chance at being questioned. He wanted the lobby cleared when the investigation team arrived.

While he waited, Jake mulled over their situation. At the very least, they would have to accept some of the blame for what had happened because it occurred on their watch. They were the security experts and they had failed. What troubled him was that whoever dumped the body was probably the same person who had beaten her to death, knew enough about their security to know where cameras were located and which light would expose the killer to detection. None of the other florescent lights were broken, just the one illuminating the trash container and its immediate surroundings.

Jake was hesitant to tell the NSA that the murderer was possibly an employee of Genetisource and maybe still within the confines of the building without more proof than his gut feeling. The evidence certainly pointed towards an employee being the killer. There was no evidence that anyone had left the building after the murder. He was confident enough in his security team and the way they ran the program at Genetisource that he was certain whoever killed Braeden was still in the building. He was also certain that Braeden's death would get covered up because of the sensitive nature of the research Genetisource performed. Under the guise of National Security, they would happily scrub away any record of her death. Conducting his own investigation was dangerous, especially since technically it was treasonous, but what could he do? He felt a duty to Wilma Braeden as well as his own people to find out what happened.

Through the windows in the lobby, Jake saw four dark colored vans enter the parking lot. Just fifty-five minutes after his phone call, the NSA team had arrived to investigate. Fifty-five minutes was great time even for them. Jake walked out and led the vans around the building to the rear entrance to the parking garage. When they arrived, Jake signaled to the guards, who pressed the button and the gates rolled up to allow the vans entry. When they were parked just inside the garage, several men exited the vans, unloading equipment from the double rear doors. One of the men, a tall, broad man who limped slightly, was obviously in charge. Jake recognized him the instant he saw his face.

Victor Roberts had been with the NSA since his discharge from the Army in 1978. Jake had known him during his days with the Agency and knew he was thorough. Vic was also a specialist at cleaning up the worst messes. They obviously wanted the situation kept as quiet as possible. Jake waited through several orders barked at the men unloading the equipment then Roberts turned toward him.

"What're you doing here?" Roberts asked, noticing Jake standing behind the van for the first time.

"My company has the contract for security for Genetisource. How are you, Vic?"

"You're doing a bang up job from the looks of things," Roberts said, ignoring the friendly greeting. "How the hell did this happen, Storm?"

Roberts, in Jake's opinion, could make John Wayne's portrayal of Rooster Cogburn look like a kindergarten schoolteacher. His team would consist of forensics specialists, cleaners specializing in the analysis and destruction of evidence, and agents who would debrief all of the employees at Genetisource, including his own.

"I wish we knew. The body was found on a routine check."

"Has anyone been told what's going on?" Roberts asked.

"Masters knows, but we haven't told anyone else."

"We'll handle it. Keep your people out of it. It's better for your health. By the way, how long do you think she was there?"

"From what I could see, not long. But I didn't look that close. I didn't want to contaminate the scene."

"It's a trash dumpster," Roberts said, smiling grimly. "Can't get much more contaminated than that."

Robert's technicians descended upon the scene like flies. Jake watched as they went to the dumpster and opened the lid. Roberts barely glanced inside, then a technician with a camera began photographing the body. When he finished, two techs climbed inside and lifted the body out, handing it to two techs waiting on the outside. Slipping the corpse into a vinyl bag, they lifted it on to a gurney and loaded it into a waiting van. Jake watched the scene unfold as the meticulous crew went about taking samples of material from everything in and around the dumpster.

Two of the technicians gathered the trash out of the dumpster and placed it into plastic bags, as the van containing Braeden's body pulled out into the early morning rain.

Leaving the team to do its job of expunging evidence, Jake took the elevator back to the main floor. He had no reason to watch over the cleaning crew, since he could do nothing to stop them.

Jake went to the security control room. Using his badge to enter, he found Cedric and Mike watching the scene in the garage. He motioned to Cedric to step outside with him.

"I need to speak to Masters before those guys get hold of him. Have someone keep watch over our friends in the garage. Let me know when they're coming."

"What about our people?"

"No one leaves until they have been debriefed. It may be mid-morning before anyone is allowed in or out of the building. If anyone asks," Jake said, nodding grimly at Cedric.

Cedric rolled his eyes and returned to the control room, retrieved his radio then accompanied Jake to the main hallway. Jake asked if Mike had downloaded the photos of the garage and Cedric nodded.

"I ran the license plates through our database and they all belong here. They were all here when the body was found and still are. No one's left during the four hours since we discovered the doc's body."

"Excellent."

Cedric turned left toward the lobby and Jake went right. The employees either returned to their offices or were waiting in the cafeteria. Jake entered the cafeteria to see Masters pacing one end of the room with his cellular phone to his ear. He was still quite agitated. Several of the other researchers were drinking coffee and looking exhausted. Jake cleared his throat and everyone turned his way.

"I know this has been a long evening and you're tired. Agents will debrief you shortly. They'll probably tell you what happened. Now, I know you have a lot questions, but that's all I can tell you for now."

Several groans issued from the crowd and Jake let them return to their breakfasts. Making his way past the tables, dodging questions, he walked toward the rear of the room where Masters ended his phone call.

"Mr. Storm, I am appalled at your security. What the hell happened?"

"I wish I knew. So far we don't have a lot of information. The NSA will be investigating everyone who was in the building last night, so be prepared for a long day."

"I haven't the time for all of this. Why are they involved?" Masters looked nervous, which caused Jake's suspicion of the doctor to rise.

"Because one of your researchers was killed inside this building last night, Dr. Masters. They financed your project and that puts them in charge. This is the way it works when you work for the government."

"I do not work for the government, Mr. Storm. I work for myself."

Jake glanced at Masters then shrugged his shoulders. "At any rate, everyone who was present last night will be debriefed before they are allowed to leave. That includes you." Jake pulled the doctor away from the rest of the room.

"Do you have any idea what happened to her, Doctor Masters?" Jake asked, quietly, so that no one sitting nearby could hear them.

Masters looked sick for a moment, then he shot Jake a smoldering look and shook his head.

"Are you insinuating that I had something to do with Dr. Braeden's demise?"

"I don't insinuate," Jake said, "I'm just asking the same questions they'll ask. If I were you, I would try not to look so suspicious. Now, do you know what happened to Braeden?"

"No," Masters said in a flat monotone. The doctor's eyes told Jake he was lying, but he had no way to prove it.

Jake waited to see if any questions arose from Masters, and when none were voiced, he turned and walked away. Passing a table where several scientists he recognized as lab staff sat, he noticed two of them fidgeting. Jake glanced at Alonga as he passed and noticed a stain on his pants. *Curious*, he thought.

Cedric caught up to him as he left the cafeteria. "The team is grilling our guys pretty hard, Jake." His concern for the men under his command was a trait that Jake had always admired in Cedric.

"One of us should be present during the questioning of our employees, Cedric. Go make certain that they don't accuse anyone on our staff of having anything to do with this. Unfortu-

nately, there is very little we can do about the way they question."
Jake leaned against the wall and sighed heavily. "I could sure use a
cup of coffee. Hell, I could use a cot and a rolled up jacket."

"Don't have a cot, but I got a small patch of cement you
can use. Don't have a jacket, guess you'll have to use Mike's gym
bag." Mike Harper was legendary for taking runs during his lunch
break, then leaving the gym bag under the counter in the security
operations room for several days. The smell could sometimes
cause a rat to puke. Jake admonished him for leaving the bag behind, but it was a habit he couldn't break.

"I think I'll pass. But maybe I could get a cup of your
special coffee?"

"That can be arranged," Cedric winked and led the way
to the operations room, where two more of his team watched the
monitors and the investigative team downstairs.

Because of the risk of espionage by foreign countries,
installations such as Genetisource required extraordinary security
measures. The security operations room was built in accordance
with all federal standards, plus a few additions that Jake added
when his firm was awarded the contract. The elevators would not
stop on the lab floor without two codes, a retina scan and a fin-
gerprint scan. The only person that could get to any level was
Masters himself. The only area Masters could not access was the
security room, which was not just Jake's idea. DARPA built that
in long before his security company won the contract.

Cedric sat on the edge of the small table at the back of
the room near the coffeepot and poured them both a mug of his
"special" coffee. He introduced Jake to the noxious drink during
their first tour in the SEAL teams. The stuff was nearly thick
enough to paint a fence with, but in times of crisis one cup would
keep you alert for hours. Jake took the cup when Cedric offered
it to him, and sipped at the lukewarm liquid. In spite of the cool-
ness of the drink, it burned Jake's parched throat as it passed.

One of the members of the NSA interrogation team entered the room behind them before the door could close. He was

making notes on a clipboard and noting camera positions. He looked over at the pot holding the "special" coffee and, without asking permission, poured some into a Styrofoam cup. He took a sip of the drink and grimaced.

"That stuff is awful. I don't know how you guys can keep it down."

Cedric smiled at Jake, "You just aren't used to real coffee. Bunch of wussies. My baby sister could take you," Cedric laughed and the man with the clipboard gave him the finger.

Indicating the monitors, the man pointed at them. "You were watching the monitors last night?"

"No," Jake said, taking another sip of the coffee. In an hour he would need antacid, but for now it was keeping him upright. "Cedric heads up the graveyard team. They were on duty."

"And you saw nothing?" The man turned to Cedric who had taken a position leaning against the doorjamb.

"No. I noticed the area was very dimly lit, but I never suspected someone had knocked out the lights. Just before midnight I sent two of my team downstairs to do a perimeter walk, which we do every two hours. One of our guys had a cup of coffee that he took with him and opened the dumpster to throw the empty cup away. That was when they found the body."

"Did they notice the broken lighting when they did the perimeter check at 10:00 p.m.?"

"No, and something like that *would* have been noted. It would have been addressed immediately."

After scribbling more notes on the clipboard, he asked a few more questions, which Cedric answered truthfully. When he finished, he placed the clipboard on the counter and asked for the security videos from the previous night. Cedric pulled out four compact disks from a rack near the rear of the room and handed them over to the agent.

"Thanks. I appreciate your help."

"Can we go now?" Cedric asked. "I've been here since eight last night and I'm bushed."

"Sure," the agent said. "If we need to talk to you more, we'll be in touch."

When the man left, Cedric pulled four more disks out of the rack and handed them to Jake. "These are the originals of the disks I just gave him. Mike figured we might need them. What do you want to do with them?"

Jake thought for a minute, then took the discs and placed them in his jacket pocket. "I'll keep them safe, for now. We'll take a look at them later."

Jake finished the coffee and tossed the cup into the trashcan near the door.

"Go home and get some rest. We'll meet later at the office to discuss what happened."

Another team of investigators arrived to interview the scientists and support personnel. Most of the people in the cafeteria were napping or watching television, but Masters still paced the back of room. Jake led the men, who identified themselves as Defense Security Agency personnel, into the cafeteria. The last man through the door politely told Jake that they would handle it from there and shut the door, leaving Jake standing in the hallway.

Jake knew that Masters would blame his team and ultimately Jake for the death of Wilma Braeden. Leaving Genetisource, he pulled the Mustang out of the parking area and gunned the engine as he rolled towards Eastgate way.

"Something here isn't right, Dr. Braeden, and I intend to find out what it is." Turning the Mustang toward Eastgate Way he made his way to the Interstate entrance ramp.

§

THREE

Jake Storm loved to drive. It was the only way he could relax at the end of a long day. He also loved it because it was his way of getting back to his roots. His father lived most of his adult life out of a car, traveling from town to town selling everything from bibles to vacuum cleaners. At the time, he didn't understand why his father was gone so much of the time, but now he did. Jake spent most of his adult life traveling around the world fighting for his country. There wasn't a whole lot of difference.

While working for the government, he would never have believed he could use the skills he had learned to make a living outside the Agency. After a few weeks of job hunting, he decided to try using his talents for personal and corporate security rather than national security. After investing a good portion of the money he had saved during his years with both the Navy and CIA, he opened Consolidated Specialty Security, Inc. In four years, he expanded the operation, opening offices in Spokane and Portland, Oregon. He now employed over sixty investigators and security specialists, over one hundred and sixty-five support personnel and billed his clients over 100 million dollars in 2008.

In spite of the growth of his business, he still personally supervised all of the larger clients employing the agency. They had directly helped him build CSS from a small security company to one of the largest domestic security contractors. Some were working on research involving the Department of Defense or other scientific projects involving national security. CSS designed each security program to fit every client's specific needs.

Jonathan Masters contacted his agency six months ago

after an incident involving one of the scientists closest to a sensitive project. The researcher had taken some valuable research material and tried to sell it to competitors, or at least that was the way Masters told it. The government stepped in and arrested the researcher, confiscating the materials. Masters took possession of his information and the researcher was deported to his native country. One of his former bosses inside the CIA recommended Jake's company to replace the security company they were using and Masters jumped at the idea. CSS rescreened all of Genetisource's employees, as well as new employees, providing building security and personal security for all of the researchers involved in sensitive projects.

With the discovery of Wilma Braeden's corpse in the underground garage of the building he was supposed to be protecting, Jake was certain that his firm would lose the contract to provide Genetisource's security. It was the first major incident any client of CSS had ever experienced. It hadn't been the fault of his program or people, but he was sure that the National Security Agency wouldn't see it that way.

After spending most of the early hours of the day at Genetisource, he went to his office, where he decided to take a nap. Cedric and Mike Harper arrived around one in the afternoon and they discussed the events and what it might mean for all of them. He instructed Mike to install extra cameras in the lab areas and to hack the entry system if necessary. Mike agreed. He didn't like being locked out of the laboratory areas anyway.

When they left, Jake took a shower in the bathroom off his office then dressed in clothes he kept for just such occasions. As the late sun made a quick descent toward the horizon, he made his way back to Genetisource.

Jake drove into the parking lot and around to the parking garage. The gates were up, and the NSA had departed, so he parked inside the garage. Every space was empty, even Masters seemed to have taken a powder. The building itself was an eyesore as far as Jake was concerned. The building was constantly updated as Genetisource added new wings. Employing many of the top scientists in the field of genetic research, they were known worldwide as the research center for genetic testing and new methods.

From the first time he met Masters, the researcher had given him the creeps. There was something about the way the man looked at him that made Jake want to wash his hands. It was more gut instinct than anything else, but when Jake looked into the man's eyes, there just didn't seem to be anything there.

"Afternoon, Boss," Cedric greeted Jake as he entered the control room from the outer hallway.

"How are things, Cedric?"

"All quiet," Cedric said. "Our friends from the NSA left a while ago. Masters apparently wasn't too thrilled after they finished questioning him. He stormed around the lobby for a while, then went up to his office, got his stuff and left. All of the other researchers are gone, too."

Mike Harper and Cedric Jaynes were the perfect Yin and Yang partnership. Jake originally recruited them directly from his own SEAL team when he started the company. They were his first employees. Each had his own unique skills and they were the best that Jake had found at what they did. They argued like children at times, amusing most who knew them, because they were really like brothers. Mike was the godfather of Cedric's one-year-old daughter and Cedric had been Mike's best man. Cedric was divorced, but his daughter stayed with him every other weekend and holidays. Mike was still married and would be for the rest of his life. They were different in size as well with Mike six feet tall and slender of build, and Cedric a monster at six-feet-five and nearly three hundred and twenty pounds. They were the perfect match, in spite of their appearance to the outside world.

Mike was a certified techno-geek, who related as well to computers as people. He was a hacker who could find out anything about anyone. Mike requested security cameras be installed in the laboratory area when they were awarded the contract for

Genetisource, but Masters refused. Now what Masters didn't know wouldn't hurt him.

"You told me to install cameras on the lab floors, but I figured I would just hack into the NSA's cameras." Mike said turning toward them for a moment, then turned back to the screen on the laptop, continuing with whatever he was working on. "They installed high-tech fiber optic cameras into his lab through the ventilation ducts."

"How'd they get in there? The labs are locked and only Masters and his researchers have key cards to access that floor."

"Those guys apparently have access anywhere they want in this building; although, they can't get in here anymore," Mike winked and grinned. "All of the labs have cameras now. I just finished piggy backing all of their feeds. Now I just have to descramble their encryption without them finding out what we are doing. It can be done with enough time. I just hope this is worth the trouble and the risk of them finding out and throwing all our asses in the brig. You know if we get caught, treason still gets you the death penalty and this, would definitely qualify."

Mike continued typing on the keyboard, trying different decryption methods. For the moment, the second video monitor remained snowy.

"I'm beginning to question whether it was such a great idea taking Genetisource as a client, Cap," Cedric commented absentmindedly as he fingered the gold chain that hung around his neck. After retiring from the Navy, he had his dog tags gold plated. The entire team, Jake included, gave him shit about it, but he steadfastly defended his decision. He insisted that he had given the Navy some of the best years of his life and deserved a reward. Jake ended up paying to have a solid gold set made to replace the plated ones.

"I can see your point." Jake cocked an eye at Cedric as he turned his chair to face him.

"Whatever Masters is working on, it must be big for the NSA to risk exposure like this. As for him, this is the first time he's left that lab in four days. He even has his meals delivered from the cafeteria," Mike said shrugging his shoulders. "I have the feeling he's losing it."

Something briefly appeared within the snow on Mike's second monitor then vanished.

"Damn it, I thought I had it that time. I'll get it and record everything they do, Boss."

"Of course you will, Mike."

Jake left the room and Genetisource, eyeing the surrounding streets for a surveillance van. He saw nothing, but he knew they wouldn't be far away.

Jake got in the Mustang and fired it up. He was curious why the NSA was all-of-a-sudden so interested in Master's day-to-day work. Unless Mike was right and they worried that the Doc had lost control. Of course if they asked him, Jake would have told them that Masters had lost it a long time ago.

Jake left the parking lot and entered the expressway, failing to notice the dark colored sedan ease into the on-ramp behind him. It followed at a distance, but kept the Mustang in sight.

§

FOUR

J onathan Masters sat in his office staring at his laptop screen. He had installed a couple of wireless cameras in the laboratory and set up secure access from his laptop, so he could keep an eye on the subject and his researchers. After fourteen years and millions of dollars in government funding, as well as some private cash donations, his project was finally showing the results they had envisioned. Between DARPA, private companies and other unnamed agencies, he knew he was running out of time. But he was certain these developments would please all of them.

After many setbacks, when he was certain that his dreams of immortality would never come to fruition, he knew the answer had been within his grasp if he just looked hard enough. Several times he thought about using someone else's genetic material but then they succeeded in getting the proper reaction thirteen months ago. After so many disappointments, they created a living creature from DNA without benefit of a living host.

Masters' office was a clash between modern and classical design. Large windows overlooked Mount Rainer to the southeast, but today thick rain clouds obscured the mountain from view. Pain pulsed behind his right eye, clouding his vision. Opening his desk drawer, he took out a bottle of pills, shook one into his hand and swallowed it along with stale water from a glass on his desk.

During his childhood, failure had never been allowed. As a young man, perfection was forced on Jonathan Masters. His father was an authoritarian who demanded loyalty along with perfection in both his wife and his offspring. His father taught biochemistry at Harvard and while he had tenure, he also spent a lot of time being disciplined by the University. The elder Masters was as hard on his students as he was his family. When Masters' older sister snapped when she was sixteen and leapt from a fifth floor window at her private school, Master's father only increased the pressure on his only other offspring, Jonathan. Young Jonathan grew into adulthood placing unyielding pressure on himself and those around him. Masters would not admit nor allow failure in his life.

In light of the recent problems they had experienced with the subject, it seemed the experiment was not a complete success. Masters wasn't ready to give up on this subject, but with the death of Wilma Braeden, one of his best bioengineers, it looked more and more like this subject was not viable. Violent outbursts, like the night he tore Braeden apart were more the norm now that it was a fully grown adult specimen. Masters couldn't believe the depth of the rage the subject showed everyone, including him. If he believed in such phenomenon, he would have sworn it was possessed.

In spite of the subject's violent tendencies, its existence was almost pitiful. It had no history before its creation; yet it insisted it had a past. Of course, that was a product of Masters teaching it about his own life because they shared a common genetic bond. It was made in Masters' image, which was the plan all along. He used his own tissue samples in the subject's creation, and fifty years of genetic history programmed into each of his cells had been transferred to the subject. Once it had gained sufficient mental development to understand, Masters had simply given it an oral history of Jonathan Masters and his many accomplishments. But even as he told the subject about himself, it seemed to already know.

Within months, the creature grew into young adulthood and appeared to understand Masters' problems deeper than the doctor himself. It often would talk with Masters and offer potential solutions. It was the only thing in Masters' life who knew about the disease that had spent the past year slowly degrading Masters' health. Having someone to confide in about his pain had given Masters comfort.

Masters married Jennifer in 2000, after enduring many conversations with colleagues about the need for family. Masters felt no real need for family because, in his experience, they only complicated one's life and hurt you when you needed them the most. But, his feelings changed when he met Jennifer. She matched his definition of the perfect woman. Her bone structure was stunning and, Masters, in his own way, loved her the moment they locked eyes.

After a courtship lasting only a few months, they married. It was the only time during the project that he wasn't totally committed to his work. Just after the twin towers fell in New York, Jennifer had told him she was pregnant.

Masters remembered his reaction to the news that Jennifer would give birth to his child. He screamed at her, then after leaving their home for several days, he returned and apologized. He was still pissed that she hadn't taken better precautions against getting pregnant, but what was done was done.

Masters had an explosive temper that could sometimes lead to violence. Empathy was not his best trait, but during her pregnancy, Masters was diagnosed with a rare form of cancer ironically linked to genetics. The propensity for the cancer was linked to his father, who died of the disease long after leaving the family. He had been forced to inquire into his past in order to find out about the link, but it was there.

When Masters told Jennifer about the genetic link, she was devastated. He did not tell her he was sick, only that he found out his father had been a carrier of the disease and so was he, meaning their daughter could also get the disease. It had taken no time for him to convince her to allow him to take stem cells from inside her womb to develop a cure for his daughter before she was born.

Without telling the other researchers, he began working

to develop a genetic editor to delete the faulty code from his unborn daughter's body. As Jennifer advanced from the second to third trimester, Masters injected a stem cell-laced concoction into her womb. After his daughter was born, he tested her and found the concoction had worked. She would never develop the disease.

While his cancer had been resistant to treatment, he had endured chemotherapy and radiation, wearing an expensive hairpiece to hide his loss of hair. The cancer finally went into remission after a year. Eventually his hair grew back, and no one ever knew. He was one of the few cancer patients that were resistant to the debilitating effects of cancer treatment. He never experienced the nausea or weakness often associated with radiation and chemotherapy. Not even Jennifer had discovered his secret.

In spite of his notoriously bad temper, nothing he did could compare with the degree of violence they had seen out of the subject. It seemed to have the same emotional swings he did, which was more than a little unnerving. It seemed to enjoy the violent outbursts almost as if it were a type of therapy. Nonetheless, it was like looking at a darker, more evil reflection of Masters himself.

Masters watched the subject on the video monitor as it paced the Plexiglas enclosure that was its home. It appeared to be throwing things at the clear walls. From the angle, he couldn't see what it was throwing, but the subject was obviously having another episode. Masters saved the mounting video footage to the server, then copied the files to a high-capacity, external hard drive that was the size of a cigarette case. He would take the footage with him and review it later.

The intercom on his phone buzzed, breaking his concentration. Masters pressed the intercom button. "Yes, what is it?"

"Doctor Alonga to see you, Sir," Janet's voice came through the speaker on his phone. Janet had been his assistant for the past year, far outlasting anyone else he had hired over the years. She was efficient and kept him on track. She was also nice to look at, which didn't hurt his libido any.   So far, he had not taken it further than the casual relationship between employer and employee, but once he delivered his research, well, that might all just change.

"Send him in."

Mario Alonga entered his office through the double, walnut-colored, wooden doors separating him from the outside, carrying a touchpad computer.   Alonga was the finest bioengineer Masters had ever encountered.   Alonga was smarter than Braeden had been by far.   Although Masters would never admit it, Alonga was far superior in skill than himself.   Alonga was, however, humble as a kitten when it came to his work.   He seemed to hide from the limelight, rather than crave it, which confounded Masters.

Alonga was just a worker bee.   Standing behind the others, including Masters, doing most of the work and innovation (the incubation tank had been his design), yet, wanting little or no credit.   Masters considered it a miracle that he met Alonga nearly twenty years ago and had lured him to Genetisource.

Alonga was Italian, wore wire frame glasses, but his face and body seemed sculpted from granite. Masters had never seen Mario work out, never even heard him talk of going to a gym, yet his body seemed hard as a rock. He reminded Masters of a younger version of Sylvester Stallone.

"Good morning, Doctor," Mario said, stopping in front of Masters' desk.

"Good morning," Masters returned, hating the pleasantries. "How is our subject today?"

"He is refusing to complete any of our tests until he is allowed to speak to you," Mario said gravely. "I have the latest brain scan results we performed after it killed Wilma. The results are, to say the least, shocking."

"I told you I will not get near it until we have the new enclosure finished. I am still recovering from the other night. I have no intention of getting that close to it again."

"I guess he'll have to wait then. He won't let us continue

testing his abilities until he sees you in person," Mario waved the folder in front of him. "We have the CAT Scan from the other night if you wish to review it."

"Sit down," Masters said, turning to his computer. Typing the keys, he pulled up the images they had taken of the subject's brain. "Maybe we can find a way to derail any further outbursts."

"As you can see, his reactions to the images we showed him of Wilma's murder and the subsequent destruction of that part of the lab seemed not to affect his brain in the least. He seems unphased by his own actions and shows no horror or, for that matter, any emotions."

Alonga seemed loath to continue, but went on. "I have to tell you everyone is very frightened of the subject. Wilma was merely checking the leads when he attacked her." Alonga swallowed hard because he was obviously as afraid of Masters as he was the being they had created. "What if that happens again?"

Masters locked eyes with Alonga, causing the researcher to look away. "We will find the problem with the subject and fix it. There is something in this data that will tell us what is causing these outbursts."

"There is a possibility, Sir," Alonga began, fear drawing his already strained features further, "we'll be forced to terminate the subject and start over."

Anger danced briefly across Masters' face, then subsided. "Mario, the problem is right in this file. We are just overlooking it. Let's get to work and see if we can find it."

They spent the next three hours going over the reports and found virtually nothing at all. In spite of the intense violence, the subject's brain waves never changed. His heart rate seemed to calm as he became more aggressive. At rest, the subject's heart rate was fifty-five. As he began to get angry and aggressive towards the doctors, his heart rate gradually slowed to fifty, then continued lower.

"What does this mean?" Alonga asked. "Why doesn't his

anger affect his heart rate or brainwaves? Hell, it's almost like violence relaxes him."

"That is the problem, old friend. When it is aggressive, his vitals appear to be normal or below. No racing heart rate, no adrenalin rushes. All our data and research says this is impossible, but the evidence speaks volumes. What flaw in his genes can produce such anger, rage and aggression, yet have no discernible effect on his biorhythms? We have to solve this problem quickly, because our time is short. We cannot keep our subject a secret much longer. Our benefactors are beginning to ask questions and we cannot allow them to know we have had any setbacks."

Alonga left the office to return to the lab and Masters turned his chair around and stared through his fifth-floor window at the rain-swollen clouds. The ironclad sky hid Mount Rainier and the Cascades from view and reflected his mood. He needed a short break from his work so that he could come back and look at this thing from a fresh perspective. Pain once again stabbed at his right eye and he absently rubbed his temples. Masters tried to relax, but the pain in his head increased, causing him to gasp. Taking another pain pill from inside his desk, he dry swallowed it.

Last year, just about the time they had realized success in the Darwin Project, he awakened one morning with a bloody nose. Being conscientious, he went to his oncologist. A few days later, he was told his cancer had returned and he was terminal. No chemotherapy would help him this time. They had resisted giving him a timeframe, but inside he knew it wouldn't be long now. That was why *this* subject must be the success. It meant his own survival beyond his death. His immortality was at stake.

Masters picked up the phone and buzzed his secretary. When she picked up, he instructed her to make reservations for one passenger traveling to Cabo San Lucas, Mexico. By this time tomorrow morning, he would be relaxing on the beach. He also instructed her not to disturb him while he was gone unless it was a life or death emergency. At the rate things were going, he would probably just get his bags unpacked in Cabo, before they called with another catastrophe.

Hanging up the phone he straightened his tie, then shrugged into his jacket and raincoat. Leaving through his private entrance, he took the stairs to the garage. Some time off would give him a better perspective on the situation and improve his chances at correcting the problems with the subject. Of course, there was the possibility that the problems were within the genetic code and could not be solved. There was a good possibility they would have to terminate the subject and try again, but Masters knew this was his last chance to get this right.

§

FIVE

Consolidated Specialty Security made their home offices on the fourteenth floor of the McManus Towers in downtown Seattle. Jake's corner office faced the Cascade Mountains and, during the summer, it provided him with a great sunrise in the early mornings. During the dreary winters, he could still see most of the way east, past Lake Washington. Today, gray clouds hung low and obscured most of his view of the lake. It was depressing.

Jake walked into his office at nine o'clock in the morning, still puzzled by Braeden's murder. He had called his contact at the NSA to inquire about the status of the investigation. They passed him over to a senior officer who had not so politely told him to mind his own business.

Questions remained that needed answers. Who or what could have beaten her so savagely, yet not aroused the suspicion of anyone in the building? Jake's first thoughts had been that a test monkey might have done the damage. They used small monkeys, nothing large enough to do that kind of damage to a grown human being. The disposal of the body was amateurish, but whoever did this had known they were being watched. There hadn't been a lot of people in the building that night, but someone should have seen something. Even the cameras had missed everything but the shadows in the garage. She was killed on a floor without cameras, which meant the laboratory. All the researchers had been in the building that evening, so who had done it? Why would her colleagues cover up her murder?

As soon as Jake reported the crime, the NSA responded immediately. That meant they had a lot to lose. Then another agency appeared and installed cameras in the labs without Masters knowing. CSS and Jake had been pushed out, so whatever had happened involved national security.

During his years in the Navy and, later with the CIA, Jake had traveled to some of the most beautiful places in the world, along with some of the ugliest, but Seattle was one of the most beautiful places he had ever been. Most of the year, the almost constant rain could be depressing. He knew it was a tradeoff, summer days among the beauty and wonder that captivated all lifelong Seattleites in exchange for the other nine months of over-cast skies and rain. Sometimes his back and legs protested, but he had endured greater pain in the past.

Jake sorted the piles of paperwork on his desk, trying to inspect and approve spending reports, so his employees would get their expense checks on time. He found it hard to focus on the mundane tasks of his work, his thoughts continually returning to Genetisource. It wasn't really his problem, yet he found his thoughts traveling back to Masters and the dead researcher.

Braeden drove an ancient Mercedes, which had been parked in the garage, yet her keys were found in her purse, inside her office. She had no reason to go to the garage without her car keys. So why was she there? This looked like an amateurish after-thought. If she was terminated by any government agency, they would not have found her belongings in her office. They probably would never have found a body at all. So, who would be stupid enough to kill someone who worked in the same building as they did, then leave behind evidence that would lead to an investiga-tion of everyone in the building? The answer kept coming back to her colleagues, but none of them seemed likely candidates. Everyone who worked at Genetisource had been cleared via back-ground checks performed by the original security company. If any of them had a violent past, they would have found out and that person would never have been hired.

Expense reports, he kept telling himself, but he couldn't focus on them. He ended up signing off on all of the reports without reading them, and then sent the authorizations for payment to accounting via e-mail. He turned his chair and stared out the window toward the mountains. *There must be a couple of feet of snow at his cabin right now,* he thought. Thoughts of escaping to the seclusion and solitude of his cabin at the base of Mount Rainier claimed his thoughts for so long he failed to notice the phone on his desk ringing until it had rung four times.

"Mr. Storm, Mr. Harper is on the line," his office assistant, Kimberly, said.

"Thanks, Kim."

Punching the flashing light on his phone console, he picked up the receiver. "Storm."

"Boss, I just wanted to update you on my efforts. I haven't been able to clean any of this video up yet."

"Keep trying. That may be our only bargaining chip."

"I'll stay on it," Mike said, and Jake could tell it was bothering him that he hadn't already figured the problem out. "Good. Let me know when you fix it. I have every confidence in you. I think that whatever Masters is doing in that lab is the key to everything."

Mike hung up and Jake stared at the phone for a moment. Mike was the best electronics and computer hacker he had ever seen. He surprised Jake more than once, but his skills were never more important.

Tapping a few keys on his computer keyboard, he pulled up the action reports from the night Braeden had perished.

"There has to be something here," he said absently.

Using a yellow legal notepad, he noted all of the significant points contained in the reports, then pulled up the photographs of the scene Mike had saved on the server. All of the evidence wasn't enough to fill two of the yellow pages. They still knew nothing and it angered him.

Jake was under no illusion that Masters would open up and tell him what happened, even under heavy interrogation. Jake was convinced Masters knew more than he was saying, but it was worth a try. He picked up the phone and dialed the main number at Genetisource and asked for Masters. When Masters' assistant answered, she told him the doctor was in a meeting and could not be disturbed. Jake hung up and checked his watch, surprised that it was already 4:30 in the afternoon. He had spent the entire day worrying over Genetisource and the problems there without noticing the passing time.

Jake decided to wait until 5:00 o'clock to try the doctor again. He hoped Mike would decode the video feed from the lab by then.

Jake stared out the window watching the rain change to snow. They were heading into dark territory where people disappeared and sometimes were sacrificed for the greater good. Jake shivered, watching the flakes pass the window.

§

SIX

At just after six, Jonathan Masters returned to his office at Genetisource. He had gone to his apartment and packed enough clothes for a few days in Mexico. He had also decided that he needed to sedate the subject until he returned. It was the only way he could keep his people safe. It was the only way they could perform more tests.

Masters watched the snow falling heavier outside his window. His flight to Mexico and his break from work might be postponed if the weather didn't let up. In addition, if the NSA showed up again with more questions, he would definitely have to delay getting away.

Transcribing notes into his laptop, he downloaded a copy into the main file residing on the project server then loaded his laptop and the external drive into his briefcase.

Masters pondered his project. He was the first person in history, besides identical twins possibly, who knew what it felt like to be in two places at once. He often imagined he could see through the subject's eyes. It was impossible, of course, but, in some ways, the idea was fascinating.

Two nights ago, he felt like he had known what it was going to do the instant before his clone had turned on Wilma Braeden, yet had been powerless to stop it. It had beaten the poor woman even after it was obvious she was dead. Masters and the other researchers had finally managed to inject it with three times the safe dose of Succinylcholine, temporarily knocking it unconscious. Succinylcholine was a powerful paralytic, but the creature had continued breathing when it should have perished.

Masters and Alonga disposed of Wilma Braeden's corpse.

The entire team cleaned the lab as if the event had never happened. They had just finished when Storm notified him they found the body in the dumpster.

While he had no experience dumping a corpse, Alonga had once again come to his rescue. They carried Braeden's body to the freight elevator at the end of the laboratory hallway and descended to the garage. Alonga covered his face and worked along the walls until he found something to throw at the lights that illuminated the dumpster. Finding a pipe, Alonga used it to shatter the fluorescent lights, leaving the area around the dumpster in shadows. They lifted Braeden into the dumpster and Alonga moved pieces of trash around to make it appear random. He explained that they should make it look like Braeden had been attacked and killed in the garage and dumped in the most convenient place the killer could find.

Masters had looked at Alonga in a whole new light after his casual disposal of Wilma Braeden. He never thought the researcher capable of such a callous act. The rest of the researchers were shocked by the incident and the casual way that Masters and Alonga had disposed of their colleague. Masters knew he was losing their trust, but at this point, he didn't care.

The pain in his head and abdomen were getting worse so he took more pain medication. He knew the pain meant he was failing. Maybe once they fixed their creation, he would get another stem cell treatment in Rio. It eased his symptoms on previous occasions. Maybe it would work again.

Having one of his own scientists bludgeoned by this beast until her body was nearly unrecognizable, and then having to cover it up, made finishing his research even more paramount. If the government rushed in now and took over the project, pushing him out in the process, nothing would be accomplished. They would just shuttle all of his research off to another of their laboratories, one more secure or on a military installation somewhere, and he would never be allowed to finish.

Of course, it would take years for them to figure out

what he had accomplished but that left him no solace. He couldn't allow the advances he made in the past two years to be flushed down the proverbial toilet so easily. He had to do something before things got any further out of hand.

The buzzer going off on his desk shattered his paralysis. He let the air from his lungs whistle through his perfect teeth, leaned forward and pressed the intercom button.

"What?" Masters yelled.

"Dr. Masters."

Masters recognized Jack Monroe's voice in spite of the noise in the background. "You need to get down to the lab right away."

"What the hell is going on down there?" Masters said, raising his voice so he could be heard above crashing sounds in the background.

"Dr. Masters, the subject is out of control again. He says he is going to destroy everything in his enclosure, then kill himself, if he doesn't see you right away. He says he knows you're planning to leave and wants to see you now or he'll *end your precious project for you.*"

"Sedate him, goddamn it." Masters knew all along that something would interfere with his plan to leave.

"He won't let us near him. He says he'll kill anyone who tries unless he speaks to you. He also threatened to kill us just like he did Wilma. Frankly, Sir, I believe him."

Masters closed his eyes and pinched the bridge of his nose between his fingers. Pain shot through his head. It was time to make a decision. If he couldn't put a stop to this, he would have to terminate the subject now. But would it end there? He couldn't keep this experiment a secret from his benefactors if bodies kept showing up. He and his researchers were not trained to dispose of bodies.

On the other hand, he could give the subject what it wanted. *Just go down to the lab and talk to it,* he thought. Maybe he could charm it into letting them sedate it until he returned. It would set the project back a while, but it was better than an all-out failure. Failure was not an option.

"Okay, I'm on my way. Please assure the subject I will not leave without making certain he is comfortable in every way."

"Thank you, Dr. Masters." Monroe ended the connection and Masters grabbed his lab coat and left his office.

"Project Darwin" was becoming a serious risk for him. If they didn't solve this quickly they would all perish under the weight of the government and his other benefactors. He would-n't have to worry about it much longer, but his legacy would be tarnished and he couldn't allow that.

Entering the lab, he noticed the agitation in his staff. They were trying to ignore the shadowy figure throwing things around in the enclosure at the far end of the room. The problem was that none of them were succeeding.

Lillith Chu, the newest member of his team sat nearest the door, typing notes into her computer. Her hands were visibly shaking and she kept being forced to use the delete key and retype what she was entering. She flinched visibly when Masters walked through the door. She glanced at him and then smiled shakily.

"What's happening down here, Lillith? Is our subject a little unsettled this afternoon?"

"That has to be the biggest understatement I've ever heard," she rolled her eyes. "That creature has been throwing shit around his enclosure like a baboon on crystal meth for almost an hour. He's destroyed nearly everything that isn't bolted down."

Standing up, she placed her laptop on the counter and hugged her arms around her chest, gripping each of her biceps with the opposite hand. "Doctor Masters, that thing is danger-ous. We can't control him and we can't sedate him if we can't get in there. I won't go anywhere near him. He's been making threats against all of us for the last few days. I think we should discuss whether he remains viable."

"Okay, I'll go talk to it and see if I can calm it down. Round everyone up for a meeting in the conference room. We'll discuss what to do next."

Dr. Chu stared into his eyes for a moment then turned away, slowly shaking her head. Masters glared at her back and walked over to the enclosure, nodding to the other researchers as he passed them. He felt their fear and it worried him.

The subject crouched in the corner of the large plasticized cell. Before creating this thing that so resembled him, he would not have thought himself capable of this much fear, but now he was certain that he hadn't discovered the depths of his turmoil yet.

"How are we today?" Masters tried to sound every bit the professional, using all the bedside manner he could muster. The condition of the enclosure was appalling and his double, standing on the opposite side of three-inch thick Plexiglas walls, was even worse.

"How's it going, Pop? Have I been a bad boy?"

"Well, you have certainly upset my staff. You know they are only trying to help you."

"I don't need their help," it grumbled, turning its head to glare at Masters, causing gooseflesh to form on the scientist's arms. "I just want to stretch my legs a little. It's inhumane to keep me in here for such long periods. All I asked for was to walk around free for a while, maybe watch the rain. These zoo-keepers keep saying that it's your decision. I cannot wait for your return. I have had my fill of these researchers and their excuses. See my point?"

"Yes, I believe I do."

Masters noted that the subject had retained a sneer on his face throughout his entire tirade. Masters also saw something odd about the stains on the subject's tunic. Among the many stains were crimson smears here and there that looked like blood. Where had the blood come from?

"So, how 'bout it, Dads? Can I take a break from my cell and go for a stroll around the park?"

"Not right away, but when I return, maybe we can..."

"That's not acceptable," the subject yelled. "I want out now."

The creature leaned closer to where Masters stood, causing him to step back. "How's the pain, Doc? Getting to you yet? I feel what you feel, even though I don't have the disease. Isn't that amazing? Wow, it must be terrible knowing you are about to die and nothing can stop it, eh?"

"Okay, you win," Masters said. "I'll get you a change of clothes so you can clean up. Then we'll go for a short walk. But you know what this means; you have to give me something in return. You have to let us continue our tests."

"Wonderful," it muttered then returned to slowly tearing apart the medical journals that were stacked knee high around the small desk on the farthest wall of the enclosure. "See how easy life can be?"

Masters paused at this statement, realizing this was exactly the response *he* used when an opponent in an argument surrendered. He smiled wanly in pure admiration of how much like him the subject had become.

"I have to meet with my staff. I will return with some clean clothes and your dinner. Then we'll take that walk."

With a wave of his hand, as if dismissing him, the subject looked more like Masters than ever. Masters left the lab and went to the same conference room where he had briefed his researchers of their new project fourteen years ago.

Nervous chatter among his team stopped when Masters entered the room. He took in the expressions of his four researchers as he sat down at the head of the large oak table. These people, with whom he'd shared a great deal of time over the past few years, were staring expectantly at him as he settled into his seat.

"I want a full report on the subject's activities. Let's begin with Dr. Alonga and continue around the table."

Mario Alonga, looking much more haggard than he had when they first discussed the experiment in the laboratory that morning two years ago, or even this morning when they discussed the problems with the subject, straightened in his chair and looked directly at Masters as he began his report.

"For the past week, when you were out of the laboratory area, the subject has grown gradually more abusive. In spite of our assurances that it is our biggest success ever, it feels it is a freak.

"The creature has also begun taking less care with hygiene and has lowered its food intake with each meal. The threats have become more graphic and bloody. Earlier today, just to prove to us that it was invincible, the subject cut a vein in its arm with its fingernail and watched as it healed. I must say that it healed much more rapidly than we first thought it would.

"Everyone here agrees that with the advanced muscle and reparative features programmed into its genetic code, the creature could make good on its threats rather easily. *If* it was released from its enclosure."

That explains the blood on the subject's clothing, Masters thought.

"And once the new chamber is finished, how do we move him?" Lillith Chu asked. "I don't think anyone here believes he will voluntarily move from one prison to another."

Each researcher expressed observations and opinions to Masters. He listened to each of them, taking notes as they spoke. When they finished, he regarded his pad for a moment. Was this how it was all going to end? Was their greatest success also their greatest failure?

"I think," he began placing his fingers in an upside down 'V' under his chin, "we should carefully consider our options and come to a decision about what to do. However, we cannot do this emotionally. We are all exhausted and need a break. So," Masters sighed heavily and continued, "What I propose is for all of us to go home, think about it and come back fresh tomorrow morning."

"Doctor, obviously we cannot let him loose. If we can't

terminate him now, then we must sedate him to keep us all safe," Mario said.

"Yes, of course," Masters said standing up, pain once again cutting through his midsection. He sucked in a breath but was successful in hiding it from the others. "I will sedate the subject and hook him up to an intravenous line. Someone will have to make sure medication bags are changed every few hours so that he doesn't wake up."

Masters walked back into the laboratory and sat near the rear wall, watching the subject from afar. While he was not visible to the creature where he sat, he felt that it knew he was there.

After a few moments, the subject looked at Masters and smiled. The gesture sent chills running up the geneticist's spine. It tapped the side of its head with a finger.

"Yes," the creature said but Masters didn't see its lips moving. The voice he heard was inside his brain. "We are closer than you realize. I have more of your DNA than any other donor. That means you and I are linked. I actually know where you are and what you are doing most of the time."

Masters felt the blood in his veins run cold. He couldn't believe what he had heard. How was it possible that the subject could communicate telepathically with him? This kind of hocus-pocus was impossible. It couldn't be explained scientifically so it could not happen. Could it?

Leaving the lab, Masters returned to his office and turned on his laptop. Writing down the details of the incident with the subject, he saved it to the hard drive and returned the computer to his bag.

There was no doubt in his mind that the subject would have to be dealt with...and soon. It wasn't something he looked forward to doing because there was no time to create another successful reproduction with the violence gene edited out. Time was no longer an option for him.

Staring out his window, Masters wished for a reasonable solution, but nothing came. He would have to terminate the subject immediately. The question was how? Even if he could sedate it with something in its food, how long would he have to inject the creature with enough Succinylcholine to stop it permanently? He didn't know, but he knew he had to try. And if the creature knew his thoughts, it would know his plan too.

§

SEVEN

S now fell heavily outside Jake's office window as he tried to phone Masters again. The call went directly to the geneticist's voicemail. *The good doctor must still be in his meeting,* he thought.

Mike called Jake at just past five o'clock to tell him he had finally decrypted the signal from the cameras on the laboratory floor. Now that they were recording what was going on in the lab they would get some answers. He hoped they would be able to stay ahead of the feds.

Needing refreshment, Jake went into the break room and grabbed a bottle of water from the refrigerator. Kimberley had gone home long ago and except for the cleaning crew, he was the only one left in the building. The weather drove most of the tenants scurrying away earlier in the day.

Leaving the offices, Jake took the elevator down to the lobby. The only person he saw was the security guard who manned the desk near the door. Jake spoke briefly about the weather to the guard, who cordially chatted with him, while keeping one eye trained on the video monitors built into his desk.

Bidding the guard a good evening, he went back to the elevators. On instinct, he punched the down button and the door opened. Inside the car, Jake used his access key and pushed the button for the basement. The basement was a secure area and only certain people were allowed access.

When the elevators opened, he stepped out into a dimly lit hallway. Turning right, he walked to the end of the hallway and made a left turn. There were utility rooms for each floor. At this end of the basement, each room contained electrical and water mains as well as junction boxes for communications. Jake found the room labeled for his floor and used his access key.

Inside, there was a junction box labeled for each suite. Finding his was not a problem since his company occupied most of the floor. Opening the access panel, he saw the computer box that controlled his phone system. Because all communications were transmitted over a T-3 trunk line, the phones for his office were controlled by a special computer system attached to the incoming line. Inside the computer, several cards controlled different parts of the system. He had watched the installers the day the system was installed. He was certain there had been three empty computer card slots in the controller. His worst fears were realized when he saw all seven slots were filled, the original system taking four, then three filled with unknown controller boards. NSA was monitoring his communications.

Taking a flashlight from his pocket, he twisted the end to turn it on. Inspecting the added cards, he recognized the technology. They were designed to tap into the phone system and mimic each line, allowing anyone with the proper receiver to listen in and actually control whether the calls got through.

Jake instantly broke out in a cold sweat. The NSA, or whoever else was involved in Masters' research, had tapped his lines. If they could monitor his phone lines, they could use the Patriot Act to gain access to their cellular phone provider as well. Jake turned his flashlight off and closed the door covering the junction box. He closed and locked the utility room and took the elevator back to his floor.

Sitting at his desk, Jake considered what he had found. The NSA or someone else had tapped their office phones and their cell phones and, one would assume, their electronic mail. That meant they were aware of what Jake and his people had found and what they suspected. That also meant they were all in danger.

Masters was involved in specialized genetic research. DARPA had been involved at one point, but now the NSA had taken control of holding Genetisource's leash. Maybe they weren't the only agency involved either. There were lots of sections of the government that financed "special projects" involving misguided ideas of making the country more secure. If the project had defense applications, the list of candidates financing this sort of research lengthened considerably. Jake cursed himself for ever getting involved with Genetisource and the psycho doctor.

Staring out at the falling snow, Jake considered taking the elevator to the roof and jumping off.

§

EIGHT

Masters entered the lab carrying a tray loaded with food. Stopping just inside the doorway, he injected the food with an animal tranquilizer. He keyed in the code that locked the lab doors. He was impeding his own escape should this turn sour, but he was certain that if the subject got its hands on him, he wouldn't be able to escape anyway. Looking toward the enclosure, he saw the creature lying on its bed, obviously content despite having thoroughly trashed his home. Masters shook his head in disbelief at the rage that had generated the destruction inside the clear, high-strength polymer walls. Quite a lot of money and time had been expended constructing the enclosure and even more on the new, more secure cells being constructed in what had once been an adjacent lab. He couldn't believe all that money would go to waste.

Handing the subject its dinner through the slot in the door would make it aware that Masters didn't trust it. The creature might realize the doctor had tainted the food. He had no choice. Masters must go inside the room with the subject, but not without protection.

Grabbing fresh scrubs and a tunic from the closet near the far end of the enclosure, Masters went back to the locked cabinet where they kept the drugs. Filling a syringe full with succinylcholine, Masters dropped it into his pocket and advanced on the plastic cage. He had to count on the creature not knowing what he intended to do. He did his best to keep his mind occupied with other thoughts. He remembered some medical terminology he had memorized once and concentrated on it while he prepared to enter the enclosure.

The cage was large enough for Masters to see there was quite a bit of damage to the walls of the structure. The walls were actually cracked in several places. In others, the panels were bowed outward from the incredible force applied from the inside. The material was supposed to be capable of withstanding a good-sized blast, but had cracked under the strain of the attacks from this thing's hands. Masters shivered again, thinking of the amount of strength it took for the subject to fracture the walls of the makeshift prison.

Terminating the creature wasn't something Masters wanted. In spite of objections from his staff, he had avoided such extreme measures; however, with the events of the past week, he had come to the conclusion that he could no longer avoid dealing with this. Maybe a post-mortem of the subject would provide answers.

Picking up the pile of clothes, Masters walked back to the entrance to the cell. The subject was no longer lying on the bed. He looked around the enclosure, but, at first, could not see where the creature was. Then he saw it standing in the farthest corner near the bed.

He picked up the plate of food and placed it on top of the clothes. Masters keyed in the code that unlocked the door. He tried to keep his fear from registering on his face. He stopped his memorized text, at this point, to seem more natural if the creature could read his thoughts. He was certain if the subject knew he was afraid, it would take advantage and attack.

Using his foot to hold the door open and never taking his eyes off the subject, Masters placed the tray on a small table near the entrance. He felt the smooth lines of the syringe in his pocket which made him feel a little more secure. His subject still faced away from him, hands clasped behind its back as if meditating on the significance of the bloody mural adorning the wall. Silence reigned in the room for several moments, long enough for Masters to contemplate stepping backward through the door and locking the door behind him.

"I thought you might like your meal before we go for that walk," Masters said, attempting to break the deafening silence and calm his own jangling nerves at the same time. Backing up to a point near the door of the enclosure, he readied himself for a quick escape if the need arose. He continued watching the subject, looking for any signs of impending strike.

"What do you think is wrong with me, Doc?" The subject didn't turn around as he spoke.

"What do you mean?"

"C'mon, Doc. Don't fucking toy with me. I know you and those other morons have been trying to figure out what went wrong with your little creation all afternoon. So give it up. Why am I so violent?" The subject tapped his left temple, but still remained turned toward the wall. "Remember, I know what you know."

Masters stopped short at this statement. Masters wished that his side of the psychic link allowed him to see what it was thinking. So far, it appeared the only limits were on his side of that link. He touched the syringe in his pocket again but left it where it was.

"I just wonder why you are so upset with us. You have made quite a mess around here and you have scared everyone half to death."

Masters was proud of how stable his voice sounded. He was sure he had succeeded in trying to keep his terror hidden.

"Oh, I guess those candy-assed researchers were a little startled by this," he said waving his arm around the room, "But I think it's kind of nice. Gives the place a little color."

The subject turned to face Masters.

"But not you, eh, Doc? You're very familiar with this kind of behavior, aren't you? In fact, you really have some anger management issues of your own, huh?"

"I don't know what you are talking about."

"Remember, Doc. I know what you know. Do you think that gorgeous piece of ass, Jennifer, would agree? How about the hooker in Rio you nearly beat to death in 2004. Maybe that little hottie in Cabo, the one with the tits from hell, that you kicked until she bled from her ears. Would she say you were a nice guy? Or would they all talk about what a sadistic piece of shit you are and how they'd all like to cut your testicles off and feed them to you with hot sauce and peppers."

Masters watched the subject advance on him slowly. He moved one foot outside the door, but held his ground. Locking eyes with the doppelganger, he admired the piercing glare in the creature's stare. Fire smoldered in those eyes. When he lost his temper, this was how Masters looked.

Once, during his college years, he had gotten into a fight in a bar near campus and had almost killed a football player twice his size. He remembered going home that night, looking in the mirror and seeing a younger version of this creature's face staring back at him. It had frightened him so much, he spent the next two days locked in his room. Not because he was afraid of killing someone, but because he could go to jail for it. Going to jail would ruin his reputation and he couldn't allow that. Masters struggled everyday with his temper, but he didn't possess the strength or bloody desires of the thing standing across from him.

Masters watched the creature edge closer to him. He was fascinated with how smooth and animal-like the creature's movements were, like a cheetah stalking prey. A moment later the subject leaned across the table, cat quick, grabbed the clothes and, unfortunately for Masters, the syringe. A second later, Masters felt the needle pierce his shoulder and the contents empty into him. His chance to react was gone now. He was just as good as dead.

Masters tried to make it outside the enclosure, but the paralytic was already hitting his system. Stumbling toward the outer doors, he tried to enter the code but couldn't remember it.

"I'll bet you're wondering where that came from, aren't you? I'm a lot faster than you might have guessed," the subject said, exiting the plastic walled prison. The creature advanced toward him, grinning maniacally. "Anyway, that doesn't matter now. You're about to go on the journey of a lifetime, Doc. Everyone wonders whether there's life after death. Well, you're about to find out. Unfortunately, you won't be around to hit the talk show circuit."

Masters slid down the wall as his legs lost the ability to carry his weight. His vision darkened at the corners, but he still saw the creature advance toward him and pick him up from the floor with one hand.

"Well, isn't that a shame. I guess nothing is going your way today, is it, Doc?" The subject hooked the chair that Lillith Chu had used earlier and lowered Masters gently onto the seat. Folding his well-built arms across his chest, he sighed as if bored by the scene.

"You were wondering what I was so pissed about, Doc? Well, let me tell you. I've been caged like an animal for months, being fed and kept warm, but otherwise devoid of meaningful contact. That's what I'm pissed about. I've done everything you've asked of me. I haven't hurt anyone; well, except for sticking you with that needle and beating that bitch Braeden to a bloody pulp, which would have never happened if she hadn't acted so smug. You see, I believe in fair treatment for what you've done to me. You've treated me like an animal, so I'm going to treat you like an animal. I'm going to euthanize you. I'll treat you with more respect than the others, though. After all, you gave me life. For that you get to die easily."

Masters couldn't believe this had happened to him. As the darkness gradually filled his vision, he realized he could no longer breathe deeply. He just couldn't expand his lungs enough.

"Doc, it's time I relieved you from duty. I thought about just letting the drug do the job, but I've decided to do it myself."

Masters couldn't move as the subject grabbed his head between his hands, bearing down with its incredible strength and sending unspeakable pain through Master's skull. Masters tried to lift his hands to fight off the creature, but didn't have the strength. Blood poured from his nose, ears and eyes as his skull shattered, sending shards of bone into his brain. Masters was beyond feeling when the subject twisted his neck violently, crushing several vertebrae, severing his spinal cord. The subject chuckled mildly as it dropped Masters' limp body to the floor.

"Now, I need a diversion so I can get the fuck out of here," the new and improved Jonathan Masters said as he keyed in the code that deactivated the lock on the outer door.

§

NINE

Cedric and Mike Harper sat in the security control room at Genetisource. Cedric had taken over watching the monitor while Mike leaned his chair against the wall and rested his eyes. Jake was counting on them to keep the situation at Genetisource in control. Cedric watched Masters enter the lab carrying what looked like a food tray. Turning to Mike, he reached his hand over and shook him awake.

"Your turn to watch," Cedric said, turning back to the monitor. "Looks like the good Doctor is eating dinner in the lab again."

In spite of the sophistication of the fiber optic cameras the NSA installed, they still could not see much of the lab. From what Mike and Cedric were able to glean from the video, there appeared to be some sort of plastic cage or terrarium at the far end of the lab, but due to its location, the camera couldn't video the entire area.

Cedric stretched, arching his arms high above his head. He turned away from the monitor and walked over to the coffee-pot at the back of the control room.

Mike eyed the cup Cedric was filling with coffee and winced, squeezing his eyes shut as if in pain. "Do you know what that stuff is going to do to your prostate?"

"I'm so tired I don't give a fuck. Want some?"

"Hell, yes." Mike laughed, handing his cup to Cedric, who filled it to the brim with his coffee. Extending his hand with the cup to Mike, he saw him peer closer at the monitors.

"Hey, buddy, I think you'd better look at this. Something… Hell, I don't know if I'm seeing what I am seeing."

Cedric turned toward the monitor and watched as Masters backed toward the camera. Someone else followed him. What had stunned Mike and now Cedric was that Masters appeared to be running from himself.

"Mike, check the doors on the lab and find out if Masters locked them down. If not, lock out all codes."

"Already on it," Mike was back at his terminal, his hands flying over the keys. Cedric kept his attention trained on the monitor.

"Surely this isn't real," Cedric said, turning away from his screen.

"Masters locked down the lab doors to the outside corridor," Mike said. "I can initiate a lockdown, but Masters' code will disengage it."

"Do it anyway," Cedric mumbled, fascinated by the scene on the monitors.

Cedric watched the double pick Masters up from the floor with one hand and place him in a chair. The subject moved just out of sight of the cameras.

"Mike, switch the camera, quick."

Punching some keys on the keyboard, Mike hit the enter key, changing the scene on the large center monitor. From this view, they could see the doctor cowering from the man who had chased him toward the exit doors. Masters' double said something, waved his hand then grabbed the doctor's head in his hands

Cedric grabbed a radio and chambered a round into his Browning .45 caliber handgun.

"I'm heading to the laboratory level. Call Jake and let him know what's happening. I'll be back."

"Watch your ass, Buddy. You have no idea what that motherfucker has cooked up," Mike yelled as Cedric ran through the security door.

"Ced, Masters' code to disengage the lock has just been entered," Mike looked at the monitor as Cedric left the room and his eyes widened. Masters was lying on the floor and the creature was standing over him. Then the double turned on several gas jets inside the lab. "Fuck me. This bastard's nuts."

Mike grabbed his radio off the console and pressed the transmit button.

"Forget the lab, Cedric, we have to evacuate the building right now. Masters is dead anyway. The other guy is turning on the gas jets in the lab."

Mike turned to the master control computer and punched up the building control functions, trying to shut down elevator access to the lab floor. All of the fire control valves were going red one by one as the double manually shut down the sprinkler valves on that floor.

Mike initiated the automated evacuation broadcast over the loudspeakers and began downloading as much information as he could to his laptop. They would need it before the night was over. Cedric came back to the security room as Mike was finishing his download.

"Time to go. Shit!" Cedric yelled as an explosion rocked the building. Several ceiling tiles fell from above their heads and Mike instinctively ducked and stared wide-eyed at Cedric.

"Masters' double shut down the master sprinkler systems for the lab." Mike said. "He used manual control and I can't turn them on from here."

"From the look of things that might not be a bad thing," Cedric said.

Mike touched a smart button on the touchscreen panel he had used to check the fire control earlier, activating the fire alarms. They were tied into the local fire department, but he had a feeling that any attempts to keep what was happening at Genetisource a secret had died with Masters.

Mike grabbed his cell phone and dialed Jake's cell number. After three rings, he answered.

"Boss, Genetisource is on fire," Mike said, relating the events of the evening as he ran for the front doors carrying all of his equipment, Cedric close behind.

§

TEN

Jake was sitting in his office when his cell phone rang. When he answered, Mike Harper began relating the most far-out story he had ever heard.

"Cedric and I just saw Masters get murdered in the lab at Genetisource. The guy that killed him looked exactly like him. I know it sounds like I've been up too long, but it's the truth, I swear. I think we now know who killed Braeden. He turned on the gas jets in the lab and closed all of the fire sprinkler control valves for the lab area. There was just an explosion. Oh, shit, there it goes."

Jake could hear sirens from the fire alarms in the background and then he heard what sounded like an explosion. He yanked the receiver away from his ear.

"Mike, are you still there?"

"Yeah, I'm here, Boss. Cedric and I are both outside the building. We activated the fire alarms and evacuation system, but we aren't sticking around to see that everyone gets out. What else should we do?"

Jake thought for a moment then came to the best solution he could think of. "Get to Master's office, if you can. Grab his laptop and as many records as you can find. Get them out of the building before it burns to the ground. Then both of you get out of there before the NSA shows up. Remember, they aren't far away and were watching the same video you were. Don't worry about what happens later. As soon as you get it, we'll meet up at the usual place. Don't trust your phone, they have them all tapped."

"The building is on fire, boss. You really want me to go

back in there?"

"If you can get in there without burning to death, yes. There may be something on that laptop we can use to bargain our way out of this."

Jake ended the call and thought about what was happening. Picking up the receiver, he dialed his attorney, Martin Boroughs. Boroughs helped him start CSS and had helped him make the business what it was. He coached Jake's Little League baseball team and had been like a second father to Jake. He advised Jake when he considered joining the Navy. Boroughs was an ex-naval lawyer with JAG before retiring and starting his own firm.

When Boroughs picked up the phone, in spite of the hour, Jake explained the situation. "If you don't hear from me by tomorrow morning, begin liquidating everything according to my instructions."

"Sure, Jake," Boroughs said. "Let me know if I you need anything."

Hanging up from Boroughs, Jake went to the safe installed behind the bookcase along the left wall and opened it. Inside he kept five thousand in cash and several documents. The safe also contained the copied security discs from the night of Wilma Braeden's murder. Removing the cash and discs, he closed and locked the safe, replacing the five books hiding it from view.

Placing the disks and cash inside his briefcase, he set the alarm and ran out of the office. On his way out, he grabbed the keys to the new Chevrolet Suburban he had just taken delivery of last week. Armor plated, with bullet-resistant glass, it could resist an attack from just about any kind of weapon.

Taking the stairwell door at a run, Jake took the stairs two at a time, down to the second floor. Every couple of floors, he stopped to listen. He didn't want to run into any bad guys coming up the stairs. He heard nothing and kept going. When he reached the second floor, he hit the release bar and ran out into the hallway. He reached the sky bridge that connected the office building with the parking garage across the street.

Seconds later, he was behind the wheel of the Suburban. It was designed for transporting clients when there was a significant threat to their lives. The diesel engine roared to life when he turned the key. Backing out of the space, he made his way from the exit ramp to the street. He needed to keep moving and make certain he wasn't being followed before meeting with Cedric and Mike.

Driving out of the parking garage, he turned right on to Fourth Avenue and went to the first light. Making another right turn, he drove all the way to the waterfront before making another left.

Snow fell more heavily now and traffic was fairly light as he drove south under the Alaskan Way Viaduct. Constantly watching his rear view mirror, looking for signs of a tail, he shifted the Suburban into four-wheel drive as it slipped in spite of its weight. Turning left on Marion, he drove back up to Third Avenue and made a right turn at the light.

Jake found a parking area that had closed for the evening. Pulling the suburban into an empty spot, he got out into the snow. He slid under the dripping vehicle and found a tracking device attached to the frame.

A bus stopped nearby to pick up one passenger. Taking the magnetized box, he stepped onto the sidewalk and attached it to the back of the bus and ran back to his vehicle.

Leaving the parking lot, Jake drove around for twenty minutes making sure no one had followed him then headed for Pioneer Square, dodging two near-collisions before parking at the curb.

When Jake first hired Cedric and Mike, the three friends had fed an intense caffeine addiction from a coffeehouse near the Square. On a normal day, it was a ten-minute walk from the office and, when the weather was warm, it offered seating outdoors.

He kept the engine running and reviewed his slowly evolving plan. It wouldn't be long before Mike called him. The thought no more than entered his mind before his phone rang.

"The Square," was all he said and hung up. Jake knew they could track his phone, so he turned it off and, opening the back, pulled the battery. Venturing into the cold snow-filled air, he tossed the phone and battery into a nearby dumpster.

After waiting for another ten minutes, he shut off the engine and locked up the vehicle. Walking the short distance to the brick-lined center of Pioneer Square, Jake continued checking for someone tailing him. The "Square" was once the main habitation for the city's homeless, but a few years before, the area had been cleaned up and most of the homeless run out.

The city told the media it was not trying to displace anyone, just beautify the city, but most of the homeless had seen it differently. Streetlights now made the park bright and frequent patrols by beat cops kept away the riff-raff. It was amazing how they missed the occasional drug deals that went down in the park. Jake figured it was as safe a place to meet as any.

Falling snow impeded the light and gave the park an eerie glow. Shadows danced in the dim light, but Jake didn't see anyone hanging around. When the weather was cold, the action moved inside. Jake walked around the perimeter of the park, trying not to look too obvious, but keeping an eye out for his men.

Jake crossed the street and stopped in front of a nearly deserted pub. Most of the time, the place would have been packed, even on a weeknight. The snowy weather had chased most of the typical Seattleites home.

Glancing across the park, he saw two shadows walking toward him. Leaving the sidewalk, he carefully crossed the icy street and angled toward the center of the square. Using the thick snow for cover, Jake advanced on the two men until he could tell who they were. Cedric and Mike were easy to pick out of a crowd, but really easy when they walked together.

"Hi, guys," Jake said as he advanced on the two men.

"Boss, we're in it deep," Mike blurted quietly. "Masters was up to some unsanctioned shit."

Jake walked east amongst the trees and the two men followed. Slush was beginning to pile up on the concrete making the going slippery. Looking around, Jake noticed the park was deserted. They were alone.

"Okay, give me the condensed version," Jake said, slipping a little on the slick concrete.

Mike told him about what they had seen, beginning with hacking the NSA video feed and ending with watching Masters' murder. He explained how the double seemed to evaporate like smoke. However, Masters' car had been missing from the parking lot when they went to the garage.

"Boss, we got as many people out of the building as we could, but some may not have made it. When we left the parking lot, a cleaning crew had arrived and begun dispersing the fire crews. They told the chief to let the building burn. Genetisource was engulfed in flames when we left."

"That's not good," Jake said, whistling through his teeth. "If they're letting it burn, they've decided to implement maximum containment. Tell me more about this double."

"The double looked like a slightly younger version of Masters, Boss. It was scary seeing them together. We couldn't get all of the stuff out and still keep track of what had happened in the lab. After the fire got going, we were busy and the double disappeared," Cedric said, stopping for a moment to stretch his left leg. "We couldn't search the place because of the fire, but Masters' Beemer was not in the parking lot."

"If he's mobile, then we have to figure out what his next move is. Were you able to get the stuff from Masters' office?"

"Boss, I nearly got my ass burned off getting that laptop," Mike said, stopping under a dripping tree. "Master's office is right above the labs on the fifth floor. I had to take the stairs down and the hallway leading to the stairwell from the fourth floor was on fire.

"I have to tell you this whole thing is giving me the creeps," Mike continued. "I don't know what Masters was involved in, but whatever it was, it was ugly. I would like to get a look at the video."

"Cedric, you and Mike and go somewhere to check out the video, but don't spend too much time. At the most, we have a few hours. It won't take the Agency long to get around to closing our part of the loopholes. Once they figure out Masters is dead, they'll want to shut everyone down who had anything to do with Genetisource."

"Boss, I brought something for you," Mike said, tossing Jake a phone. "I stopped off at Wal-Mart and bought several burner phones, so they can't track us. These will be safe for a while. I've already programmed in our numbers."

"Thank God for Wal-Mart," Jake grinned. "Get done as quickly as you can, then call me. Avoid confrontation if you see anyone following you, but if they bring a fight to you, take them out quietly. We need to keep the locals out of this if we can."

Leaving the two men walking toward their vehicle, Jake made his way back across the park to the Suburban.

What the fuck had Masters been doing? He knew from the records and the one new staff member he'd added since Jake began doing security for Genetisource that he was involved in biological gene research. But what kind of evil was he involved in that could bring down this much heat?

§

ELEVEN

Master's creation had found the plane ticket to Cabo. He knew from his benefactor's experiences he could have a lot of fun there. In Cabo, there lived a certain young lady who could certainly ease his tension.

Loose ends. He needed to take care of the researchers quietly. They were the only people who could identify him as the clone. He had to remedy that situation at once. They would either be on his team or out of the picture entirely. Then he was off to Mexico for a well-deserved rest. *He had been working too damn hard lately*, he thought, chuckling.

After sneaking out of the building, he took Masters' BMW, leaving the inferno in his wake. Driving the car had not been a problem. He seemed to instinctively know what to do. Leaving the parking garage, he drove south on the access road, parking for a moment to watch the show. The havoc caused by the fire insured no one saw him exit the building. Genetisource would be rebuilt when he returned, better than ever. After all he was superior to the original Masters in every way. In fact, it was time for him to begin thinking of himself as Jonathan Masters and not his double. He almost felt giddy, watching as the building burned, flames licking the night sky, turning the low-hanging, iron clad clouds bright orange.

The double had just missed running into Mike Harper when he had gone to Masters' office. Mike had run in, grabbed the laptop and retreated from the advancing fire, while the double, unconcerned with such trivialities as fire, had taken his time, exiting the elevator as Mike entered the stairwell. With Masters' corpse reduced to bone fragments, the Agency would have a hard time separating his remains from the debris. This should enable his resurrection upon his return from vacation.

The first thing he had to do was clean up so he went to Masters' nearby love nest. His clothes were filthy and burned so they had to go. The apartment was nearby and offered him shelter while he planned his mission. He didn't have a lot of time, but was confident he could take care of the loose ends quickly and get on the plane by midnight.

Bellevue's south side was home to many contractors for the government as well as several drug companies and engineering firms. Most people thought aerospace when referring to the Northwest, but in many ways, the Seattle area surpassed the Silicone Valley in California in its attraction of high-tech innovation. Much of the eastside area was home to some of the wealthiest people in the world. Masters kept his apartment close to the office as a place to rest during long nights spent in the lab.

Parking on the street, he left the car and walked through the blanket of snow to the apartment. The clone saw no one as he made his way to the front door. It was much colder and windier here than at Genetisource.

In spite of the fact that he was dressed in thin slacks, a short-sleeved shirt and Masters' sport coat and with temperatures hovering just below freezing, he felt like a million bucks. When he climbed the set of stairs leading to the apartment, he was nearly skipping across the slick concrete. Using the keys that he had taken out of Masters' pocket before torching the lab, he opened the door and went inside.

Lights came on as soon as he entered the doorway and he noticed a rectangular panel. Motion sensors installed in every room turned on lights when anyone entered.

In thirty minutes, he had showered, shaved and dressed in Masters' best casual clothes. He selected warmer clothes, only because it was what was expected. The cold weather didn't seem to affect him anymore than the fire had affected him. Topping off the ensemble with a brown leather bomber jacket, he admired his reflection in the mirror and thought he would easily pass for the deceased doctor.

Removing the airline tickets from the sport coat, he grabbed Masters' wallet and slipped both inside the jacket's inside pocket. Once he was finished dressing, the creature realized he was hungry. He went to the kitchen to raid the refrigerator.

Finding a bag of egg rolls and some won-ton soup in the refrigerator, the double tossed them into the microwave and heated them up. When he had cleaned out the refrigerator, he found he was still hungry, but there was nothing edible left in the apartment.

Leaving the apartment, the creature checked the Rolex watch he had found in the bedroom. Jennifer had bought that for Masters. Then the subject double-checked his thought. No, she bought it for me. The other was the imposter. The imposter had thought the watch ostentatious and not his style, but the subject thought it fit him nicely. The diamonds circling the watch's face twinkled even in the low light outside the apartment.

Making his way through the gathering slush, he fired up the BMW and pulled away, making a U-turn in the middle of the deserted street and driving back down the hill. The creature's first stop was Mario Alonga's house in Juniper Hills Estates a few miles south.

Steering the BMW on the on-ramp to Interstate 90, he took the first exit to 405 southbound. One exit down, the double exited the freeway and turned left, driving up the narrow, snow covered two-lane blacktop to Juniper Hill.

§

TWELVE

Jake knew they would need more tools if they were to make it out of this situation alive. Leaving Pioneer Square, he drove east to Fourth Avenue then north, turning right onto Aurora Avenue. Aurora Avenue ran along the west side of Lake Union. Carefully driving through the mounting snow, he made his way north until he crossed the Aurora Bridge. Two streets up, he made a right on to a side street, stopping at a self-storage yard. At a kiosk outside the main gate, he input a code that opened the gate. He entered the yard, driving between the buildings until he found the one he wanted. Parking the Suburban, he zipped up his coat enough to keep out the cold wind, but still allowing him access to his gun.

Removing his keys, he locked the doors to the Suburban then, using the remote, started the engine. A fence and a line of trees separated the storage area from a public golf course, so the area was very private. Entering the warehouse- sized building, he pulled the door closed behind him.

Twisting a knob on the wall, lights came on throughout the building. Jake moved quickly, making his way toward a storage room near the far end of the building. When he reached it, he used another key on his ring to unlock the big Schlage that secured the sliding metal door. Removing the lock, Jake thought he heard a noise other than the hasp grating on the metal latch. Stopping, he held his breath listening for a repeat of the noise, but after a few seconds figured it must have been an echo.

Sliding the door up, he turned on the light within the unit. Inside, several boxes lined one wall and several cabinets with pegboards reaching toward the ceiling, lined the opposite wall. On one of the boards, several MP-5 assault rifles were attached. Jake had used the storage facility because it was hard to store this kind of equipment in a downtown high-rise office building. Taking the assault weapons down, he placed them on one of the boxes and opened one of the drawers in the cabinets.

Jake removed several flak vests from inside, including an extra-large for Cedric and placed them on another box near the door. Closing the drawer, he once again heard movement inside the building. Pulling the Glock from under his jacket, he stepped out of the unit into the hallway. Mirrors hung in the corners of the hallways and he could see someone moving along the west wall. Backing up, he grabbed the duplicate light control for the building and twisted the knob to zero, plunging the building into darkness.

Stepping inside the storage unit, he turned off the lights in there as well. The interior of the building wasn't totally black; a small amount of light was supplied by skylights in the metal ceiling. It was dark enough to allow Jake a little freedom of movement. Grabbing up one of the assault rifles, he opened the drawer of one of the metal cabinets and took three loaded magazines and put them in his jacket pocket. Taking a sound suppressor as well, he screwed it onto the barrel of the gun.

Moving toward the hallway he had just vacated, he glanced in the security mirror and saw two figures moving towards him close to the wall. Waiting until they were close, he moved into view and shot them both before they could react. He stepped to the side, avoiding their bodies as they fell. He advanced silently down the hallway until he could see in the other mirror. Here he was more visible under one of the skylights.

Jake checked the mirror but didn't see anyone, so he moved past the storage room toward the other hallway. Before rounding the corner, he peered into the darkened hallway and saw two more men moving toward him. Stepping around the corner, he fired two bursts from the gun, hitting the lead man in the face, but the other man jumped back, sliding down the wall and scrambling backwards into the cover of an adjacent hallway.

Jake moved quickly to the storage room and stepped inside. He was now 30 feet farther from his attacker and backed against a wall with no chance of escape.

"We have this place surrounded, you know," the man said from the other hallway. Jake heard clicking sounds that sounded like the man was having trouble with his firearm.

Moving into the hallway, Jake advanced toward the man he had shot. He was close enough to the corner that he could hear the second assailant breathing. Leaning down, he found a flash-bang grenade attached to the dead man's vest. Removing it, he didn't pull the pin, but simply tossed it towards the end of the hallway.

"I'm not that stupid," the assailant said, then instantly regretted it when Jake stepped around the corner and placed the muzzle of the assault rifle against his forehead.

"Yeah, but you are stupid enough to talk. Drop your weapon, quietly." Jake had him cold and the man complied. Backing up, Jake grabbed him and shoved him into the hallway.

"How many?" Jake asked, shoving him against the solid metal wall.

"Why should I tell you?"

"Do you like your knees?"

"Do you have any idea of the shit storm headed your way?"

"I've got an idea. Now, how many?" Jake said, stepping back as he aimed the rifle at his knee.

"There were only four of us. We followed you and decided to take you here because we could make it look like you surprised burglars."

"Fine. What was Masters up to?"

"We were just sent to clean up the mess. The details are left to the higher ups"

"So, you don't know anything?"

"No," the man spat.

"Okay," Jake said and fired once, the bullet ripping away part of the assailant's head.

Grabbing a cart from the end of the hallway, he loaded up the bodies and rolled it into one of the open storage units and shut the door using his jacket to avoid leaving fingerprints on the metal surface. If they sent a team for him, it meant the Agency was planning on taking out everyone who might know what was going on at Genetisource. He took a second cart and returned to his storage unit loading up everything he could take in one load.

Rolling the cart full of weapons toward the door, advancing slowly through the darkness, he stopped when he reached the door. Using one hand, he pressed the door open a little, checking both ways, but saw nothing. Stepping out into the falling snow, he checked the Suburban and found it empty as well. He pressed the button on the remote control and the rear cargo door rose. In minutes, he loaded the cargo area from corner to corner with the stuff from the storage. Opening the driver's door, he felt the impact and then heard the bullet hit the resistant glass and ping upward.

"Goddamn, what am I, a shit magnet?" Jake said. Pulling the Glock from inside his coat, he fired twice in the direction of the gunfire as he slid in behind the wheel.

Several rounds slammed into the windshield leaving impressions in the surface, but not penetrating the glass. Pulling the shift lever into reverse, Jake jammed the accelerator to the floor, throwing snow toward the front of the vehicle as he shot backward. Someone jumped from behind the building, directly into the path of the Suburban and Jake heard the thump as the SUV rolled over the person. From the front side of the SUV, three armed men ran toward him, but he was backing away too fast for them to keep pace.

Turning the wheel to the right when he reached the corner, he hit the brakes and spun the front of the car to the left. Shifting into drive, he glued the accelerator to the floor and headed for the exit. Knowing the vehicle wouldn't survive a collision with the gate, he knew he would have stop to input the code.

Near the end of the last building, someone stepped into the vehicle's path. Jake hit the brakes, sliding to a stop. The man raised his rifle and Jake slammed the accelerator down. The first round careened off the bumper, the second was stopped by the hood as the big SUV slammed into the assailant, pinning his body against the gate.

"Four my ass," he said. "Does anyone tell the truth anymore?"

Rolling down the window, Jake punched in his code to open the gate. Several rounds smacked into the side of the Suburban and he saw figures running toward him through the snow as he waited for the gate to open. When he could get the Suburban through the opening, he sped into the night.

Heading south on Aurora, he looked behind him, but no one followed. With that kind of attack, he knew they were branded. They would be considered domestic terrorists by now with a shoot-on-sight order. He had to prepare Mike and Cedric for what was about to land on them.

§

THIRTEEN

As snow piled up from the late winter storm in the lesser-traveled areas of Seattle, the streets had begun to freeze over. Icicles hung from the bows of Douglas firs as well as the overhead power lines. By early morning, several thousand residents would not have power because of the ice. A slight breeze filtered through the trees, causing ice to fall from the branches into the street.

Through the falling snowflakes, a dark red BMW coupe made its way through the rapidly icing streets. The vehicle moved slowly, as if its driver was afraid of driving on the icy street or looking for an address. Because of the weather, few people were on the streets of north Seattle at this time of night, so the car seemed out of place.

Masters' double slowed to a stop, looking at the numbers on the front of the small house. The street dead-ended not far from where he sat, so this had to be the place. Easing the car to the curb, the creature turned off the engine. He had a mission to complete and this was the second of four stops.

He had already spoken to Mario Alonga, but the doctor had been most uncooperative. The double, acting as Masters, had fired him, but when Alonga threatened to expose the subject to the government, he decided on a more permanent solution. Sadly, Alonga was now a statistic. He tied the researcher to a chair to make it look like someone had interrogated him before killing him.

The Masters' double was covered in blood when he finished with Alonga, so he spent a little extra time cleaning up before leaving the researcher's home. The creature needed to make sure he didn't leave DNA behind this time. He had to pay more attention to detail if he was to finish his mission.

Alonga had shot at him with a handgun, but missed. Masters' double had brought the gun along, for use in the next three visits. He would dump the gun when he was finished.

He left the BMW at the curb and walked down the sidewalk to Marie Jenkins' home. The house was in dire need of repairs, including the identification numbers because the creature had passed it three times before locating the address. The double would give her time off to make the repairs if she made it through their meeting.

He climbed the stairs to the front door. Snow and ice made traction a problem, but by balancing just right, the creature was able to compensate for the slippery surface. Most of the homes in this area averaged around eighty years old, with none of the modern conveniences found in newer homes. The front yard was adorned with an ancient maple tree on one side and younger, but larger firs lined the other. Obviously she enjoyed lots of shade and privacy.

Masters' double rang the doorbell. He expected to wake the young scientist, but could see light glowing behind the curtains covering the front windows. Moments passed, then two deadbolt locks snapped open and the door swung inside.

"Dr. Masters, I thought you might be coming around, so I waited up," she said motioning him inside. "Please come in out of the cold."

Marie was dressed in a simple terry cloth robe and fuzzy slippers. The slippers were tattered around the toes and the robe faded and somewhat threadbare. Maybe Masters didn't pay her enough.

"Why were you expecting me?" the double asked and then saw the television displaying video from the scene at Genetisource. "Oh you've heard about the fire." he said, wiping the snow from his shoes and crossing the threshold. Marie closed the door behind him and walked into the living room.

"I was watching television when they broke in with the news about the fire. Do you have any idea what happened?"

"As a matter of fact I do," the double searched for any sign of disbelief in her face before he continued. This was the point where the creature had slipped up with Alonga. He didn't want it to happen here. "The subject tried to escape. It nearly made it, but I fought it off. I locked it in the lab, but the creature started the fire using the gas burners. It was able to turn off the master fire control inside the lab. I barely escaped before the whole place blew."

Marie appeared to think about what Masters' double said for a moment and then a puzzled look crossed her face. It was something that the double had seen in Mario's face as well. Even the refined version of the story seemed deficient.

"Would you like a cup of coffee, Doctor Masters? It's freshly made."

"No, thank you, my dear," he said gripping the pistol in its coat pocket.

"I had a feeling I was going to be up for a while, so I made some. I think I'll go pour a cup for myself." Marie left Masters' double standing in the small living room and walked down a hallway to the kitchen.

The double noted the simplicity of the small bungalow. The living room was furnished with a worn sofa and chair; a few photographs of what he assumed were members of Marie's family adorned the walls. A newer, flat screen television hung from a metal bracket bolted to the wall. The hardwood floor was immaculate and a handmade Persian rug covered the floor beneath a small, oval shaped wooden table. He left the living room and walked into the kitchen. He found the back door ajar and Marie Jenkins gone.

The double ran through the kitchen toward the back door. The phone was hanging off the hook and he could hear the operator on the other end asking who was on the line. The creature jerked the receiver out of the phone as he passed it.

Marie made her way carefully down the back stairs, her slippers offering her very little traction on the slippery surface. She fell, screaming as she slid to the bottom on her side. She was trying to get to her feet when he reached her.

The double grabbed her by the throat and hoisted her off the ground. She beat at his arms, but couldn't break the hold. Dragging her up the stairs, he tossed her through the doorway, her body landing in a heap against the refrigerator. Masters' double didn't have to worry about her screaming because she could only squeak after the damage he had done to her throat. Gaining her balance, she scurried along the floor toward the front of the house heading for the front door. He reached her before she managed to get halfway down the hallway and stepped in the middle of her back. Something crunched and she stopped struggling.

"You see, I can't have any naysayers on my team who don't agree with my philosophy. Now you have always been very efficient, Marie, one of the best assisting researchers I've ever known, but this development is very disappointing."

Marie struggled to move her arms and push her broken body away from him, but she couldn't get leverage. She knew she was dying at the hands of the subject, but it was too late.

"Marie, I haven't much time. I must go and see our other colleagues before the night is out, so I must be leaving. But you needn't worry; I won't leave you in this predicament."

He turned her over so he could look her in the eyes. Fear registered deep within those beautiful orbs and the creature could almost feel it. She trembled at the sight of him standing over her, making the double feel very powerful. He almost felt sorry for her. She was such a beauty; he never meant to end her life in this manner. The subject smiled at her and then placed one hand on her chin and one on the back of her head and turned it slowly until the bones in her neck gave way. He continued applying pressure until her head was nearly turned backward, facing the floor. The creature dropped her head to the hardwood floor with a thump.

Returning to the BMW, he sat for a moment in the cold. Jenkins' scream had alerted the neighbors and someone called the authorities. He heard sirens approaching, so he had to leave before the police arrived. It was important to finish this soon, before they were hunted him down. The subject would not be able to take time to talk to the others; he would have to just dispense with them. It was time for new blood. He started the engine and pulled the BMW away from the curb and out into the snow covered street. At the bottom of the short hill, he turned right and sped up, the sanded road giving the BMW better traction.

The next stop was Jack Monroe. He lived in Magnolia and would probably be asleep at this hour, but after all, as Masters, he'd called him many times in the middle of the night, so a visit wouldn't be out of the ordinary. Somewhere in the back of his mind, the double realized that he had never visited his employees in their homes, not the old him or the new him.

"Tonight is a night for firsts," he said aloud chuckling at his wit.

§

FOURTEEN

While Masters' clone made his way to Magnolia, Jake drove to Gasworks Park. The park wasn't far enough away from the scene at the storage unit, but he figured this was the last place they would expect him to go. He didn't intend to stay long, so it was as good a place as any. After escaping the assault at the storage facility, he phoned Cedric and told him to meet him at the park.

Parking on the street, Jake changed the magazine in his Glock, then took a box of cartridges out of the glove compartment and reloaded the empty one. With the weapons he took from the storage facility, he and the other two ex-SEALs could hold off any assault team the government sent for them. Pulling on a pair of fleece-lined gloves, he went out into the cold and walked into the park.

Gasworks Park is located on the north end of Lake Union. In warmer weather, joggers ran and mothers with young children walked along the fir-lined trail. Students from several nearby Universities hung out here to smoke pot and hide from their instructors for a few hours. A few years back, a series of attacks had nearly closed the park, but the cops increased their presence and the attacks stopped. The police caught the rapist, eventually, but the patrols continued.

The park was closed at this time of the night. A number of exhibits were open to the public during the day, but at night, they closed the park in an effort to keep vandalism under control. He watched vigilantly for park patrols, but saw no one.

Walking slowly along the path, Jake stopped at one of the exhibits and looked around. Continuing down the pathway, he heard someone clear his throat behind him. Whirling, he pulled the Glock from under his coat, ready to shoot his attacker. Mike Harper and Cedric Jaynes were standing near the exhibit, watching him with smiles on their faces.

"Keyed up a little tight, aren't we, Boss?" Mike said as he stepped from the shadows.

"You're fired," he said glaring at both of them. "You're both fucking fired."

"Oh, now, don't get pissed. We come bearing gifts and information," Cedric said coming out of the shadows, joining Mike and Jake on the path.

Jake had nearly fired on them, but luckily he recognized them before squeezing the trigger. After what happened at his office, he had a right to be keyed up.

"You wouldn't say that if you knew what I was guilty of."

Concerned looks crossed both of their faces and Mike stepped forward.

"What happened?"

"I went to my storage unit to retrieve some toys and got hit by an entire fire team. I barely made it out."

Cedric whistled through his teeth. "Damn, this means they're hunting all of us."

"No kidding. What did you find on Masters' computer?"

"Nothing yet," Mike said rolling his eyes. "Bastard secured everything, but I'll get it. Each folder has a different password. It's going to take a while to crack this and time is something we really don't have right now."

Jake nodded his head. Masters had been obsessed with security, so it wasn't surprising he would have found a way to lock down everything relating to his work on the laptop.

"Boroughs has assumed control of CSS. When the government comes looking for us, he'll tell them he was the silent partner and show them paperwork backing it up. He'll tell them he has no idea where we've gone."

"One other thing," Mike said as Jake finished. "We were listening to the scanner earlier. Apparently someone is taking out the docs from Genetisource. Jenkins made a 911 call and they found her dead. No details, but it wasn't pretty by the sound of the stuff coming over the radio. We called Monroe and no one answered. I hope he's just out on the town."

Jake thought about this development. Was the NSA taking out the researchers or was it Masters' double from the lab? If the latter, who would he go after next?

"Cedric, call and warn the other researchers from Genetisource. Tell them Masters' experiment has escaped and is coming for them. That should give them all the information they need. If this is the double doing this then he'll probably go for Masters' family when he is finished with the docs."

Cedric moved away from them so he could have some privacy. Mike stared into the darkness for a moment, his arms crossed over his chest. "My family is also in danger, aren't they, Boss?"

Jake nodded his head. "Call your wife and have her pack a bag. We'll pick her up on our way out of town. We have to get some place safe, somewhere away from here. I own a cabin near Las Vegas, but that's a long way to go on short notice."

Jake handed Mike a thousand in cash from the money he had taken from his safe. "If we have to, we'll split up and you can get them out of here. Cedric's family is in Connecticut, so they are safe for now."

Cedric came running across the parking lot toward them, shaking his head. It always amazed Jake at how easily the big man moved.

"Nobody answered, Boss. He may have gotten to them or they figured out what happened and ran for the hills. I tossed the burn phone after I made the last call, just in case our friends were tapped into their phones."

Jake nodded grimly. "Did you try calling Masters' wife?" He had a wife and daughter as I remember it. He might head there next."

Cedric shook his head. All three men ran toward the street where the Suburban was parked at the curb. A breeze rose, moaning through the Douglas firs, dislodging snow from the branches and raining it down on their heads. Jake realized he needed to make a decision now.

"Cedric, drive to Las Vegas. Mike and I will go and get Masters' wife and kid and get them to a safe place. We'll contact you as soon as we can. When you get there, call my caretaker. His name is Ben and he'll set you up at the cabin. Get the place ready for company," Jake said, writing the address of the cabin on a piece of paper. "When you get to Portland, call Gunther and have him get you a different vehicle and some cash from the emergency account."

Paul Gunther ran the Portland offices of CSS. He was an able person, but was not a part of this situation and Jake wanted to keep it that way. Cedric turned and left Mike and Jake standing by the SUV. Snow was collecting on the cooling windshield of the vehicle and beginning to freeze.

Backing out of the space, Jake turned north and made his way to the interstate. Mike took a laptop with a Wi-Fi adapter out of his bag and turned the power on. Similar to the burn phones, it was untraceable.

"Find Masters' home address."

§

81

FIFTEEN

Genetisource no longer burned, but smoke hung heavy in the frigid air as it smoldered. The inversion layer hanging over the Puget Sound kept the smoke close to the surface and it was beginning to affect those trying to sift through the ashes. Chemicals had fueled the fire which quickly engulfed the entire building. There wasn't a whole lot left other than a twisted steel superstructure and the now blackened stone façade on the first floor. The stench left behind by the burning building made James Kelly's eyes tear up and his lungs feel as if they were going to burst. The snowstorm had finally begun to lift, but the soot from the fire turned the falling snowflakes from white to grey.

Kelly surveyed the scene around him, shaking his head. What a fucking mess this turned out to be. He was the lone agent on the scene. He sent his support team to debrief the researchers from Genetisource and inform them of their unemployment. There was no way to keep the fire under wraps, but he still felt they had a chance to keep Genetisource's research a secret.

News vans from local stations lined the perimeter of the parking lot and he ordered his agents to keep them back. When Kelly arrived, the fire had been burning brightly. He immediately called in a tech team and had them turn off the gas supply, eliminating some of the fuel Fire suppression teams applied retardant chemicals to put out the still burning debris within the collapsed structure.

The local reporters spouted theories about the cause of the fire and how many victims had perished. Containing the story would be a nightmare. Kelly's plan was to lay the blame at the feet of Masters himself. They assumed the doctor had perished in the fire. Kelly hoped he had. A dead doctor was easier to blame than a live one.

Once the fire was out, it would take several hours before they could enter the remains. Kelly would have to deal with the EPA as well when they arrived. And he was certain they would.

Kelly sat on the wet hood of the car, eyeing the local firemen who watched as his own fire crew poured water on the flames. The fire chief had been pissed when Kelly sent them away, but he had invoked Homeland Security and the chief immediately backed off. Kelly loved the Patriot Act. It made cops and other local agencies listen without fail. Kelly smiled at the thought of how much power he wielded under the guise of national security.

Kelly lit a cigarette and shivered, trying to keep warm. He was dressed in a wool overcoat with leather gloves, but the cold still got to him. Living in Florida for the past few years had softened him. In his younger years, he had spent a lot of time in more frigid climates, but now he avoided those assignments religiously.

Just yesterday morning, Kelly had been on his first vacation in over four years, languishing on a beach in Miami, when he received an alert to return to Washington D.C. Two hours after landing at Dulles, he was boarding a Gulfstream Jet bound for Seattle. His superiors suspected Masters wasn't telling them everything about his progress and had been watching his activities for the past few months. They were becoming increasingly suspicious that their interests were not being served. Kelly's mission had been to perform a surprise security inspection on Genetisource later today.

He reviewed the Genetisource file while on the turbulent five-hour long flight. His plane finally touched down in Seattle. Upon his arrival, Kelly was notified of the fire. Now he was performing the mop-up action. If Masters or anyone else had been inside the building when it burned, there would be nothing but bone fragments left of them. The fire had produced enough heat to twist steel. They would search for Masters, presuming he wasn't killed in the fire, because they needed answers. If they couldn't find Masters, he hoped the researchers could provide the information he wanted. Kelly had a gut feeling the doctor was still around somewhere, and he had more than cursory involvement in the fire that destroyed his own building.

Kelly also wondered what Jake Storm's involvement was. Kelly had known Storm for years. They had a history. Kelly knew Storm's company provided security for Genetisource, but Storm was nothing if not meticulous. Kelly was certain Storm had files on every Genetisource employee, including Masters. Storm would also know he and his employees were in trouble, which meant they were on the run.

Kelly had always been jealous of Storm, even though he wouldn't have admitted it to anyone but himself. Storm had left the CIA and founded a successful security agency without the help of anyone in the government. Kelly didn't like anyone who was allowed to leave the fold so easily; it just didn't fit in with his image of how things should be.

"Agent Kelly." Kelly saw Harley Williams and Specialist Charadan Chelnik approaching from outside the yellow tape. Williams was a good agent who followed orders well; Chelnik was an espionage expert who worked as a consultant for the Central Intelligence Agency. He was on loan to them and had ridden in the jet with Kelly. Kelly had a feeling they were not bringing him good news.

"Where are my doctors, Gentlemen?"

"Well, it appears someone has killed at least two. We have Garrett and Hammond checking on the other two."

"What the fuck do you mean two are dead? Who killed them?"

"Do we know?" Williams said sarcastically. "We just came from Alonga's house. It isn't far from here and we found him in the kitchen, tied to a chair. If I didn't know better, I would say he died during enhanced interrogation. But this was too sloppy. Like someone trying to mimic something they had seen in a movie. Hammond found local law enforcement crawling all over Marie Jenkins' house. They used national security to get inside and found out someone had tried to unscrew her head like a bottle top." The disgust registered in Williams' face as he finished his report. He blew into his bare hands then glared at Kelly, as if he was to blame for bringing him out on a night like this.

"This is just fucking terrific. Have we found Masters yet?"

"We rang his house and spoke to his wife, but she said she hadn't seen him in weeks. We have a team checking outgoing flights and we're checking local hospitals, but if he was in this," Williams said, waving his hand at the remains of Genetisource, "He didn't make it out."

"You're so sure? I'm beginning to think he set this fire as a diversion."

Kelly walked away. Reporters screamed questions at him over the noise of the equipment and his agents struggled to hold them back. This wasn't going to be his night, and he doubted things would improve by morning.

Kelly wished he were still lying on a Florida beach instead of freezing his ass off in this shithole. Maybe his ex-wife had been right; his addiction to duty often went against his best interests.

Walking toward the burned out hull of the building, he stared at embers as they traced their way into the sky. Between the noise of the equipment and the growing wind, he almost failed to hear Williams yelling his name. When he finally heard the agent calling, he turned away from the flames, but his vision was now clouded with dark spots from the firelight.

"The other team found Masters at Chu's house. He fired at them when they tried to stop him. He got away, but it sounds like a massacre took place."

§

SIXTEEN

Jake and Mike Harper drove silently through the gradually diminishing snowfall. As the night drifted into the early morning hours, the air temperature had gotten colder, turning already snow-slickened streets into ice rinks. Mike navigated from the passenger seat while Jake tried to avoid the few morons out driving the icy streets. Nearly four inches of snow had fallen, not a lot, but enough to make traffic chaotic and travel slow. Jake was more concerned about the macabre events of the evening and what came next.

"Take the first exit on the other side of the bridge and go south."

Jake was approaching the east end of the Evergreen Point floating bridge. He saw the sign marking the exit and left the expressway. At the stop sign, the Suburban slid to a stop before he applied the accelerator and turned southbound. The snow was deeper on the roadway here. There were few travelers and the plows hadn't made it here yet.

There were spooks from agencies both named and unnamed coming at this situation from all sides. Jake had been one of them and knew they would want to contain the situation with Genetisource. They would rely on the news cycle to move on quickly to other things. Propaganda was an illusionist's game the Agency played with precision. It meant terminating anyone involved with what Masters was doing, but what was wrong with a few assassinations for the security of the good 'ole USA?

"My gut tells me that if we don't protect Masters' wife and kid, that either Masters or a cleaner team will get to them and make them and there won't be any reason to protect them. They'll be dead or sent somewhere that no one will ever see them again."

"You have to remember, Boss," Mike said with a degree of sadness in his voice. "We all know what they're capable of when they want to keep something secret. The way they took over the Genetisource scene tonight tells me they are serious, but what do we really know? Should we take it upon ourselves to save the world?"

"I don't know about you," Jake said glancing from the road to look at Mike briefly before returning his attention to the snow-covered two-lane, "but whatever Masters was doing scares the fuck out of me. I've worked with guys like him and I know that whatever we think was happening is only a small slice of the actual story. If DARPA and the Defense Department sanctioned it, then they're responsible for the outcome. It's their mess and they intend to clean it up. No one can get in their way and survive. Trust me, we have to do this."

"So you think we'll have to expose this to the press at some point?"

Jake thought about this, but had no answer. "I think we need to find out what Masters was up to and then make the decision. We may need to use it as a bargaining chip for our lives."

Mike shut the laptop and returned it to his backpack. "Coming up on your right is a driveway. Pull in there."

Jake slowed and turned into the driveway. The heavy vehicle slipped once but the four-wheel-drive stabilized it. He drove down a thirty yard entry road and his lights when he approached a large double iron gate. Surrounded by trees they could see nothing of a house further on. The driveway veered to the left fifty feet beyond the gate. He rolled down his window and punched the call button on a panel near the gate. A few moments passed then someone answered.

"Can I help you?" The voice was female, but whoever it was sounded impatient.

"Hello. My name is Jake Storm. I run security for Genetisource. There's been a problem there."

There was a pause at the other end; then a bright light came on in the panel. "Place your identification in the light."

Jake placed his license and one of his business cards in front of what was obviously a camera mounted in the panel. After a moment there was a buzz from the panel and the gate began to open.

"Proceed up the driveway to the house," the voice said.

Jake rolled up the window and waited for the gate to open. When it had opened enough, he drove through. Within two hundred yards, they entered a clearing containing a large house. Floodlights grasped the perimeter in a two-hundred-foot radius so anyone entering would be easily seen. Stopping at the apex of the circular driveway, he turned the engine off.

Masters had quite a home. The design was a mixture of modern architecture and classic northwest style. The outside of the house was covered in stucco, but the roof was peaked and covered in cedar shakes. Large Douglas Firs bookended the home and small patches of grass were visible in spite of the snow. It appeared from the lack of snow on the driveway, that it was heated from underneath. The house was a stark contrast to the surrounding flora and Jake thought it looked garish. Mike chuckled as he took it in.

"Masters wasn't much on sticking to one style, was he?" Mike said as Jake stopped near the front door. "He might as well stick flamingos in the front yard."

Leaving the car, they walked up a set of stone steps into a small courtyard, then up to the front door. Jake noticed there wasn't a doorbell, so he waited. When the woman opened the door, she wasn't what Jake expected.

"It's late, Gentlemen. What brings you here?" She was direct, and Jake noticed she was dressed like she was about to leave.

"There was an incident at Genetisource this evening. Ma'am, were you going somewhere?"

"No," she answered curtly. "Whatever happened at Genetisource is my husband's problem."

"Well see, that's the problem. We think you and your daughter may be in danger and we can't find your husband. May we please come in and explain?"

Jennifer Masters glared at him for a moment then backed inside, motioning them to follow. Once inside, she closed the door quickly and turned, leading them into a small receiving room to the right of the foyer. The inside of the house was elegant and altogether different from the outside. A huge staircase descended from the second floor, winding down to the marble-tiled floor of the entryway. Jake was impressed with the decor and had a feeling that Jonathan Masters hadn't been involved.

Jennifer Masters was beautiful. Tall, with blonde hair and blue eyes, but not cold like her husband's. Her eyes were deep and radiant, giving a hint of intelligence and warmth even when she was clearly upset. Motioning them to a sofa, she sat down across from them in an overstuffed leather chair. Jake noticed her shoes were wet, yet she hadn't stepped out onto the porch when she greeted them. Dressed in black pants, a dark blouse and a leather jacket similar to his, Jake still thought she looked ready to leave.

"What I have to say is going to come as a shock," Jake began, but she waved her hand as if to say nothing could shock her about her husband. "There was a fire at Genetisource tonight. We think your husband was killed inside."

"Really. Well, I think you must be mistaken. The son-of-a-bitch just called fifteen minutes ago and said he was coming home."

Jake and Mike looked at each other, and as if Jake had given him a silent command, Mike stood and went back into the foyer. Things were happening faster than Jake had thought they would.

"Ma'am, the person who called you tonight wasn't your husband. I really cannot prove this right now, but you're in grave danger. We need to get you and your daughter to safety."

"Look, I don't give a damn either way because I intend to get the hell out of here before he shows up. Now if you'll excuse me." She stood and turned toward the front door.

"You don't get it, Mrs. Masters. The person who called you tonight, he looks like your husband, sounds like him, but isn't him. My associate watched this man kill your husband tonight in the lab. He's responsible for at least two more deaths that we know of. We're pretty sure he means you harm. We can help you, but you have to work with us."

Jake heard an engine outside and Mike came running into the room. "He's here, Jake."

Jennifer Masters stared at Jake for a moment then ran for the stairs.

"Get your daughter. We'll leave together."

"I don't think so. I don't know you. Why should I trust you?"

"Look, we can argue about it later. If you want to leave once we get out of this, then you can leave. For now, you have to trust us." Jake said this while removing two pistols from under his coat. She saw the guns and ran up the stairs.

"Jake, he went around back."

"The garage is back there," Jennifer yelled as she climbed the stairs two at a time.

Mike was looking in every door as the proceeded down a hallway to the left of the staircase. He finally found one with stairs leading down. As he opened it, he heard the engine shut off and a door open.

Mike flanked the opening on the other side.

"Go help her get the kid downstairs and ready to run," Mike said, pulling the slide back to chamber a round. "I'll watch our backs."

Jake turned and ran back toward the foyer. Running down the hallway into the foyer, he saw Jennifer Masters dragging a suitcase in one hand and leading her daughter with the other. Jake grabbed the suitcase on the run and ushered them outside, into the waiting Suburban. Using the remote, he opened the rear of the vehicle, tossed the suitcase inside then used the remote start button to fire up the engine.

"Get in. We'll be back in a minute." Jake saw the fear in her eyes as she climbed into the back seat and began securing her daughter.

"Whatever you hear or see, don't go back inside the house," Jake said running for the front door.

Jake ran into the house and heard gunfire erupt from the hallway. He found Mike aiming his MP-5 down the hallway firing in neat bursts, backing toward the foyer. The assault weapon clicked empty as Jake came up behind Mike. There was no doubt that this was the double they saw kill Masters. The double's weapon clicked empty as sank to his knees. As Mike moved toward the creature, he abruptly rolled to his feet, grabbed Mike by the throat and shook him violently.

"Kill him, Jake," Mike strangled out the words as Jake approached.

"Drop him, Motherfucker. Now!" Jake screamed as he tried to get a clear shot at the clone. Mike was in his line of fire, trying to pry away the hands gripping his throat.

"If you insist," Master's double said, smiling past Mike's head at Jake.

Jake heard a loud snap as Masters twisted Mike's head to the side, breaking his neck. Jake knew he would never forget that sound as long as he lived. The creature threw Mike's now lifeless corpse away as if it were a rag doll. Jake fired the Glock repeatedly until it was empty. The impact from the slugs knocked Masters' double backwards, sending him crashing down the staircase into the garage. Jake tucked the Glock into his waistband and removed the forty-five from his shoulder holster, backing toward the front door.

Jake stared in disbelief as the double came out of the stairwell, stepped over Mike's corpse and ran toward the front of the house. What the fuck was he wearing for armor? Jake emptied the Browning into him then ran for the Suburban.

Yanking open the Suburban's driver's side door, Jake climbed in. Turning the key, he started the engine and put the vehicle in gear, squealing the tires down the driveway. As they made the trees at the east end of the property, he saw the creature standing on the porch. The front of his shirt was soaked with blood, confirming that Jake's bullets had hit the mark, but amazingly he was still walking as if he hadn't been injured. Jake knew Masters double had taken nine slugs from Mike's gun and nine from the Glock, plus seven from the forty-five and countless rounds from the MP-5. Even body armor didn't give that much protection. Yet, there he stood, watching the fleeing SUV. If he had not seen it with his own eyes, he wouldn't have believed it.

Jake remembered the gate at the last minute, but Masters' wife pointed a remote control from the back seat and the gate swung open. Turning left, without slowing down, the tires protested, but he held control of the heavy vehicle as it entered the roadway.

"Mommy, what's happening? Where's the other man?"

Jake looked at the woman in the rear view mirror and shook his head. She seemed to sense what he was saying and closed her eyes. "Honey, he couldn't come with us."

"Why not?"

"Shush, honey. Let this man drive. We'll talk about it later."

Holding the wheel with one hand, he ejected the empty magazine from the Glock and replaced it with a full one, then did the same for the Browning, chambering rounds in both. His eyes went to the rearview mirror and looked at the woman riding in the back seat. Once again he was struck with awe at how truly beautiful she was. What the hell had Masters been thinking when he chose his work over this woman. The man had obviously been a fool.

"We have to find a safe place to stay the night."

Jennifer Masters eyed him curiously in the mirror as he spoke to her. Jake could discern nothing from her featureless expression. She seemed in shock, but he was betting that her mind was looking for a way out. Her daughter stared out the window, watching tiny flakes of snow whipping past.

Jake was wired because he had no idea why the twenty-five bullets didn't put Masters down. After nine bullets pierced his body, Masters had possessed the strength to pick Mike off the floor and snap his neck like a toothpick. How was that possible? What gave this thing the ability to withstand that many shots and still live?

§

SEVENTEEN

The creature watched Masters' wife and child drive away with the man in the black SUV. The man would suffer for taking his wife and child, but revenge would have to wait. Intense heat grew within him spreading quickly throughout his body. His body was healing faster than ever, but pain racked every breath. The bullets in the creature's chest and abdomen had penetrated several important organs. He could feel the vessels healing as he stood watching the driveway. While the feeling was not unpleasant, he was aware of the damage the bullets had done. Blood dripped from twenty wounds onto the snow-covered porch. Pain wracked his body with every breath. One of the bullets punched through his breastbone, burying itself and several bone fragments deep in his right lung. He coughed raggedly, spitting blood into the snow. Coughing again, he spewed two of the forty-five caliber slugs on to the walkway.

Heat in his muscles made him feel like he was going to burst into flames. If he didn't get nourishment soon, his body would begin to feed on itself. He needed the fuel to accelerate the healing process.

Leaving the front walkway, he ran back inside the house, kicking the front door closed. Making his way to the kitchen, he stepped over Mike's body, kicking it as he went. Opening the refrigerator, he found it stocked with leftovers. Emptying the contents, he set the containers on the granite countertop. Tearing into the items without regard to their packaging, he swallowed without chewing, casually tossing the empty containers on to the marble tiled floor.

After he finished with the cooked items, he moved to several uncooked cuts of beef, eating them raw. Plastic meat containers littered the floor as he lost himself in the tender morsels of beef and chicken. When he had consumed all of the contents of the refrigerator, he emptied the freezer, filling the sink with hot water and tossing the frozen items in to thaw. Moving on to the cabinets, he emptied them of their contents, as well, until he consumed every piece of food he could find. When the frozen items had thawed enough to chew, he crunched the half-thawed meat as it were ice cubes.

Looking around at the trash littered kitchen, he chuckled at the mess of empty food containers and boxes of cookies he'd left. The kitchen now looked as if a tornado had somehow spawned within the kitchen and ripped everything from the shelves, leaving nothing but waste in his wake. Leaving the disaster area, he went to the front of the house, stepping over Mike's body again and looked out the front window. He would get his family back, one way or another.

Turning from the picture window, he walked across the foyer. He picked up Mike's corpse and tossed it down the stairs into the garage. Climbing the stairs two at a time, he went upstairs to the bedroom he shared with Jennifer.

Inside the closet, he found more clothes that fit him. Stripping, he took a quick shower, washing the blood from his body. He dressed quickly. He could already feel the heat building within him again. He would need to get more food on his way to the airport.

Gathering up his blood-soaked clothes, he tossed them into a garment bag he found in the closet. Blood was everywhere, having dripped from him as he walked through the house. He would come up with a suitable excuse later. Grabbing the garment bag, he left the bedroom and went to the garage.

Loading Mike's corpse into the trunk, he tossed the bag filled with bloody clothes in with him and slammed the trunk lid.

The double checked his watch. He would need to hurry to make his flight to Mexico. Backing out of the garage, he drove around the house. It had stopped snowing, but globs of wet snow fell from tree branches hitting the Beemer's windshield in wet plops. Turning south on Lake Washington Boulevard, he headed for the airport. Within a few minutes he saw a strip mall containing an all-night grocery store and a McDonalds.

He drove through the parking lot, continuing around to the rear of the store, searching for a place to dump the body locked in the trunk of the car. He found what he was looking for near the loading dock. Stopping near a green trash dumpster, he left the car running and looked around to make sure no one was watching. He saw no one. Masters double opened the trunk, pulled Mike's body out and, using his free hand, he opened the lid on the dumpster and tossed it inside. Grabbing the garment bag, he tossed it in quickly, and closed the lid.

He got back into the BMW and glanced at the McDonald's. Frustrated and in pain, he drove to the drive-thru and eyed the menu.

"Give me ten Big Macs, six extra-large orders of fries and three chocolate shakes, please." He was afraid his gravelly voice was too loud, but it may have been the constant drumming in his head and ears that made it sound too loud.

"Will that be all, Sir?" The voice from the speaker sounded normal, easing his worry. "Please pull forward."

Masters eased the vehicle forward to the pick-up window and waited for his order. He needed nourishment so badly he was dizzy. He waited impatiently for his order. After five minutes, the clerk came to the window with four large bags of food and the shakes in a cardboard drink carrier. Masters paid him and took the food.

Screeching through the drive-thru, the BMW exited, parking across the lot. Tearing open one of the hamburger containers, he stuffed the contents into his mouth, consuming it in three large bites. After swallowing three of the burgers, he drove out of the parking lot on to the street.

While he ate, the double couldn't think about anything but feeding the fire that burned within his torn body. He could feel his broken ribs, an injury suffered when the bullets passed through his chest, knitting under his skin. He knew that his body healed according to a schedule, first the deep tissue and internal organs would knit and expel the shrapnel from the bullets, then his protective skeleton and finally the external wounds would close up, leaving the excreted lead lying on the outside of his body. Finishing the first bag of food, he pulled the plastic lid off one of the shakes and drank it in three long swallows.

By the time he reached the expressway, ironically not far from Genetisource, he had finished all the food and tossed the empty cartons and bags into the back seat. He set a more leisurely pace and concentrated on his driving. The last thing he needed right now was to be pulled over by an over-zealous cop looking to bust him.

Seeing the lights of an intersection ahead, he turned right and into the onramp to the 405 expressway. Picking his speed up a little, he headed south toward the Seattle-Tacoma Airport, knowing he would have to hurry to get there in time for his flight.

§

EIGHTEEN

After leaving Masters' estate, Jake drove in silence back across the floating bridge to Seattle. With the murder of Mike Harper still on his mind, he just couldn't believe his friend was dead. Mike's death was his fault. Mike wanted to go with Cedric, but he died protecting Jake and Masters' wife and kid.

He would call Boroughs in the morning and have him notify Mike's wife about her husband's death. He wanted to do it, but he couldn't risk getting caught. It sickened him that he was already thinking like a fugitive. He had left Mike in the house with that monster. It violated everything he was taught as a SEAL. Turning southbound on the interstate he headed toward Tacoma.

The city of Tacoma lies at the south end of the Puget Sound, thirty miles south of Seattle. While not considered a suburb, it is another in a series of cities that runs together on the east and south side of Puget Sound.

As he passed Safeco Field, the cell phone on the passenger seat rang. Jake picked up the phone and pressed the answer button. Cedric began talking, but Jake interrupted before Cedric could get far.

"Mike's dead, Cedric," Jake said quietly.

"WHAT?"

"Mike's dead. The creature got him and it was over in a second. Mike emptied his gun into him, but it grabbed him and broke his neck."

"Are you sure he was dead?" Cedric asked, not believing what Jake was saying. He and Mike had been close friends for so long, it would take Cedric a while to get used to the idea.

Jake explained what happened at Masters' home. After a generous amount of cursing on Cedric's part because Jake had to leave Mike's body behind, Jake tried in vain to calm his friend. SEALs never leave anyone on the battlefield;

"Jake, if I get the chance to whack this piece of shit, I'll cut him to pieces."

"I know, Cedric. Look, we need to continue with our original plan. Head to Nevada and find Ben. He'll get you to the cabin. I have a few things I need to take care of; then we're right behind you."

"Who's we?"

"Jennifer Masters and her daughter are both with me."

"Outstanding," Cedric said sounding disgusted. "Just what we need in the middle of this. You're wearing your big red S. Boss, I know this is your deal, but we can't protect anyone when we can't protect ourselves."

"Look, I get it, Cedric, but we have very little wiggle room on this. Just get to Vegas and I'll call you as soon as I can."

Without explaining any further, Jake told Cedric he would contact his caretaker in Nevada and tell the old man to expect him.

Jake felt worse than Cedric did. Mike had been his friend too. He was an integral part of their team. He could still see Masters' double grinning at him as he snapped Mike's neck. Jake had lost friends before, but he never thought it would happen in this business.

Corporate security was normally a fairly safe trade; it wasn't every day that you even had to wear a gun. For the most part, it was a relatively boring job. Considering the events of his earlier life, that was just fine

"What do we do now?" The woman asked from the rear seat. Her daughter had fallen asleep on one side of the rear seat.

"First, I get us squared away for the night. Then I call the agent in charge and try to negotiate our way out of this. If there's no way to negotiate, then we'll head for Nevada. I have a place there. We can hide out and try to figure out what to do next."

"He killed your friend, didn't he?"

Jake closed his eyes again, then opened them and turned toward her.

"In a way I guess he did. But, your husband wasn't at the house. The thing at your house was something your husband made. It took nine rounds from Mike, then I emptied both of my guns into him and it barely slowed him down."

"How is that possible?"

"I have no idea. I only know that he was coming there for the two of you and if we hadn't been there, you both would probably be dead."

Jennifer considered this for a moment and then nodded her head.

"If he was anything like his creator, I can guarantee it."

Jake looked at her for a moment, somewhat shocked by her statement. Her gaze screamed "Don't ask", so he decided to let it go.

The lanes on the freeway had been sanded, but there was still quite a bit of snow along the sides. Watching Jennifer in the mirror, he saw her wipe a tear away; then she leaned forward.

"My husband didn't think we were entitled to any consideration in his life. Every once in a while, he would come home frustrated with something at the office or some other part of his life and he would take that frustration out on us. He never hit Amanda but I was often the target of his temper."

"It started about a year after we were married, while I was pregnant. He came home one night, brooding about some failed experiment and slapped me when I offered to help. The hitting became a daily thing until about two years ago when he stopped coming home as often. The times he was at home, he was always distant. He didn't communicate with me, and the longer I stayed, the less I cared. Living with him was bad, but I was afraid that if I asked for a divorce, he would take Amanda, so I stayed to protect her." She put her hand on Amanda as she spoke.

"Tonight, when I heard about the fire, I decided to leave. Take Amanda and just disappear. God forgive me, but I hoped that he had died in the fire. No such luck." Jennifer gazed out the window and brushed a tear away.

Jake drove south, through sparse traffic in the darkness. *The farther they were from the city, the better,* he thought.

"Anyway, when he called, I realized something was wrong," Jennifer continued. "It was in his voice. Now I know what it was. It really looked like him?"

Jake nodded without saying a word. The memory of the attack kept coming into his mind. He couldn't believe he was responsible for Mike's death. He should have gone for the headshot before the double snapped his neck. Maybe Mike would still be alive.

Taking the downtown Tacoma exit, he drove to the Marriott Hotel. Pulling the SUV under the portico, Jake grabbed the suitcase. Jennifer carried her daughter and Jake waved off the parking attendant, pressing the lock button on the remote.

Jake went to the front desk and rented a suite. He paid cash for the room and refused to open an account for the telephone. He wouldn't need the room phone and couldn't risk using it anyway for fear of leaving a trail.

Once Jake registered, he led Jennifer and Amanda to the elevators. He had used an alias to register for the room, so there was little chance they would be disturbed by their adversaries.

Once they were inside the room, Jake went back downstairs and moved the Suburban to the self-park lot across the street from the hotel. Making his way back inside the hotel, he took the elevators back to the fifth floor, using his key card to enter the room.

When Jake returned, she was sitting on the sofa, drinking vodka from a small water glass. She had apparently raided the mini-bar.

"Can I fix you something, Mr. Storm?"

"No, thank you. I don't drink much anymore."

Jennifer looked at him as if she thought the night's action required lubrication; then she sat down. Mixing tonic into her glass, she tucked her long legs underneath her.

"Tell me something, Mr. Storm," Jennifer began, swallowing half her drink with her first sip. "Why should we trust you?"

Jake sighed and thought for a moment. He wasn't sure that he had a suitable answer. Why should they trust him?

"I guess I can't think of a reason why. I only know that, right this minute, I'm the only person who can protect you."

"It certainly didn't look like you handled the situation at the house all that well."

Jake felt his temper rise. He had lost a good friend tonight while trying to help her, and she was questioning his motives and abilities?

"You know, you could try thanking me. My friend and I saved you and your little girl tonight, and it came at a very high cost. I could just leave you here to fend for yourself."

Jennifer glared at him for a moment; then her face softened.

"I guess that was unfair. Thank you for saving us. I just don't know what you can do for us." Swallowing the last of her drink, they locked eyes briefly and Jake was surprised at the rage he saw burning in hers.

"I know that thing is a threat to anyone who gets in its way. He has already killed five people. Maybe more. Every researcher your husband worked with is dead. I believe you and your daughter are next on his list."

"Why?"

"I wish I knew. I *can* tell you this. Protecting people is what I do. I can protect you and your daughter now. I won't let that thing get to you *or* her. But if you don't trust me, or my abilities, you can leave in the morning and go your own way. I can only offer my protection. I can't force it on you."

Jennifer stared at him for a moment, then placed her face in her hands and began to cry. She sobbed quietly for nearly five minutes. Jake watched, not knowing how to comfort her. Taking her glass, he retrieved another bottle of Vodka from the honor bar and poured it in. Taking the glass from him, she looked directly at him, then away, draining the vodka in one gulp.

"I wish things hadn't happened this way, but remember I'm trying to help you."

Jennifer nodded her head. Using a tissue from a dispenser on the lamp table next to her, she blotted the tears from her eyes.

"So, my husband is trying to kill his own wife and child reaching up from the grave?"

Jake hadn't expected the question and it seemed foolish for him to comment on it, but he sat next to her anyway and took her hands in his.

"Look, I just feel if we stick together, we all have a better chance of coming out of this alive. I'll do my damnedest to see that you stay safe. Right now, I think you should go in there with your daughter and try to sleep. I'll watch things."

Jennifer eyed him curiously again, stood and walked silently into the adjoining bedroom, closing the door behind her. In a few moments, all was silent and the light under the door extinguished.

Jake sat watching the occasional snowflake drift past the window. After what seemed like hours, he went over to the sofa and stretched out. He would catnap a little while, but he knew that deep sleep wouldn't come to him tonight, if ever again.

§

NINETEEN

Snow drifted past the window in Kelly's hotel room in downtown Bellevue. The sky brightened along the horizon as dawn approached, but the only thing it revealed was a gray, ironclad sky. He was no weatherman but he thought the worst of the weather had passed.

The agents Kelly sent to the homes of the researchers reported back. All the researchers were dead. The press got the news before he could quell it and the murders were the lead story on every broadcast. The team he sent to Masters' house found blood everywhere, but no wife and kid and no bodies.

Just after leaving Genetisource, Kelly learned that a fire team was dispatched to terminate Jake Storm. They failed and several people perished in the process. He hadn't issued the order and offered to castrate the agent who issued the order.

They still had a lot of cleanup work to do at the burned out building that had been Genetisource. With precious little time and even fewer resources to handle the task, Kelly put at least one four-man team at the scene to assess the security risks. A team in Washington was working on a good cover story. The agents were just getting inside the building to look for victims. The Agency had their own pathologist at the scene and would take any remains to a secure facility to perform tests and determine identity.

Kelly turned toward the ringing phone. He stood and walked slowly to the desk where it sat, sighing heavily. Dreading more bad news, he picked up the receiver. "Kelly," he said.

"Kelly, this is Jake Storm." The voice on the other end sounded weary, making Kelly wonder what his nemesis had been up to all night.

"Waddya want, Storm? And how did you get my cell phone number?"

"I Googled *dashing spy* and typed in 'synonym', and there you were," Storm answered.

Kelly thought he could actually hear a grin coming across the phone line.

"I think we need to talk."

"Really? Well, only if you intend to bring me everything you have on our good doctor, and turn yourself in for the murder of several federal agents," Kelly said, squeezing the bridge of his nose with his fingertips.

"I don't have that much on him, really. As far as the agents go, they attacked me first. They tried to kill me."

"Well then, you have nothing to worry about."

"Yeah, right. Do you want to talk or not? If you do, meet me at ten o'clock this morning at the Pike Place Market on the second floor, near the elevator to the pub."

"Fine with me. Make sure you bring everything you have, Jake," Kelly sighed again. "You better have some answers for me."

"What kind of answers?"

"Like why all of *your* people have disappeared. Like where the hell Masters' wife and kid are? Like, why you and *all* your employees were nowhere to be found after the fire last night? Questions like that."

Silence pervaded on the line then Storm spoke in a strained voice.

"I'll tell you everything that we know for sure. You're just going to have to work for everything else. I want to discuss how I can get out from under this with a minimal amount of bloodshed. I don't want any of my people charged with any crimes, or otherwise sanctioned, because *your* mad scientist fucked up."

The phone went dead. Kelly sat for a moment, thinking about the call. What kind of information did Storm have? Why would the man think his people were in danger unless he felt the NSA would supersede his own authority on this? Would they order termination of all those involved with Genetisource? If that were the case, the orders would have already been issued. As far as he knew, no other agencies were involved. He would have been notified if terminations had been ordered. The only time he wouldn't be notified, was if someone else was running the show.

Trudging into the bathroom, he relieved himself, then returned to the hard hotel bed and stretched out. He hated strange places and hated trying to sleep on uncomfortable beds. He was starting to drift off when the phone rang again.

"We have news."

Kelly recognized the voice as Agent Chelnik.

"Lay it on me," Kelly answered wearily.

"The local police are pissed about us ordering them to stand down. They want answers."

"Just tell them that under the Patriot Act we have the right to suspend their involvement as a matter of national security. Tell them anything, but tell them to butt out. Take anyone who bitches into custody." Kelly was getting a headache.

Kelly sighed and watched the sun rising above the mountains in the east. He needed a couple of hours of sleep. His jetlag was killing him but this needed his attention.

"Tell them I'll meet with them in an hour. Then send some agents to check out the Pike Place Market. See if we can get people in there."

"What for?"

"I'm meeting the head of the security agency who worked at Genetisource. I need backup in case it goes sour."

"Oh, one more thing, Sir. We have some visitors from another agency poking around the building. From all reports from headquarters, there's a man waiting for you there who claims he is taking charge of the search for Masters."

"What agency?"

"DOD, Sir. He said that they were taking charge of all of it."

"Great, I'll be right there." Kelly hung up the phone and looked at the clock. It was just past six in the morning and he knew that getting any sleep was out of the question. Rubbing his tired eyes, Kelly dressed.

Now he had one of the DOD's agencies breathing down his neck. What did they want? Fucking Masters and his gene splicing operation was turning into the mess he had envisioned. He wondered how long it would be before he was replaced and a cleaning team sent to insure the project's continued secrecy. Kelly grabbed his cell phone and left the room, heading for Genetisource.

§

TWENTY

Jake awoke to the sound of the door being opened. Jumping off the sofa, where he had fallen asleep at just past six-thirty in the morning, he grabbed his gun off the coffee table and aimed it at the opening door.

Jennifer Masters walked in carrying several white bags. Jake smelled the food as she turned to face him. She stopped when she saw him pointing his gun at her.

"Where have you been?" Jake asked, placing the pistol back on the coffee table.

"I figured we might have a little breakfast to start the day."

"So you thought you would just dance down to the coffee shop and get some?"

"Well, I didn't dance," she smiled weakly at her joke, as if expecting him to laugh too, but her smile faltered when he didn't.

She placed the bags on the small table in the corner of the room near the window. "I just thought…"

"Let me explain something. Do not leave this room unless we're together. There are bad people looking for us and if someone recognizes you, they'll find us. Hotels are the first place they'll look. I wouldn't have brought us here except it's the only place where I could leave you while I try to get us out of this mess."

Jake could see the defiance rising in her eyes again and he clamped his mouth shut. It was neither the time nor the place for a fight.

"Well, in that case, I guess you're not hungry. I need to wake Amanda so she can eat."

Jake checked his watch and saw that he had been asleep less than an hour. Less than three hours until his meeting with Kelly. Kelly had always hated Jake. That made the meeting even more dangerous. Jake felt he could handle Kelly, as long he was prepared, but he also needed Kelly to understand their situation.

Something Jake gleaned from their conversation was that Kelly himself didn't understand, nor was he aware of, what Masters had been doing at Genetisource. Masters had gone off the reservation, but how could they not have known? If Kelly hadn't been read in on the program, then the Agency had not been involved before today. Which meant Kelly was here for the clean-up only and someone else was pulling the strings. DARPA didn't kill people. So the question remained, for whom had Masters been working? Could he engineer a deal to get them out from under the consequences?

Jennifer glared at him from the table as she nibbled at her breakfast. Amanda sat next to her mother, dressed in a pair of pajamas, her blonde hair sticking out in all directions, eating in silence. Jake felt bad about the way he treated her but still felt he had been right.

"Listen, I'm sorry if I came on a little strong," Jake said, eyeing the third plate of food sitting on the table. "There are a lot of things we don't know right now and we can't take any unnecessary chances."

"I understand," Jennifer said quietly. "You're the knight on his white horse and we are the damsels in distress."

"That isn't it. I just don't want to make any mistakes. We can't afford it. Right now, our lives depend on making the right decisions. We have to have as much information about your husband's project as possible. You are the only link I have to your husband. You know him better than anyone."

Jake tried to emphasize the last two words of the statement and it seemed to do the trick. She turned and looked directly into his eyes.

"I'm sorry if I endangered us. It won't happen again," she paused, holding out a cup of coffee to him. "I don't know why, but I trust you. If I didn't, Amanda and I wouldn't have been here this morning. I don't mean to make you think otherwise."

Jake accepted the coffee and regarded her for a moment. He couldn't figure out why she had stayed with Masters so long when he had treated her so badly.

"Join us for breakfast?"

"I guess so," he sighed, smiling back at her and taking the cover off of the plate of bacon and eggs.

They enjoyed small talk about his years in the military while they ate. Jennifer entertained him with a few anecdotes from her years in college. They stayed away from the subjects of her husband and their current predicament.

When they finished breakfast, Amanda adjourned to the bathroom for a shower. Jake pulled Jennifer aside and spoke quietly to her.

"I have to go out and deal with a few things. I've put the "Do Not Disturb" sign on the door, so if anyone knocks, don't answer it. I'll use my key to get in."

"Got it, Boss." She looked at him with laughter shining in her eyes. He chuckled and shook his finger at her.

"I wish you would take me seriously."

She sobered, but still retained the glint in her eyes, which he found appealing. "I do take it seriously, but one of us has to retain a sense of humor."

"Are you saying I don't have a sense of humor?"

"You just need to lighten up. I know you're good at this and I am placing our lives in your care. Just make sure you don't let us down."

Jennifer Masters suddenly reached out to him, placed her hand on his cheek, and then abruptly pulled it away.

Jake looked at her for a moment longer, and then left the room. Walking outside to the parking lot, he dialed Cedric's number on the burner phone. It rang three times before a groggy answer greeted him.

"Cedric, is everything going according to plan?"

"Yeah, I got to Portland this morning and arranged a private flight to Vegas. I'll get a car and head for the cabin. So, how did you find this place, Jake?"

"A few years ago I had to protect a witness involved in a treason case. When we found we had a mole inside the Agency, they told me to find a safe place to put her until she went before a Congressional hearing. That's the place."

"So the CIA owns it?"

"Yes, but they don't know they own it. I had to buy it under an assumed name. They never asked about the expenditure, so I never told them about it."

Cedric was silent for a moment then he chuckled.

"What a plan. Gee, if they only knew that you planned to hold their fugitives in a place that they, by all rights, own outright. How are you making out on your end?"

"Our old friend, Kelly, is heading up the cleaning team. I'm meeting him later. He wants to debrief our people, and then take all the evidence. Right now, I'm pleading temporary amnesia."

"More like permanent insanity. I guess it's a waste of time for me to tell you to watch your back, right? You can't trust Kelly, even though you were once a member of the same agency. What the hell have we gotten ourselves into, Jake?"

"That's what we have to find out."

Jake told him he would drive to Vegas with Jennifer and Amanda, arriving in three days.

"Be careful, Boss."

"Don't worry, Cedric. Remember, I was a spy once. I've played this game before."

"Just watch yourself," Cedric said. "This is no game to them and they want to hurt us."

Cedric disconnected and Jake walked back into the lobby. Stopping at the newsstand, Jake bought a copy of the *Seattle Times*. Looking around for anyone who was paying more than casual attention to him, he saw no one. Folding the newspaper, he tucked it under his arm until he was safely inside the elevator.

The blaze had made the front page. A huge color photo of the fire-ravaged building emblazoned the front page. The story said Genetisource had been involved in private research and recounted their breakthroughs in cellular reproduction, but said nothing about government ties. The sidebar of the story was about the five murdered researchers who had worked at Genetisource.

Jake used his key to enter the room. He found Jennifer and Amanda watching cartoons on television and arguing the importance of doing homework. They both glanced at the door nervously when he entered, then returned to their argument.

Jake retired to the bathroom for a shower. Shedding his clothes, he turned on the water to hot. When the water warmed, he climbed in, sluicing off the grime he had collected the night before. He couldn't change clothes because he couldn't risk returning to his place to pack.

Jake was certain Kelly was as much in the dark as he was about Masters' project. That meant the people who installed the cameras in the lab were possibly from some other part of the government. If this was correct, Kelly's control of this was an illusion and someone else was steering the ship from the sidelines. That meant no deals would be made. The only way he could keep them safe was to find out what Masters had been doing and threaten to release it. If the agency in charge decided the risk of keeping them alive outweighed the reward, they were dead.

Turning the water off, he stepped out, dripping on to the tile floor. He dried himself, and then dressed.

If he hadn't seen it all before, he would have thought the idea of the government killing its own people was paranoid delusion. While working for the Agency, he had seen unknown enti-

ties come in and wave a hand, causing the deaths of more innocent people than he cared to remember.

By 8:15 he was ready to leave the hotel and head off for
his meeting with Kelly. He would have to really hurry if he
wanted to check the area before the meeting time.

Jake left the bedroom and went into the front room. Jennifer and Amanda both watched as he entered the room, then
Jennifer smiled approvingly.

"You clean up well," Jennifer said.

Jake smiled and pointed at the door. "Remember what I
said. I don't think they have any idea where we are, but just in
case don't open the door for anyone. Keep as quiet as possible.
I'll be back as soon as I can."

"What if you don't?"

Jake had been dreading this direct and certainly pertinent
question. Taking a piece of the hotel stationary, Jake wrote a
phone number down on it.

"Call this number if I'm not back by one in the afternoon. I need time to deal with this, and the traffic will be murder.
This is my attorney. Martin Boroughs will help you get to a safe
place. After that, you'll have to tell the press what happened."

"But I don't know what my husband was doing," she said
sounding hopeless.

Jake was about to reply when Amanda asked him another
question he would have preferred to avoid answering.

"My Daddy is dead, isn't he, Mr. Storm?"

Jake looked at Jennifer and saw her eyes tear slightly.
Her watery glance said that he should tread lightly on this subject.

"Honey, we're not sure. My men saw an argument in
your daddy's laboratory last night. In fact, I'm about to go find
out more information about that right now. So I really can't give
you an answer."

Amanda returned to her picture for a moment. She
turned to Jake with a teary glance and said, "He's dead. I know it.
I can feel it." She sobbed softly and Jake wanted to take the little

girl in his arms and make it better, but he knew it was a waste of time. He had lost his parents at a young age and no amount of consoling helped. Even though Masters had been a piece of shit, his daughter loved him.

Amanda crawled into her mother's lap and put her arms around the woman's neck, burying her face in Jennifer's shoulder. Jake went to the bedroom, checking his Glock, careful to keep it out of Amanda's sight. Returning, he grabbed his jacket and walked to the door.

Jake looked back once as he opened the door, and then left the room. He would do his best to keep any harm from coming to this little one and her mother. The child wouldn't be able to hold up if she lost both of her parents.

§

TWENTY-ONE

Blue sky and sunshine had replaced the dreary clouds that pushed eastward over the Cascade Mountains during the early hours of the morning. In spite of the clear skies, the temperature at nine o'clock remained below freezing. It was rare for the weather to be this cold in Seattle during the first part of February, but then again the weather in the Northwest was often unpredictable under the best of circumstances.

Jake parked the Suburban in a lot near Pier 20 at just past nine-thirty, walking the rest of the way to Pike Place Public Market. Jake felt that approaching from the waterfront would keep him from being seen. If Kelly and his men had scoped the place out and planted men inside, and Jake was sure they had, he would have to stay loose.

Pike Place was a huge attraction for tourists from all over the world. Several attached buildings were filled with clothing and tourist shops. There were art galleries, ethnic shops and a couple of travel agencies. Fishmongers, restaurants, shops selling fresh fruit and vegetables and fresh flowers inhabited the rest of the public market.

Jake bought a cup of coffee at a small restaurant across the street from the building and watched as people came and went. Fifteen minutes after sitting down, he spotted Kelly and six other men approaching the Market from the East. Kelly acted casually, but with a few words, directed the men inside. Jake noticed, even from a distance, the grey hair creeping into the formerly blonde hair at Kelly's temples. Kelly turned in place, searching the area with eyes that were both cunning and alert, and then disappeared into the gathering crowds.

Jake stood up and saw another group of four men. They were led by a tall, thin man with white hair wearing a long black coat. There was something familiar about him and the way he ordered his men around, but Jake couldn't remember where he had seen the white-haired man before.

Jake identified two more shooters milling within the throngs of people moving through the market. Part of him wanted to run, but he knew that would only make him look guiltier than he was. He had the element of surprise and he was in control of the timeframe for revealing himself to Kelly. By the looks of things, they had read his file and weren't taking any chances.

Jake left a ten-dollar bill on the table and went around to the south side of the building. The wind blowing off of Elliott Bay was frigid, but his gloves blocked most of the cold. Entering the building, he unbuttoned his jacket and freed up his Glock.

The shops in this part of the market were relatively empty during this time of the morning. Most didn't open their doors for another hour. A few lonely tourists window-shopped. Once inside the building, Jake proceeded to the first staircase he came to, and climbed to the second floor.

On the second floor, he waited until a crowd of tourists went past and joined them. Two of the men he had seen enter the building earlier were standing near a closed shop dealing in Asian silks. Stepping inside an open souvenir shop, he bought a baseball cap and a pair of cheap sunglasses. The smell of candles and incense mixed with the smell of old wood and fish was heavy in the air as he left the store and made his way toward the pub. The hat and sunglasses made him look like any tourist.

Jake saw Kelly standing near the open area where a brewers' vat poked through the second floor. He checked each of the few people walking through this part of the market carefully, trying to pick Jake out.

Jake saw nothing of the white-haired man he had spotted earlier. He might have been mistaken, placing the man with Kelly's crew, but he didn't think so. Jake pulled back until Kelly turned away then moved across to the opposite side of the hallway. Leaning into the doorway of a closed candle store, he waited until Kelly passed then fell in behind him. When he was close enough for only Kelly to hear him, he quietly spoke.

"Kelly," Jake said with his hand under his jacket. "Keep walking. Don't make any sign you're talking to me and turn off that transmitter."

"What the hell?" Kelly said stopping.

"Keep walking," Jake whispered then repeated. "And lose the bug. I know you're wearing one, so do it."

Kelly reached under his jacket and flipped a switch, turning off the transmitter he was wearing underneath.

"Well, Jake. It's been a long time, hasn't it?" Kelly said continuing to walk down the corridor.

"I thought this meeting would be just between us, Kelly." Jake said, nodding his head toward the art gallery.

"You know I couldn't meet you alone. Anyway, I'm not in charge anymore. I was relieved this morning and another agency took control."

"I guess I don't have to ask how bad things are then."

"You killed agents, Jake. What did you expect them to do? Give you a medal?"

"I expected you to play this straight. You know damn well I had nothing to do with Masters and his experiments."

"That may be, but you know too much. You know how this works. You're either on the inside or you're not. For all we know, you might have concocted this whole situation."

When they reached the staircase at the end of the hallway, he told Kelly to take it. As they descended, Jake thought something seemed out of place. Kelly was entirely too calm. When they reached the bottom of the stairs, he saw the man with the white hair standing at a newsstand counter near their end of the hallway.

"I assume he's your new leader?" Jake said, wondering how he could have made such a horrendous blunder. The meeting had seemed like a good idea at the time, but now he was quickly running out of escape plans. His only advantage, the reason he chose the market, was his knowledge of the building.

"Yeah. He says he's from DOD, but I think he's from some place even they aren't aware of."

Jake knew what Kelly was saying. There were hundreds of small black-ops groups that no one knew about, but were paid for with government money. Before he could back away from Kelly, the man noticed them and walked toward them.

"This is…" Kelly began, but the other man cut him off.

"I work for an agency within the Department of Defense."

"No kidding," Jake said facing Kelly again. "Well, my deal was to speak only to Mr. Kelly here, so if you don't mind…"

"Mr. Storm, I don't think you realize…"

"I don't think you realize. I'm here to speak to Kelly only. I have no intention of dealing with some "spy" who works for someone who can't help me."

White Hair's eyes narrowed, then he backed away, speaking into a microphone hidden beneath his left coat lapel. White Hair stood against the wall, glaring at Jake, a smile twitching at the left corner of his mouth.

"Was that necessary?" Kelly asked, turning to Jake.

Jake pulled the Glock from under his coat and pointed it at Kelly's midsection. The gun was shielded from public view by his jacket, but Kelly saw it and the color drained from his face.

"Absolutely. What the fuck are you pulling, Kelly?"

"He arrived this morning," Kelly said, shaking his head. Leaning close to Jake, he spoke in a low voice. "We were told he was in charge. He had authorization from the Secretary of Defense, Jake. You're in deep shit, my friend. They don't care what you know; they don't intend to let you leave here."

Jake glanced down the hallway and saw several men working their way through the crowds. He also heard footsteps behind him on the stairs. He moved a little closer to the door and the exit just behind and to his right. He was now hidden from view of anyone on the stairs.

"Look, I didn't have to come here. I could have let you and your people flounder for weeks. If that man tries to detain me, I will resist. And you know me better than he does. If I decide to resist, I *will* walk out of here."

Kelly moved toward Jake so that he was now past the staircase as well. Jake saw Kelly raise his hand as if telling someone on the stairs to stop.

"What do you know about Genetisource and the fire?"

"Not a Goddamn thing."

"Bullshit, Jake. Your people saw everything and we know it. If you don't give me the information you have, I can't help you."

"From the looks of things you can't help me anyway," Jake said, nodding his head and smiling at the men gathered around the white-haired agent.

Even if he gave them everything he had, their lives were over. Jake wished he hadn't come here and desperately wanted to leave, but knew the only way out was by force or in a body bag.

"I tried to be the right kind of guy, Kelly. Now you leave me no choice." Jake had been working his way away from Kelly and now leaned against a nearby exit door. Jake had spent enough time in the Market to know the door led to a service hallway then down three floors to the street. Smiling at Kelly, he winked, leaned against the door and disappeared through it. As soon as the door closed, he turned the dead bolt.

Running down the hallway, he took the stairs two and three at a time, winding down three floors to the street below. He didn't hear anyone following him which seemed odd. Jake, ran across the street at an angle heading toward the bay. As he came to the end of the building, he slid on a patch of ice while turning the corner and collided with two men running down the sidewalk.

The man nearest Jake moved his right hand under his suit coat, trying to pull a gun, but the impact from running into Jake had pinned his hand in front of him. Jake reached forward and grabbed the man's arm, pulling him forward and brought up his own right arm, catching his opponent across the windpipe. Momentum carried the agent forward and he was swung off his feet, his body slamming to the concrete sidewalk on his back. Jake kicked him in the temple ending his fight instantly. Jake vaguely heard the gun the man was trying to pull clatter across the cement.

Surprise continued to favor Jake. The swiftness of the attack combined with the force with which it was applied caused the second agent to hesitate. Jake didn't give him an opportunity to recover. Jumping over the fallen man, he grabbed the second man, hitting him across face with the edge of his hand, shattering the bridge of his nose. The man screamed as blood sprayed from his wounded face and Jake grabbed him by the chin, forcing him backward into a steel pole, slamming the back of his head into it. The second agent slid to the ground.

Jake heard movement behind him and tried to turn but was grabbed roughly and hoisted into the air, his arms pinned to his sides with great force. He saw another man approaching from the same direction the first two men had come and knew he would be done if he couldn't break this hold. Jake threw his weight forward, causing his opponent to drop his feet to the ground, trying to get control of his squirming prey. As Jake's feet met the walkway again, the approaching big man swung a straight jab at his face, connecting with his nose. Pain exploded though Jake's head and blood streamed down his face. His consciousness slipped for a moment but before the big man could finish the job, he was hoisted off his feet again, causing a second blow to glance off his chest. Jake pistoned his feet outward connecting with the big man's knees and Jake heard the snapping of bone and carti-lage. The big man screamed falling backward to the sidewalk.

When his feet hit the ground again, Jake threw his weight backward shoving his captor into the wall of the building. Pain spread across his chest as the man tightened his grip. Reaching his right hand back, he found the man's crotch. Grabbing hold of the bear hugging bastard's nuts, he squeezed with all the strength he could muster. The man's arms dropped from around his chest as Jake yanked forward on his testicles. When he doubled over in pain, gasping for breath, Jake grabbed his neck and twisted up and to the left. He heard a snap and the man's body went limp. *Well, they asked for it,* he thought.

Jake ran toward Elliot Bay. The ice was very bad along the sidewalk and he was running downhill slipping more than once before reaching the bottom. He heard footsteps behind him and a car's engine revving nearby. Turning the corner at the next street, Jake headed to the Aquarium. He heard squealing tires as he reached the corner and turned to see a black sedan rushing toward him. Jake pulled his gun and opened fire on the car. Bul-lets hit the windshield and punched through into the driver's area beyond. Jake had to jump into the street as the car careened out of control and slammed into the pole where he had been stand-ing.

With no time to catch his breath, Jake ran across the street and down the hill. The cold air burned his lungs but he didn't stop until he was well away from the scene of the collision. He no longer heard anyone pursuing him. Near the parking lot where he had left the Suburban, he stopped long enough to catch his breath and see if he was being followed. No one in the build-ings or on the street seemed to be paying attention to him so, straightening his jacket, he walked casually to his car.

Jakes nose gushed. He took a handkerchief out of his back pocket and dealt with the blood. Getting behind the wheel, he started the engine and backed out of the parking space. Turn-ing right at the exit, he followed the street down to the waterfront, then turned left at the light and followed the street south until he was in the industrial district.

Safely away from the city, he quickly headed south along Marginal Way to Route 99. At a gas station in Burien, he used the sink in the bathroom outside to clean the blood off his face. Taking his nose between the palms of his hands, he simultaneously pulled and squeezed, setting his broken nose. The blood from his nose had soaked his shirt and covered his pants but there was nothing he could do about it.

As Jake left the restroom, he used the burn phone to call Martin Boroughs. He instructed the lawyer to liquidate as many of his holdings as he could and move the money to an offshore account. Once Jake had new identification, he could forward it to Boroughs and get access to the funds, provided he lived long enough.

§

TWENTY-TWO

Every Navy SEAL has an escape package; at least those who survived the training and actually lived longer than a few missions. Jake had several. One was in Germany, one France and two others in credit unions near the airport.

Jake stopped at a mall as he got closer to the airport and purchased several pairs of jeans, several sport shirts, denim shirts, socks and a heavy coat. Changing into a pair of the jeans and denim shirt in a dressing room, he dropped his bloody clothes in a trashcan as he left the store. The clerk had eyed his clothes but said nothing when Jake paid cash for his purchases.

At a Nike outlet store, he purchased two pairs of running shoes. Stowing his packages in the SUV, he walked to the credit union across the parking lot and accessed his safety deposit box. When he left, his briefcase was considerably heavier. Driving to another bank in Kent, he cleaned out an additional stash. Two hours after his encounter at the Pike Place Market, he returned to the hotel room with over forty thousand dollars in cash.

Jennifer and Amanda looked up as he walked into the room and gasped in unison when they saw his face. After placing the briefcase on the couch, he went to the bathroom to see how bad it really was.

"What happened to you?"

"Ran into a door. It hurts, but I'll live."

Jennifer eyed him curiously for a moment, and then shook her head.

"Guys… Why is it that you always have to display the machismo?"

"It comes with the penis, babe."

"I take it your meeting didn't go very well?"

"Several dead government agents tell you anything?" Jake shook his head slowly and took a tissue from a wall-mounted dispenser to wipe fresh blood from the tip of his nose. "It's worse than I originally thought. We have to leave right now. Get all your stuff together."

"I hope they look worse than you do." She smiled and Jake chuckled.

"Something like that."

Jennifer hesitated, as if wanting to say something more, then turned and gathered up the clothes not already packed in her suitcase. Jake went out to the front room.

Jake found blood had leaked from his nose and stained his new shirt, so he took another from one of his bags and re-moved the tags. Removing his shirt, he rolled it up and stuffed it in the bag with the other new shirts. Taking the clean shirt from the bed, he heard a gasp from behind him. Turning, he saw Jennifer staring at him from the other side of the room. She had seen the pattern of scars crisscrossing his back, from the shoulder blades to his belt line.

"I had an accident when I was in the Navy. I'll tell you about it sometime. Right now we have to get going."

Pulling the shirt over his head, he tucked the tail into the waistband on his jeans. He changed into his new socks and shoes then reloaded his pistol. When Jennifer finished packing, he performed a final check to make sure they hadn't left anything behind. Once he was certain things were clean, he shouldered their bags, as well as his new clothes, and led them downstairs. His nose began bleeding again as they reached the elevator. He wiped at it with a damp towel from the room.

Jake hadn't intended to stick around long, so he had parked under the portico in front of the main doors. They weren't very busy so the attendants had told him not to worry. Step-ping into the cold, he used the remote to unlock the vehicle's doors, then raised the deck lid and loaded the suitcase. Stepping around to the driver's side he got behind the wheel.

"What about checking out?" Jennifer asked as he closed the door.

Jake smiled and shook his head. "Doesn't matter. The maids will figure out we're gone."

Leaving the parking lot, Jake drove east and caught the Interstate heading south. Jennifer sat next to him, with Amanda playing in the back seat. In the silence, he remembered Kelly's reaction when Jake told him that his own agency had placed cameras in Masters' lab. Kelly hadn't known about the cameras, which meant someone else was responsible for them. Who had Masters really been working for?

White-Hair undoubtedly worked for the agency responsible for the cameras. That worried Jake. This guy had not been bothered by the fact that they might have had a firefight in the middle of a crowded tourist attraction. In fact, he seemed to want it to happen.

Jake smiled at Jennifer, turning his head to look at the little girl. She eyed him curiously and smiled back. Jake turned his eyes to the slick roads ahead and saw water as the sand-covered snow along the edge of the freeway began to melt and run across the concrete lanes.

South of Olympia, the air warmed. A few hours later, as they passed over the Columbia River into Portland, Oregon, the roads had cleared and the sun was shining brightly.

§

PART II

Trial by Fire

TWENTY-THREE

L as Vegas is a booming metropolis in Nevada's southern desert. What had once been a small town with very little outside the casino areas of the downtown area had become a sprawling metropolis. Throughout the '60s and '70s, growth in the small city had been slow and mercurial, with nearly as many people leaving the city as coming to it. Until the mid '70s, organized crime had a strong foothold in Las Vegas where their interests included casinos, construction companies and transportation. The mob had controlled the city government, as well as a good portion of the police force, and made criminal activity in the city other than their own, nearly non-existent. Of course, in the late '90s, Las Vegas elected a former mob lawyer, Oscar Goodman, to the Mayor's office. Even now, when you ask a local who was in Las Vegas during the '50s, '60s and '70s, most would look wistfully at you and say they were the best times for the city.

Gaming regulators and Federal investigations eventually rid the gaming industry of most of the organized crime element, bringing in business owners who were not connected to any "families". The population of the town remains transient but corporate vision began to shape both the city and its skyline. More businesses not associated with casino gaming moved to southern Nevada. During the late eighties and early nineties, more and more people began to migrate to the desert city. What was once a small, dusty town full of casinos and vice, quickly became the fastest growing city in the United States.

By 2008, the population in the Las Vegas valley swelled to more than three million people. When the housing bust hit, foreclosures were the new business, with Las Vegas leading the nation. People still moved to the oasis of the desert, but many left as well.

During the summer, the temperatures in the valley often reached over 110 degrees. People searched for places to get away from the intense heat. Because Las Vegas is at the center of a small valley formed by higher desert all around, a lot of residents were forced to pack up the kids and head for a cooler spot.

Mount Charleston is just forty minutes from the heart of Vegas at roughly eight thousand feet in elevation. While the city scorched under the desert sun, temperatures on the mountain rarely rose above the eighties. Campgrounds, where one could pitch a tent or park a small motor home, provided a place to escape the heat of the desert.

Vacation homes and permanent residents live in relative seclusion on the mountain. The Bureau of Land Management or one of two families who had settled the area in the early twentieth century owned much of the land. One of the families owned a small café that was a hit with the locals because of its Bavarian styling, traditional food and light atmosphere. On the other side of the mountain, another family owned a small ski area that was a favorite year-round with Las Vegas residents.

During the summer of 2003, Jake was protecting a witness in an espionage case for the Department of Justice. Although CIA personnel were not allowed to work within U.S. borders, they were often "loaned" to other agencies for special projects. During that summer, the Agency investigated the existence of a traitor within its ranks. Two "safe" houses had already been compromised, so Jake and his team hid the witness, but didn't disclose her location to his superiors.

Jake found a listing for the cabin in the pages of a "Homes for Sale" magazine on a paper rack. After visiting it, he found it had everything he needed. The place was remote enough to make getting to it hard and finding them, damn near impossible.

He had purchased the place from a couple who wanted a quick sale. They lived on Charleston while he was stationed at Nellis Air Force Base and she had worked as a promotions director for Caesar's Palace. When the husband was transferred, they had to sell. The cabin sat in the middle of a five-acre parcel of land leased from the BLM. They had a 99 year lease, which wouldn't be up for renewal during his lifetime. Jake had purchased the place, using a cover account for a front corporation he'd established, for just over $175,000.

Fences had been installed before he bought the place but Jake had spent a week extending them and installing security cameras, as well as a remote control gate that could be operated from inside the cabin. The witness had watched him and three other agents working in the warm summer sun. She had even pitched in several times to help when they needed an extra hand. They kept her safe, delivering her to the Marshall's service but she was killed during a firefight after the swap. Jake never identified who sold them out.

Jake kept the cabin after the case was closed. He paid for the property with Agency money, but they hadn't asked for a receipt or title, so he had never told them about it.

Jake hired a local man to take care of repairs on the cabin when he wasn't around. Ben Thomas was a cantankerous old man who had won Jake over the first time they met. Jake was looking for someone to help repair the roof. Someone suggested Ben.

During their first meeting, Ben called Jake a pansy, climbed on the roof and repaired most of the wooden shakes himself. By the time they finished, the old man had endeared himself to Jake. He traveled around the area with an old semi-domesticated grey wolf.

Ben had once told Jake that he'd found the wolf on the side of the road in Montana during his days of crossing the country in his Kenworth. After being severely injured during an encounter with a fast moving vehicle, the wolf had been left for dead. Ben had taken it to a vet and then nursed the animal back to health. When he tried to release the animal, she wouldn't leave his side. One generally didn't argue with a wolf.

After leaving Kelly behind in Seattle, Jake drove eighteen hours to Las Vegas. The weather had cleared south of the Washington state line but remained cold. They rented a hotel room for a few hours in Reno, six hours northwest of Las Vegas. Jake took a cold shower to wake up after only three hours of sleep. The short nap made him long for a much longer rest but he needed to reach their destination and plan their next move. He loaded them back into the Suburban and hit the road again.

Driving past the exit off of highway 95 north of Las Vegas, leading to Mt. Charleston, they entered the outskirts of the city. Sunshine and blessed seventy-five-degree heat rained brightly on them as they proceeded from the high desert. Driving past the first few casinos on the northwestern outskirts of Vegas and into the center of the valley, traffic became denser as he neared downtown. Merging into the southbound lanes of Interstate 15, Jake glanced back and saw Amanda staring with wonder at the tall, multicolored buildings along both sides of the freeway. Taking the Flamingo Road exit, he stopped at the Rio Hotel casino.

The Rio was a large resort with red and blue colored glass panels that climbed high on both of the towers of the hotel. The décor on the inside was just as colorful, a paisley patterned red, blue and gold colored carpeting and neon lights covering the entire expanse of the gaming floor. Paying cash for the room, he rented a suite and took the ladies upstairs.

Leaving Jennifer and Amanda in the hotel room to rest, Jake went back downstairs to the casino and called Cedric on a burn phone he bought at a Wal-Mart in Eugene, Oregon.

Jake figured that the clone had taken Masters' seat on the flight to Mexico. Masters told Jake about the trip during his investigation into Braeden's death. It seemed logical, at least to Jake, that they keep someone tracking the creature's movements.

That meant they were at least two days behind the creature and had to catch up soon.

Jake called Cedric's burn phone but there was no answer. With Mike dead, he needed a tech to crack the security on Masters' laptop so he dialed Nicolletta Vencensa. When she didn't answer, he left the burn phone number on her voice mail. Nicolletta had taught Mike just about everything he knew about hacking when they were in the SEALs. She was working as a contractor for a company that supported several military installations. She had also been very sweet on Mike at the time.

Jake walked around the casino, watching the gamblers and noting the various security cameras. It wasn't impossible to steal from a casino but it wasn't the easiest thing to do either. The garish colors, scantily clad cocktail waitresses and flashing lights hid a very elaborate security system that could detect all kinds of cheating. The places always impressed him but too much time inside them gave him a headache.

Leaving the slots untouched, he returned to the room. Jennifer and Amanda had fallen asleep on the bed. Taking a cue from them, he hung the "Do Not Disturb" sign on the door, secured the deadbolt, placed his gun on the table next to the sofa and lay down. He needed time to get over the fast trip and nearly fourteen hundred miles he had driven.

When he awoke, two hours later, Jake went back downstairs and called Cedric. After trying twice, there was still no answer. Jake began to worry about the wisdom of coming to the desert. Maybe they had already figured out his plan and beat him to the cabin. Maybe he was taking Jennifer and Amanda into a trap.

The third call was finally successful when, after seven rings, a panting Cedric picked up the phone.

"Where have you been?" Jake asked.

"This crazy dog has been playing keep away from me all morning. He stole all my tools then decided to wrestle me when I tried to get them back. I'm getting too old for this crap."

Jake chuckled and could see in his mind Cedric trying to wrestle with the 150-pound wolf.

"Well, I guess you won't mind if I take you away from here. Meet me at Caesar's. I'm sending you on another mission. Mike told me that Masters purchased tickets to Cabo. I need you to find him but don't do anything. We need to keep an eye on him and know exactly where he goes from there. Can you do that without trying to take him down?"

Silence dominated the phone line as Cedric struggled with his answer to this question. Jake knew that his love for Mike Harper was clouding his judgment, but he had to know if Cedric was up to leaving it alone until they could figure out a way to kill it.

"I can." Cedric finally answered. "You know you're asking a lot of me, Jake. But if things happened the way you said they did, and I have no doubt they did, then guns are useless against this thing. Plus, I don't want to end up in jail in Mexico over a piece of shit."

Jake almost laughed at his partner's assumption that he would live to be placed in jail should he go up against the clone alone. Jake wasn't certain they could deal with the clone at all but there had to be a way to stop its regeneration.

"You have to remember this thing isn't normal. I saw what it did to Mike and you saw what it did to Masters, which means we both know what it can do. We have to handle this right, Cedric, or none of us are gonna to make it."

"I know."

"Meet me at Cleopatra's Barge in Caesar's at 5:00 p.m. Bring your bags. Meanwhile, I'll purchase your ticket. There's a travel agency here."

Jake hung up and went to the travel agency. He booked the next flight out to Los Angeles, connecting to Cabo San Lucas, Mexico. Jake paid over two thousand dollars for the round-trip, which was more than he would have liked, but it was his only choice.

Once he had the tickets, he went back to the phones and dialed Nicolletta's number in LA. Again, it was answered by the computerized equivalent to her voice and he left a second message. Once he hung up, he walked back to the elevators and went up to the room. The two Masters were still asleep. He checked his watch and decided a change of clothes would be necessary. He had time before he met Cedric.

§

TWENTY-FOUR

As Jake drove across Northern California, cloaked in darkness, Nicolletta Vencensa was trying to avoid getting her ass shot off six hundred miles south in North Hollywood, California.

Nicolletta, or "Nick" as most of her friends called her, was a freelance computer and network specialist. Mostly, she analyzed programs for bugs, working for very high-profile companies. But sometimes she took a job based on the payout, occasionally for disreputable individuals who wanted her services for illegal activities. Ultimately, she was a hacker who worked for anyone with the money to hire her. She was very good at her job, and her services weren't cheap.

Most of these jobs were remote enough that she never met her employers, and she liked it that way. It gave her what politicians liked to call *plausible deniability*. She didn't leave tracks that anyone could follow. This time, Nick had gotten too close to her employer and was about to pay for it.

Two weeks ago, a friend had referred her to Big John Toscani. Toscani called her and told her he needed a secure network set up in his home. After meeting with Toscani, she agreed to design and build the secure network. It would be used to keep track of all of his businesses. All his "businesses", meant the hoods he employed making false identifications, running drugs, guns and hookers and even a couple of legitimate operations including a Porsche® dealership in the valley. After a week setting up equipment in his home and training his men to use the tablet computers Nick bought for them, she was just about finished. She installed a server with a security algorithm that would keep all of the information transmitted over the internet secure. Toscani's men possessed the only computers containing security keys.

Because of her other activities, Nick chose to work during the evening hours. Tonight, shortly after arriving to complete her job and get paid, all hell broke loose. Now, Toscani was dead on the floor, just feet from her hiding place behind an overturned sofa, a pool of his blood soaking into a Chinese rug. Any thought of how she would collect the balance of her $50,000 fee was far from her mind as she tried to find a way out of her situation. Glass rained all around her as bullets ripped through the room.

Big John's men were scattered throughout the room, firing volleys through the shattered windows, trying to protect their boss. Unfortunately, they didn't realize the mission was a lost cause.

Nick never went into any situation like this unarmed, but Toscani's bodyguard had stripped her of her gun when she entered the residence. The bodyguard was lying beside his boss, a dark hole having replaced his left eye and several more piercing his torso.

Nick crawled toward the two men trying to get to her pistol, which protruded from the bodyguard's trousers. Staying low to the floor, she managed to get within reaching distance of the gun and used her long arms and fingers to pluck the weapon free. Sliding back to her original position behind the sofa, she pulled the slide on her Baretta, chambering a round.

The gunfire ceased for a moment and she heard someone running outside the shattered remnants of the picture window. Two of Big John's men were crouched nearby, peering outside to see where the sounds were coming from. Nick decided to make her exit.

Sliding across the hardwood floor, she rolled to her feet and fled through the open double doors into the hallway. Staying low was more than an average problem for Nick. Standing six-feet-three-inches tall in her socks with curly black hair that descended nearly to her beltline, it took a lot of effort to conceal her. Easing through the door, she found the hallway empty.

Graced with a photographic memory, Nick remembered the layout of the house from the tour Toscani had given her when they met. He had been very proud of his achievement and showed it off with a twinkle in his heavily-lidded eyes. He acted like he had hammered every nail himself. For someone who worked in a business that generally shunned attention, Big John spent a lot of money trying to get noticed.

Halfway down the hall, she heard a burst of gunfire then glass shattering further down. Advancing into the gloom, she saw a man lying on the floor in a halo of glass, a growing pool of blood beneath him. Beside him, a pump shotgun lay near his right hand. Nick knelt and grabbed the scattergun. Checking his pockets for extra shells, she found six and dropped them into the pocket of her leather jacket.

Kneeling by the dead man, she listened for any sounds of movement, but heard nothing. Walking through the open sliding glass door the dead man had protected, she saw shards of glass littering the marble tiled floor on the inside and the concrete outside. Drops of blood covered the cement walkway and splattered the sidewall next to the door. Apparently the dead man had hit someone.

Outside the chilly night air was damp. Staying as close to the wall as she could, Nick moved toward the pool house. Past the glare of the pool lights, she saw movement in the bushes near a short rock wall separating the pool area from the rear yard. Aiming the shotgun in the direction of the movement, she squeezed the trigger and flame shot out the end of the barrel. Buckshot ripped through the bushes and whatever was hiding in them. Someone screamed.

Nick didn't pause to find out how much damage she had done. Moving cautiously to her left around the pool, she struggled to remain cloaked in the shadows. She silently thanked the dead gangster for allowing her to come to his house dressed casually. The jeans and black silk shirt she wore were comfortable, but the jogging shoes were a true blessing. She had a feeling she would need them. Her car was parked in the parking lot of a mall 10 miles away. She had taken a taxi from there to keep anyone from identifying her car.

Hiding in the thick foliage on the opposite side of the pool, she reloaded the shotgun. Racking a round into the chamber, she prepared to move on.

She trained her eyes on the foliage surrounding the pathway as she moved away from the pool. Staying as low as possible, she saw the lawn sloping away from the pool house. A tall concrete wall bordered the property with thick hedges and several oaks in front of it. The wall was eight-feet high, sculptured and beautiful but also functional for keeping the property separated from the world beyond. The only way in or out of the property she knew of, was a double wrought iron gate on the south side of the property. She was moving toward the wall at the farthest northeastern point. As far away from the shooting as she could get.

Stopping at the side of the pool house, she surveyed the open ground between where she stood and the wall at the far end of the property. At least 50 yards of open ground stood between her and the hedges lining the wall. The land sloped downward, making staying low much harder.

Nick heard sirens approaching and noticed that the gunfire had ceased. Whoever had staged the midnight raid was either counting coup on those inside the house or had split when they heard the sirens. Getting caught inside the perimeter of the property by the cops could lead to unpleasant things for her.

Moving away from the side of the pool house, a shadow approached from the other side of the building stopping only steps away from where she stood. She silently cursed her luck and waited for the figure to move away. Peering around the corner of the wall, she saw him standing in her escape route. He appeared nervous, shuffling his feet, swinging an assault weapon back and forth, trying to cover every direction at once.

Nick heard the sound of something snap under her feet and the man spun around to face her. Leveling the shotgun at his midsection, he raised the rifle as she squeezed the trigger. The blast hit him in the chest knocking him off his feet, his body sliding across the concrete walkway. The roar of the shotgun had been deafening in the narrow area. Stepping over him, she heard him groan but she didn't bother to check how much damage the shotgun blast had done to him.

Leaving the seemingly dead assassin lying where he was, she ran for the northeast corner of the property, keeping the shotgun level in front of her. Reaching the hedges, she worked her way to the wall, pausing to look back at the pool house. The man must have been wearing body armor because he was trying to roll to a sitting position. Tossing the shotgun aside, she jumped and caught the bottom of the iron railing at the top of the wall. Using her feet to walk up the wall, she swung her legs over the top, dropping into the darkness on the other side just as gunfire erupted behind her. Nick heard several rounds smack into the wall behind her.

She hoped that whatever was on this side of the fence was better than what lay on the side she had just left. But when her feet hit the ground, she quickly found that she was perched on a hill covered in strands of creeping ivy. As Nick tried to gain her balance, her feet became tangled in the vines and she fell, rolling down the hillside through the clinging plants. Forty feet below the wall, she slammed into a tree, knocking the wind from her lungs.

Nick lay next to the tree, trying to catch her breath. When the pain subsided and she could draw breath, she tried to sit up but stabbing pain raced through her right side. Deciding that sitting up was a bad move, she rolled over facing the starlit sky and tried to catch her breath. Cursing her clumsy feet, she pulled her legs up scooting her ass against the base of the tree.

Once her back was vertical and she stopped moving, the pain eased and she was able to slowly move her extremities. Being careful not to twist, she reached across her body with her left hand and felt along her right side. Although the entire right side of her body was sore to the touch, she didn't feel anything that hinted at broken ribs so, gritting her teeth against the pain, she grabbed the tree and pulled herself up.

Glancing up the hill, she saw a flashlight appear then disappear at the top of the wall. The sirens were much closer now; too close. Without further delay, she moved around the tree and continued down the hillside.

Nick ran as fast as she could, while keeping her balance, through the dense foliage. Apparently no houses faced this side of the property so she was alone. Reaching the bottom of the incline, she found she had another problem. About a hundred yards away was a residential street where cars moved noisily. She was separated from the street by a drainage culvert with walls that sloped twenty feet to the bottom. A six-foot barbed wire fence blocked access to the culvert. She would have to go through the fence.

She tucked the Beretta securely into the back of her jeans and approached the fence. She took out the multi-tool she carried everywhere and cut strands of barbed wire until she could pass through. In spite of her best efforts, one of the barbs caught her shirt and cut her left breast. The sting was instant but brief and she eased the rest of her body through without further injury. On the other side, she descended into the culvert before unbuttoning her shirt to see how much damage the cut had done. There wasn't much blood but it stung like crazy.

"That's what you get for having big boobs, my dear," she said, doing a very passable impression of the Wicked Witch from the Wizard of Oz, her favorite movie.

Rebuttoning her shirt, she climbed up the far side of the culvert and found that the concrete barrier, separating the culvert from the street, was blocking her way. Running south along the wall, she gained enough speed and leapt, clearing the cement wall with room to spare. Landing on the street side of the culvert, she rolled on her shoulder, fresh pain bursting through her ribs and got up on her knees.

Closing her eyes, trying to shut out the pain, she regained her balance and leaned against the concrete wall. Surveying her surroundings when she opened her eyes, she walked south along the street she identified as Hilltop Drive.

She saw the lights of an all-night mini-market down the block. Nick had turned her cell phone off before leaving her Escalade at the mall and had no intention of powering it up. She didn't want to leave a trail for the cops to connect her with the massacre she had just escaped.

When she reached the store, she bought a burner cell and a two-hour card. The red headed young man behind the counter, who looked eighteen but was probably older in spite of the acne that marked every inch of his face and neck, could only stare at her breasts as he was rang up her purchases. Outside, she inserted the battery and SIM card, then powered up the phone and registered the phone card. When she finished, she dialed information and asked for a cab company. The operator connected her immediately. The cab dispatcher gave her an ETA of fifteen minutes, so she hung up the phone and returned to the store.

Purchasing two beers and a Snickers bar, she walked outside to wait for her taxi. She knew that fifteen minutes was really forty-five minutes, so she would have plenty of time to finish the beer before her ride arrived. She finished the first bottle in three long swallows, tossed it in a plastic recycling bin by the entrance to the store, belched, then opened the second bottle and tore into the wrapper on the candy bar. Her taxi arrived just as she was finishing the second beer. Discarding the bottle and candy wrapper, she climbed into the taxi and told the driver to take her to the Casa Grande Mall in Glendale.

Fifteen minutes later, she was sitting behind the wheel of her black Cadillac Escalade in the empty parking garage across from the mall. Her ribs were still screaming, so she took off her shirt and bra and inspected the damage aided only slightly by the dome light. Colorful bruises overlapped the entire left side of her ribcage and part of her abdomen. Wincing, she slipped back into her blouse, leaving the bra sitting on the passenger seat and put her leather jacket back on.

Starting the engine and locking the doors, tears flowed down her cheeks and she folded her arms around her upper body being careful not to irritate the bruised portion. She had been standing close to Big John when the first shots had crashed through the window. Had the shooter fired a little to the left, Big John would still be alive, trying to figure what to do with her corpse instead.

Wiping her face on a tissue from the dispenser in the floorboard, she turned on the radio. Punching the seek button on her satellite radio, she found a station playing fusion jazz and backed the Escalade out of the parking space.

Warm, humid nights were so rare this time of year, Nick couldn't resist opening the sunroof. Leaving the parking garage, she made her way to the entrance to the Ventura Freeway. Using a roundabout route, she took the 134 to the San Diego freeway. Heading south, she connected to the 110 through South Los Angeles. When she hit the 105, she headed west toward LAX.

Sepulveda Blvd. eventually turned into the Pacific Coast Highway south of Manhattan Beach. Stopping at an all-night burger joint in Redondo she bought a burger, fries and shake, eating them on a picnic table outside the restaurant as the ocean breeze moved the palm tree limbs above her head. Gradually her mood improved and she could no longer feel tears trying to wedge their way into the open air.

She finished eating and checked her watch. It was past one in the morning. Leaving the restaurant, she drove south along the PCH through Seal Beach and Huntington Beach. Changing the station to an adult classic station, she tapped her fingers on the steering wheel to the Surfaris, Smokey Robinson singing "Cruisin'" and the Beach Boys with "Catch A Wave".

Nick had moved to Los Angeles from Brooklyn, New York at the age of nineteen. By that time her Sicilian parents had washed their hands of her for good. She was the overly-intelligent child, bred from over-intelligence. Her parents were both instructors at Cornell University. Her father had immigrated to the United States from Palermo, Sicily, when it was clear that he needed a better education than could be had there. He studied at Harvard, graduating with a Master's Degree in mathematics, at the age of twenty-four. He had accepted a teaching position with Harvard until he met her mother, a student majoring in Physics. After a whirlwind courtship lasting six months, in which time her mother had gained her doctorate, they married.

Six months later, they were both offered jobs at Cornell. Moving into a flat in Hell's Kitchen, four months after they married, her mother discovered she was pregnant. Little Nicolletta had amazed even her own parents by talking and walking at six months. By the age of three she was already far ahead of most fourth grade students in reading, math and science. Admitted to a private school for the gifted, her parents had scrimped to provide her tuition.

Nick graduated high school at eleven years old and by the time her seventeenth birthday came around, she graduated NYU with a Master's degree in computer science. She spent her eighteenth birthday in Riker's Island, charged with hacking into off-track betting parlor computers. She was placed on probation but her parents couldn't stand the fact that she had embarrassed them and told her to leave. She stayed in Brooklyn in her own apartment for six months, working odd jobs, finally gathering enough money to buy a ten-year old Pontiac. A day later, she left Brooklyn for the sunny beaches of California. She hadn't seen or spoken to her parents in over twelve years.

When she arrived in California, she found that her New York ways were a constant barrier. Most people found her

Brooklyn accent funny and often she hid behind her shyness. Soon, however, she found that she could market her skills with a computer effectively enough to make money without a lot of human contact. She formed a business that specialized in information security and even gained a couple of government contracts.

After more than twelve years in the southland, her accent had faded. The only time it came out was when she was drunk or angry. She traded her glasses for contacts and lost nearly sixty pounds, replacing it with muscle earned by sweating through hours at the gym. She had a boyfriend who was a member of the SEAL teams long before she changed her appearance. He showed her how to shoot; she taught him how to crack electronic locks and hack computer systems. Their relationship had been an even trade, but hadn't lasted long. She wondered what Mike would say if he saw her now.

Pulling the Escalade on to Cliff Drive, she parked in the lot north of Heisler Park, just a few miles north of Laguna Beach. Making her way out to the sand, she sat and watched the tide roll in. As the surf broke, she thought about Mike Harper again and wondered what he was up to these days.

Watching the waves break on the sand, she dreamt of spending time riding the surf and sunning on her beach. She had made a lot of money over the years and owned a beautiful beach house just a few miles south of where she now sat. Purchasing the house two years ago, she had remodeled it, installing a secure wireless network that allowed her to work anywhere, even on the deck, or sitting on her private beach.

Coming back to the present, she saw the sky steadily getting lighter. Checking her watch, she found it was nearly six o'clock in the morning. She also realized that her butt was wet, covered with sand and she was cold. Nick got up, walked back to the Escalade and started the engine. Making her way down Cliff Drive, back to the PCH, she turned south and drove through the city of Laguna Beach.

Navigating past quaint shops that were dark in this early hour of the morning, she drove toward her home. At the south side of Laguna, she turned right onto the coast road and three blocks down, drove into her driveway. Parking in her garage, she went inside the house and made sure that no one awaited her return.

The sun had risen above the eastern horizon by the time she had checked out the house. Nick locked the doors, engaged the security system that she had designed then climbed the stairs to her bedroom. Stripping out of her filthy clothes, she took a shower, letting the hot water soothe the ache in her ribs and back. She wrapped her hair in a towel, disinfected the cut on her breast and put a butterfly bandage over it. She plugged in her cell phone to charge, but didn't turn it on. She needed a break after tonight. Tossing the towel on to the floor, she slipped her long nude form between the sheets and was asleep in minutes.

§

TWENTY-FIVE

L ate afternoon in the desert during winter is an interesting dichotomy of bright clear sky bathed in sunlight and, at the same time, the temperatures can be rather cold. Sunlight glared off the golden windows of several strip hotel towers as it made its gradual descent toward the horizon. Jake had slept only a short time, but the nap helped drain away some of the stress and tension of not sleeping for the past few days.

Five days after Braeden's murder they were no closer to figuring out the circumstances of her death. They assumed that the double had killed her, but why? And why had Master's created the monster in the first place?

After changing clothes and drinking some coffee to help him stay awake, Jake headed off to meet Cedric. Jennifer Masters was awake by the time he returned from calling Cedric and they talked for a while about their situation.

Jake told her the truth, without glossing over the worst parts, and now she knew how grave their predicament was. She took the news without emotion but then cursed her dead husband for putting them in this impossible situation.

Hailing a cab in valet, Jake told the driver to take him to Caesar's Palace. As they crossed the bridge over Interstate 15, he caught glimpses of new construction along the "Strip" and shook his head. Las Vegas had evolved into a family destination according to the press circulated by the Chamber of Commerce, but Jake always saw the place in a different way. A nice, shiny coat of paint covering graft and misery all wrapped up as an entertainment burrito.

Making his way across the casino floor, he walked directly to a bar. He had spent time chasing women here, in his younger years. Cleopatra's Barge was generally thought of as a meat market among locals, built to look like an Egyptian boat bearing a carving of the Egyptian temptress on its bow, with the entrance made to look like the gangplank. The club was geared to the successful twenty-something crowds and the music was often more than Jake could take. This early in the day no music played, but the bar was open and right now a drink sounded pretty good.

Jake crossed the gangplank on to the barge, taking a seat at the bar. The place was empty except for a cocktail waitress who was off work for the day, and the DJ setting up equipment for karaoke night on the stage near the far wall. He ordered a Scotch neat and watched the crowds filtering past. Tourists stopped and took pictures of Cleopatra then moved on. At just past five, Cedric walked in and sat down on the stool next to Jake.

"Damn, this place is hard to find."

"Didn't you ask for directions?

"Hey, I'm a guy, remember?" Cedric said with a laugh. "I don't ask for directions to anything."

Jake laughed and ordered another Scotch; Cedric ordered a gin and tonic. Jake passed Cedric an envelope containing five thousand dollars and an airline ticket to Cabo.

"Is it bonus time already?"

"I expect receipts, buddy. This is my own money."

"If this thing doesn't go right, tax right-offs will be the least of your worries."

Jake nodded grimly and sipped the single malt the bartender brought him. He watched the cocktail waitress gather her belongings, smile at them both and walk down the gangplank.

"My, my, they are pretty here," Cedric said, his eyes glued to her behind as she wiggled out on to the casino floor.

"Buddy, she probably costs more than what you have in that envelope."

147

"They can't resist my charm. You don't have to pay them when they can't resist you."

"Nothing in this world is free, my man."

Cedric turned to him and gave him a strange look.

"You're a cynical motherfucker, ain't you?"

"Not cynical, man, just realistic."

Cedric turned back to where the, now departed, waitress had been but she had disappeared into the crowd. Turning back to Jake his expression sobered.

"Okay. What do I do when I find this thing that looks like Masters?"

"Just follow him and be careful. I'm going to have Nick keep an eye on flights and see when he leaves Cabo. It's very important to find out what he's up to and where he goes. I have a feeling we'll be seeing him again."

"Nick?" Cedric asked, raising an eyebrow. "You mean Mike's ex-flame? The chubby computer nerd who followed us around like a mascot? That Nick?"

Jake nodded, grinning. "She's quite expensive, but I figured what happened to Mike would lower her fees a bit."

"Speaking of that, did Boroughs take care of Allison?" Cedric asked. Allison was Mike Harper's widow.

"He called yesterday and said she was safe. They moved her out of state and she has twenty-four hour security. I don't think Kelly would go after her but you never know."

Cedric nodded. "As for the double, have you found anything more about what it is? I would say you're at the top of his shit list right now. You've got his woman and his daughter."

"Yeah, well, your job is to protect me, because I am protecting them.

"That's my priority, other than securing the safe house. How are the repairs coming?"

"Done. Ben is something else," Cedric said, finishing his drink.

"Did you pick up your escape pack?" Jake asked, taking another sip of Scotch.

"Yeah," Cedric said gravely, staring across the casino. "What if we can't take this thing?"

"Hey, I'm leaving that up to you. I can't do everything," Jake said, grinning at Cedric, who grimaced.

"Shit rolls downhill; is what you're saying?"

"You got it, Buddy," Jake laughed and Cedric rolled his eyes.

"Well, I guess I'd better get my ass to the airport, Boss. Don't want to miss my plane," Cedric said, laughing at his choice of words.

"Take care. And remember what I said. You can't take that thing alone, so don't try."

Cedric stared into his eyes for a moment, and then slapped Jake's back and turned away. Cedric walked across the casino floor, melding with the crowd. Finishing his Scotch in one swallow, Jake paid the tab.

The glow from the winter sun faded in the west as he walked into the valet at the Rio. Jake had walked the mile between the two casinos, basking in the setting sun. Jennifer was playing a game with Amanda when he entered the hotel room. He told them to get dressed and he would take them out to dinner. Jennifer asked if it was safe and he nodded, telling her a change of scenery would do them all good.

While Jake waited for an hour for the girls get ready, he made reservations at the Rainforest Cafe inside the MGM hotel. On the way to the hotel, Amanda saw a sign on the Mirage advertising the tiger preserve. She begged them to stop so she could see the tigers. The taxi pulled into the valet and Jake paid them then led the two ladies inside.

Walking through throngs of gamblers and tourists, Amanda saw a huge waterfall cascading under a bridge and ran to it, dragging her mother by the hand. Jake asked a valet where the tiger exhibit was then followed the two women.

The indoor waterfall mystified Amanda and Jennifer seemed somewhat taken aback by it as well. Jake stayed here on a trip once and found the hotel incredible for watching people and listening to music, but it was merely glitz that drew in gamblers. The moving water made it a nice place to escape the summer heat.

Waiting patiently until they finished enjoying the cascading water, he led them across the casino to the tiger exhibit. Amanda stopped several times to look at flashing signs, but they finally made it across the main floor to the tiger habitat.

The two magicians who used the tigers in an act for many years had closed their show following an incident with one of their tigers. The hotel maintained their tiger exhibit because of the long-standing relationship. The crowd gathered around the large Plexiglas enclosure surprised Jake. After waiting behind several families, they finally made it to the front of the crowd and could see the tigers within. Amanda exclaimed breathlessly as soon she could see them clearly.

Jake took time to point out the role that the tigers once played in the magic show that played at the hotel, but Amanda seemed uninterested.

Leaning close to the plastic barrier, Amanda stared at one of the tigers. The big cat had been lounging near the pool, ignoring the crowd of people staring in at it. Suddenly he got to his feet and padded over, sitting down in front of her. Jake wondered if the window was a one-way mirror, the kind used in interrogation rooms around the country. Jake and Jennifer both flinched as the tiger pressed his nose to the clear plastic wall and locked eyes with the little girl. Amanda stared quietly at the tiger just as intently as the animal watched her. For one creepy moment, everything went silent as the crowd noticed the experience between Amanda and the animal, then the tiger opened its mouth and gave the glass one long lick. Amanda giggled and the tiger stood and walked to the other side of the pool, climbing up to a perch above the water.

Several of the onlookers pointed at the threesome and murmured too low for Jake to hear. Amanda turned to Jake and he took her hand, quickly leading them outside.

Jennifer looked at Jake and he shrugged his shoulders. He had never seen an animal act like that. What caused the tiger to lick the glass? Most of the time, the tigers just slept as people gawked at them, their contempt hidden behind their closed eyes. Maybe it was just a coincidence but he wondered if there wasn't something more to it.

As dusk deepened, darkening the desert sky, they stopped in front of the Mirage long enough to watch the man-made volcano explode for the first time of the evening. Amanda stared wide-eyed at the sight until it finished, and then they walked south along the strip. Jake flagged a cab and they rode in silent awe past the Bellagio's fountains, the Paris hotel with a scaled down replica of the Eiffel Tower in front and finally reaching the MGM hotel at the south end of the strip. Jake was pleased the women were having such a good time seeing the sights of Las Vegas. He paid the cab fare and they entered the MGM, making their way to the Rainforest Cafe just in time for his reservations.

The hostess seated them, at Jake's request, by the center waterfall, where animatronic animals from all over the world made noises and moved. Amanda sat watching them in awe until dinner arrived. After they finished dinner, they walked across the sky bridge to the New York themed casino across the Strip. Amanda had seen pictures of the real New York City and nearly squealed as they walked along the replica of the Brooklyn Bridge. When Jennifer and Amanda began to tire, Jake haled a taxi and they rode back to their hotel.

When they returned to the hotel at just past eleven, Jake was carrying a sleeping Amanda. Jennifer took her from Jake and carried her to their room, while he phoned Nick again from his burn phone.

The phone rang twice before she picked up.

"Hello," came a distinctly familiar feminine voice.

"Nick, this is Jake Storm, how are you?"

"Nursing some wounds, but fine otherwise. What do you need?"

"Look, I need help. I need someone who can crack the security on a computer without destroying the files."

"Mike should be able to do that, if you're still in contact with him."

"That's the problem. I can't really get into it right now, but we had a confrontation a couple nights ago and Mike didn't make it. I'm sorry, Nick."

Silence dominated the conversation for a moment then Nick cleared her throat.

"What do you need?"

"We're in Las Vegas. This is a dangerous situation. The CIA and other defense and homeland security agencies are chasing us. There are other dangers as well that I can't get into over the phone. You need to know what you're getting into."

"That doesn't matter. I'm assuming you're calling me on a Wal-Mart special. I'll bring secure smart phones that bounce from one network to another and a few other gadgets that might come in handy. I'll also create new identifications for everyone when I arrive. We may have to run, so that will be a necessity."

She told him she would drive to Vegas as soon as she could get everything she needed. Jake asked her to run a trace on Masters through the airline ticketing databases, then thanked her and hung up.

Jake was amazed that she wanted anything to do with him, considering what they were involved in, but Nick hadn't hesitated. He looked forward to having her on the team.

Entering the hotel suite, Jake noticed the light on in the bedroom. Jennifer came out and motioned him inside.

"She woke up and wouldn't go back to sleep until she thanked you and said goodnight."

Jake walked over to the bed, taking a seat on the edge. Amanda gazed up at him with dreamy eyes filled with sleep and smiled at him.

"Thank you for showing me the tigers, Mr. Storm. I loved it all. Goodnight."

"Goodnight, sweetheart," Jake said, tucking the blanket in around her.

Amanda abruptly threw her arms around Jake's neck and hugged him tightly, then settled back into the bed, as he sat stunned. He couldn't believe that Masters had been such a fool.

Jake turned out the lights and shut the door behind him, joining Jennifer in the front room. She was standing by the window watching the cars roll by on the interstate below. Jake asked if she wanted a drink and she nodded.

Buying a small bottle of Vodka for Jennifer and a Scotch for himself out of the mini bar (for a guy who didn't drink much, he sure had his fill today), he poured the contents of the bottles into two glasses. Handing one to Jennifer, he sat on the couch while she stood by the window, staring out at the neon lights.

"Tonight was wonderful," Jennifer said finally turning away from the window and sitting on the sofa beside him. "It felt almost like we were a family on vacation rather than running from government agents and a killer."

Jake nodded and sipped his Scotch. Jennifer leaned over and kissed him on the lips. He jumped as if he had been shocked. Blushing, she rose, swallowed the rest of her Vodka and went into the bedroom and shut the door.

Sometime after one o'clock in the morning, he fell asleep on the sofa with his clothes on.

§

TWENTY-SIX

Darkness was passing into the first light of morning as James Kelly sat on the king-sized bed in his hotel room at the Westin in Seattle. Facing the window, he watched as the sky first turned gray, and then golden as the sun crested the Cascades to the East.

The combined forces of Kelly's NSA agents and the DOD team had accomplished nothing in the search for Storm and the others. Masters was booked on a flight to Mexico and someone had used the ticket. He sent an agent down there to track him but, so far, the man had reported nothing new. It was as if they had all dropped off the face of the earth.

During their search of what remained of the Genetisource building, they discovered bone fragments. The fragments had been reduced nearly to dust during the incineration of the building, but lab technicians were performing DNA tests on the remains. The problem was, they had found the bodies of the four people who died in the fire. The lab floor had partially collapsed but only one body had been found. The remainder of the deaths had occurred on the main floor as the victims tried to escape. So to whom did the bones belong?

Bellevue Police found Mike Harper's corpse in a dumpster behind a local grocery store. When his team heard the dispatch, they tried to take possession of the body, but the locals had been there and gone. Later in the day, his team went to the city morgue and confiscated the remains. Over the course of the past few days, so many people had threatened him, he was certain the situation was going to blow up in his face.

Overnight they performed an autopsy, which revealed that Mike died of a broken neck and severed spinal cord. Much like Marie Jenkins, his head had been nearly turned around on his body. Who could have done that to a fully armed, former Navy SEAL?

Kelly couldn't find Mike's wife and the attorney took over CSS and was able to get a sympathetic federal judge to sign an injunction, keeping Kelly and his team from searching their offices. He spent a day in court trying to get the injunction lifted, to no avail. In the end, Kelly released Mike's body to the attorney for burial.

While he was still pissed at Jake Storm for meddling in this, he had no doubt that Jake hadn't left Mike's body in the dumpster. Kelly had no idea who had attacked the man, but he intended to find out.

After the incident at the market, Hindeman, the white-haired specter now in charge of the retrieval and cover up, had been so pissed he broke a window of one of the stores with his fist. His white hair was splattered with his own blood as a medic from their team bandaged his hand. Kelly asked what Masters had been researching, but was told to butt out.

Hindeman took over the chase and pushed Kelly and his team out of the loop. Kelly had orders to support Hindeman, but nothing more. That worried Kelly. He was certain that if his superiors were telling him to keep out, this situation was a career killer. But he wasn't willing to support Hindeman. The whole thing smelled bad and Kelly wanted out. Let Storm and his buddies take the shit for this situation.

Hindeman ordered him to research Storm's background to try and discover where he might have taken Masters' wife and kid. Over the past two days Kelly searched records they had confiscated from Jake's home but found nothing. Threatening Jake's attorney, Martin Boroughs with Gitmo, had gone nowhere. Borough just smiled and told him to get a warrant or go fuck himself. Kelly got the warrant and Boroughs had shown him Jake's power of attorney, effectively making him majority stockholder in CSS.

Kelly searched city and county records for western Washington and found the cabin near Mt. Rainier but when they searched it, the cabin appeared to have not been used in quite a while.

Boroughs only had orders from Jake to liquidate his assets, which Boroughs had accomplished before Kelly could stop him. The short time it had taken Boroughs to eliminate Jake's involvement with CSS was nothing short of amazing. The money from the sale of the assets had been transferred to an offshore account and Kelly could do nothing about it.

Kelly received a warrant earlier in the day for Storm's bank records. After several hours of searching, he finally found a clue. He had been paying the salary of someone in Nevada. Kelly tracked the man down and found that he lived on Mt. Charleston, near Las Vegas. Kelly knew that Jake would need a place out of sight to stash the woman and her child, so he began searching the tax rolls for Clark County. It had taken him a while, but he found out that there was a cabin on Mt. Charleston; owned by a dummy corporation the CIA used as a safe house. Kelly thought it could be the perfect place for Jake to hide.

Kelly knew Hindeman was given orders to contain the situation at all costs but he thought the man was a little too eager. He also knew if he failed to hand over Storm's location to Hindeman, he risked being jailed for treason, ending his career at the Agency and possibly landing him in prison.

Storm had gotten to him. The way he handled the situation at the Market and the fact that he seemed to be a step ahead of them had gained Kelly's respect. He wasn't prepared to hand Storm's location over just yet because he knew the man well enough to know he would be prepared to stand off an army. Kelly's love for his own ass far outweighed any loyalty to his job and his government.

Kelly smoked and watched the approaching day dawning outside his window. The sky to the west was overcast again, and threatening rain, but the temperature had risen above freezing, so they were only expecting light rain showers instead of snow. He hated the overcast skies and the way they drenched the city in darkness and shadows. In fact, he hated everything about this place and silently wished he could get on a plane and fly back to Florida.

Clouds of smoke circled his head as he paced back and forth in front of the window. In spite of not liking Storm, he couldn't let Hindeman bulldoze them without attempting to warn them. Doing some digging, he found a number for the guy Jake was paying to look after the property.

Kelly heard of Storm's exploits at the Agency when he was still in training. After about two years of working together, Storm's team had been tasked with keeping a witness to several murders safe until federal prosecutors could indict a group of espionage co-conspirators. When an attempt had been made to terminate the witness, Storm took the witness and went into hiding, leaving the Agency blind as to their whereabouts.

After the witness testified, they were supposed to transfer the witness to the Marshal's service. Just after the transfer, the Marshalls were ambushed. The witness was killed and Storm resigned his position. Kelly heard Storm's superiors held him responsible for the failure, even though they had already handed the witness off to the marshals.

Finishing his cigarette, Kelly made his decision. He would warn Storm that they were coming for them. He couldn't keep the cabin's location a secret for more than a couple of days, but the delay would allow Storm time to prepare.

Kelly showered and dressed, then left the hotel. Parking his car near Pier 46, he was lucky to find a pay phone inside a nearby restaurant that was just opening for the breakfast rush. Reading the number off a slip of paper he had taken from his jacket pocket, he punched it in and waited while the phone rang.

After four rings, a message played repeating the phone number, then a beep. Kelly disguised his voice as best he could and left a message detailing what he knew.

Kelly couldn't wait any longer to go into the office, so he paid his bill and left the restaurant. He just hoped the caretaker would deliver his message soon. He called Martin Boroughs and told him to call Jake and have him contact Kelly as soon as possible. Boroughs told him to fuck off and hung up.

Driving to the Federal Building, Kelly parked his car in the parking garage. Taking the elevator to the third floor, he went directly to his temporary office. They had taken over some unused space that was once utilized by a DEA task force working the Philippine gangs in Seattle. Reading over the situational reports on his desk, he found that nothing had changed since he left last night. They were still trying to identify the bone fragments from the Genetisource fire and no one had any idea where Jake and the woman were.

Looking out his office door, he saw Hindeman headed toward him. Kelly thought he would have the situation contained if they hadn't saddled him with the white-haired bastard but instead they had five dead agents, not counting the two men that Masters' double had killed the first night and an unresolved manhunt with no clues. Kelly thought Hindeman was a hired killer who enjoyed his job way too much.

Hindeman and two of his goons came into Kelly's office and shut the door. Kelly folded his arms across his chest and leaned back in his chair, staring at the white-haired devil. Taking the chair across from Kelly, Hindeman sat while the other two men stood silently behind him. The position was meant to intimidate Kelly but all it did was bore him.

Hindeman looked as if he hadn't slept in a week. His white hair was greasy and unwashed. Kelly appreciated that the man was so unraveled.

"We went over Storm's place again last night," Hindeman said, staring his sick gray eyes into Kelly's.

"Find anything new?"

"Not a fucking thing. This guy is like smoke. How could a man just take off like that with a woman and child in tow and leave no trace?"

"Look, Storm is a warrior. If he's gone underground and doesn't want you to find him, you won't. He was trained to avoid capture and detection. Hell, he could be in this room right now and if he didn't want you to know, you wouldn't."

"I thought you hated this guy," Hindeman said, looking surprised at Kelly's obvious admiration.

"I'm not fond of Storm, but that doesn't prevent me from respecting his talents. He is resourceful and an absolute bear when cornered. What you have to worry about with Storm is not so much finding him, but dealing with him once you do. When he recognizes an enemy, he will go out of his way to destroy that enemy."

"One man can't stand up against all of us," Hindeman made a sweeping gesture at the men outside the office. "He can't stand off an army."

"If you believe that, I suggest you look at his military record again. That's what they train SEALs to do and he is especially good at it. You need to accept that taking him won't be easy."

Hindeman snorted and stared at Kelly. "Just concern yourself with finding him and let me worry about how we'll take him down."

"What about Masters?"

Hindeman stood but when Kelly mentioned Masters, anger flashed across his face, giving Kelly a true look at the madness looming behind his eyes.

"Mind your own business. We'll find Masters. You just find Storm."

Hindeman got up and left his office, the other two men following in his wake. Kelly watched them leave then decided that he needed a walk. Leaving the building, he walked down the

street to a deli and bought a cup of coffee. Watching office work-
ers pass by on the sidewalk outside, he contemplated his next
move.

§

TWENTY-SEVEN

M asters' double walked along the sandy precipices of the Pacific Ocean in Cabo San Lucas, searching for Marcella, his mistress. It was the end of his third day in Cabo, land of the ever-present party. Cabo was full of stars, wannabe golf pros and sun worshipers fighting to get their share of the radiation raining from the sky. Men and women were tanned so brown they almost looked like locals; they littered the beaches and walked the streets.

Marcella was not there when he arrived but was due to return from an emergency trip to Mexico City today. She was beautiful but, in her absence, he kept himself busy with other readily available female companions. It was no wonder his creator had loved coming here.

During the evening, the beaches gave way to the tide as sun worshipers moved inside for parties that never seemed to end. Tequila and sex flowed around Cabo like water from a tap.

The clone stared westward as the sun drifted behind a distant cloud making its ever-consistent descent toward the horizon. Small crabs leapt wildly on the sand in the waning sunlight. Grey shadows formed, surrounding the last vestiges of the early spring beachcombers.

After Marcella's departure, he picked up three beauties in a bar. When he got too rough, they tried to leave so he killed them, dumping their bodies into the ocean from the high cliffs that bordered Marcella's small house. They wouldn't wash ashore for a while, if ever, and when they did, the damage he had inflicted would make their bodies nearly impossible to identify.

The creature walked along the beach, deep in thought, wondering what made people spend so much time lying in the sun. It seemed an incredible waste of time. While the effects of sunbathing were pleasing to the eyes, eventually they made a mess of the skin. He was the only person that could survive long-term exposure to the sun and not get cancer.

Masters' double saw two sun-baked women approaching from the north end of the beach and stopped walking. One was tall and slender, small breasted, wearing a white bikini adorned with what appeared to be shark's teeth on the strings tying the pieces together; the other, shorter with huge breasts, spilling from all sides of her black spandex two-piece. The tall one saw him first, nodding at him and leaning in to whisper to the shorter girl. They walked toward him, the taller girl's blonde hair whipping from one side to another. She reminded him of Jennifer.

The creature was thinking how he could play with these young beauties when he heard someone call his name. Turning toward the voice, he saw Marcella walking toward him, shoes dangling from her right hand. Once he noticed her, she ran to him, pushing all thoughts of the two bikini-clad beauties from his mind. Marcella threw her arms around his neck.

"How is my man?" Marcella asked, pressing her soft lips to his, her accent almost negligible.

"I've been lonely without you."

"Oh, you say such nice things."

Lowering her to the sand, they turned north, walking slowly down the beach toward the path that led to her small bungalow. Marcella told him of her mother's illness and that she had only forty-eight hours before she would return to Mexico City. Masters' double smiled as the two women he had seen earlier pouted as they passed them. They had no idea of the fate Marcella's arrival had spared them.

"So, have you missed me?" Marcella asked as they entered the path to her cottage.

"Of course, Darling. I always miss you when you're gone. I've awaited your return patiently, longing for your touch every minute."

Marcella turned and stared at him for a moment, then continued walking up the path.

The double wasn't sure if he had said something wrong or just out of place. His creator must never have spoken like this to her. He had to concentrate on remembering his creator's mannerisms if he wished to live Masters' life.

"You're such a romantic. Keep that up and you'll get more than you bargained for in a little while," she purred as he stroked her long, dark brown hair. "Would you like an appetizer before dinner, my love?"

"That sounds like a smashing plan," the double said. He found he liked sex. His creator had only used the event to relax or for entertainment. The new and improved version saw the fun and sheer enjoyment of carnal lust.

Climbing the steep slope to her cottage, they admired the flowers and the sunset along the horizon. The path was half a mile long, climbing more than a hundred feet above the rocky ocean. There was nothing to keep someone from falling over the edge of the cliffs.

Marcella kissed his chest and looked into his eyes as they climbed the steps to the front porch of her house.

"When are you going to get rid of your wife and move here permanently?"

"Sooner than you think, my darling. Genetisource burned down three nights ago. I'll stay here for a few days then go back to the States to tie up some loose ends. When I finish, I'll have nothing keeping me there." Of course, he had no intention of giving up his family for this tramp, but she wouldn't live long enough to find out the truth.

Marcella's deep brown skin glowed in the dying sunlight and he picked her up off the porch steps and carried her inside the house. Once inside, she stripped off her tank top and shorts, revealing the treasures underneath. He had intended to kill her as soon as she returned, but after careful consideration, decided to have some fun first. He carried her to the bedroom and pushed her down on to the mattress. He would take her one more time, then dispose of her.

After Marcella was gone, he had to fly to Mexico City to kill the doctor who treated his creator's cancer. Once he destroyed the records of his illness, he would slip into his old life completely healthy.

§

TWENTY-EIGHT

Nick phoned Jake at eight in the morning and told him to meet her in the main bar at ten-thirty. When Jake asked how he would recognize her, she chuckled dryly and said she would know him.

Just before she was due to arrive, Jake wandered downstairs and checked out the sparse crowds lining the blackjack and crap tables. It amazed him that people gambled this early in the morning. Jake felt there were other ways one could gamble that were much more meaningful.

He sat on a stool at the main casino bar, not far from the hotel lobby and ordered a cup of coffee from the bartender. Ten years ago, Nick taught a class in hacking electronic locks and computer security countermeasures at the SEAL training base in San Diego. Jake remembered a very tall, plump young woman with stunningly clear olive skin and long curly black hair native to her Sicilian heritage. She was cute and Cedric was correct when he called her their mascot. She followed them everywhere but it was obvious the target of her affection had been Mike Harper.

Jake watched the double doors leading to the valet stand whenever the door opened, checking to see if he recognized the person entering. At ten-thirty an Amazon with curly dark hair walked through the double doors and removed her sunglasses. Looking around, she glanced at Jake then continued her visual search of the casino. She was a sight, dressed in black leather pants and a black spandex blouse that hugged every curve. Black, knee length spike heeled boots rounded out the impressive ensemble.

Jake stared for a moment then looked away, not wanting to seem creepy. A few moments later, he caught the scent of *White Diamonds* perfume and looked up. The tall woman, who had been surveying the casino, walked past and sat down on the stool to his right.

"How are you doing?" She asked, a faint Brooklyn accent in her voice.

Jake glanced at her thinking she looked a little familiar then dismissed at as wishful thinking.

"Do we really have the time to sit at a bar this time of morning? Couldn't we find something better to do?" The tall woman said, placing her hand on Jake's thigh.

Jake was stunned at how forward she was. She stared at him with a huge grin on her tanned face. Her white teeth were even and incredible. Once again he was struck by déjà vu; then her identity hit him like a brick dropped from the twelfth floor of a building.

"Nick?"

"Geez you're slow. I even let my accent through figuring it would give me away."

"Wow, you look great."

"Thanks," she grinned again.

Jake was floored by the change in her. When they had last seen each other, she had been soft featured, because of her weight, and dressed conservatively. This stunning woman could walk the runways in Paris. But looking at her face, he saw the same young woman he had known so many years ago.

Reaching into the large shoulder bag that she carried, Nick removed a small cell phone and handed it to Jake.

"This is totally clean. It's rigged to encrypt communications so they can't be tapped or traced to either source."

"Great." Jake realized that he was still staring at her.

"Been a long time, Jake."

"Yes, it has. I wish you'd come to work for me a long time ago."

"I hate the rain. There are no real beaches in Washington, not like California anyway. I would have hated it."

Leaving the bar, Jake led her to the elevators. Inside the car, he punched the button for his floor and she remained silent. When the elevator stopped, Jake led Nick down the hallway to the room. When they entered, they saw Jennifer sitting on the sofa, Amanda next to her, reading from the Las Vegas tourism guide. Jennifer glanced at Nick, making a face at Jake, as she rose from the cushions.

"I thought you said that your friend's name was Nick?"

"Nicolletta," Nick said duplicating the Italian pronunciation of her name perfectly, sticking out her hand. Jennifer took it and they shook while Jake gathered their bags. "Nick to my friends."

Carrying the suitcases out the door, Jake led them to the elevators where they descended to the main floor. After paying the bill, Jake dropped the bags near the door and walked out to the parking lot to get the Suburban. Nick watched him leave then pressed a button on her remote to start the engine on her Black Escalade sitting just beyond the sliding glass doors.

"So what role do you play in all of this?" Jennifer asked, staring up at Nick.

"I just got here," Nick said, keeping her expression placid. "My guess is, I'll find out soon enough. From the sound of it, it won't be a fun and exciting gig."

When Jake pulled the SUV up to the doors, Nick grabbed both bags and tossed them into the opening rear hatch. Securing Amanda in the back, Jennifer, for the first time since leaving Washington, climbed in next to Jake.

"I'll follow you," Nick said, walking to her Escalade and stepping inside. She didn't even use the steps on the side to get in.

Jake drove northbound as fast as he could without attracting attention and, once they were out of the city, he relaxed a little. Taking the Mt. Charleston turnoff, he made sure that Nick was following then picked up his speed, the diesel engine growling as he climbed into the foothills.

Jake was surprised at the lack of snow on the ground at the hotel which was located about halfway up the canyon. A golf course had also been added since his last visit.

As they crested a hill near the top of the canyon, they came to a hairpin turn that hid an intersection with another road. Taking the right turn off the main road, Jake drove into the residential area. Climbing up the narrow road between homes that would sell for almost a million dollars, Jake continued for almost a mile. Turning sharply left where the pavement ended, the Suburban thumped up the dirt road, climbing even steeper into the trees. Jake tried to avoid the worst of the potholes, but Jennifer almost hit her head on the ceiling after a couple of major divots.

They passed several large homes, each with a satellite dish and lines, both electrical and phone, descending from poles near the street. He turned right onto an even narrower dirt path hardly wide enough for one car and ascended steeply through a thick stand of pines. Within a few hundred yards, they passed a slight bend in the road and were confronted by a large chain link gate, razor wire encircling the top.

Rolling down his window, Jake slid a magnetic card into the slot on a reader near the gate. The gate swung slowly inward. Moving through the gate, they climbed the bumpy path for another quarter mile, finally breaking into a clearing. Jake parked in front of the cabin in the center of the clearing. Nick pulled up next to him and cut her engine.

"Nice place, Jake," Nick said, stepping up beside him as he slid out of the Suburban. "Just the sort of place I would have imagined you living in."

Jake unloaded the bags as Ben opened the front door of the cabin. Taking the luggage, Ben took them inside reemerging a moment later with two wolves heeled at his side.

The moment Amanda hit the ground and saw the wolves, she screamed "doggies" in a high-pitched voice and ran to the animals. Jake started to grab her, but she was too fast. The wolves moved toward the little girl, licking her face, nearly drowning her in wolf drool.

Jake noticed a lot more grey in Maggie's coat than the last time he had seen her. Once the wolves had calmed down, both sat at Amanda's feet. For a long moment Amanda locked eyes with Maggie, dangerous when dealing with wolves, but the animal sighed once, then craned her neck forward licking Amanda's face.

Jake was stunned by the way the wild animals immediately took to her. Jennifer watched nervously as the canines pinned her daughter to the ground taking turns licking her already drenched face, careful not to injure her.

One wall of the family room was adorned with a painted picture of the mountain, much as it looked now with a small cap of snow at the very top, and in one corner a wood stove sat with a fire crackling neatly inside its belly. Jake gave them all a tour and told them to choose their bedrooms.

Nick went to the den across from the family room. Removing a small box from within her bag, she tested the phone jacks, shaking her head. She told Jake and Ben to unload the crates from the rear of her Escalade. He and Ben unloaded the heavy boxes and took them inside, placing them on the floor in the den. As they gathered the last box and shut the doors behind them, Jake saw Nick sitting in the rocker on the porch, removing her spike heels, exchanging them for a pair of Caterpillar work boots with deep treads and steel toes.

"I have to set up a cellular repeater tower. We'll need to boost the coverage up here. Where is the highest point around here?"

"About five miles up that trail," Ben said pointing toward the mountain.

Nick stared for a moment along Ben's arm and nodded her head. "Any snow up there?"

"Not much to speak of. Why? Are you serious about hiking up there?"

"We need secure communications. This is the only way. Are there other towers up there?"

"Yeah, but they're secured behind a fence. You'll need power."

"This baby is solar powered. I just need to get a pack ready and head out."

Nick had to duck under the beam as she stepped off the porch. Opening one of the crates, she extracted a brand new pack. Stuffing some oatmeal bars and a couple of bottles of water inside, she readied the pack as if she were going on a two-day hike. Opening a second crate, she retrieved a small dish and case that resembled a satellite transponder. It looked heavy, but Nick handled the apparatus easily.

"Be back in a while," she said shrugging into a jacket. Smiling at the stunned men, she walked out the front door, disappearing up the trail.

When she was gone, Ben offered Jake a beer, which he gladly accepted. It was past noon, and Jake noticed the old man fixing sandwiches from a plate of roast beef he took from the refrigerator. Jake sipped from his beer and went looking for Jennifer and Amanda.

Jake found them inside one of the bedrooms, unpacking their clothes. Maggie stood guard by the door, glancing at him when he approached. The wolf woofed once, then returned her stare to Amanda who sat on the bed, refolding their clothes.

"Bathroom is down the hallway on the right, along with two more bedrooms. Make yourselves at home. Ben is making sandwiches if you're hungry."

"Thanks," Jennifer said, not looking at him.

Jake returned to the dining room with Jennifer, Amanda and her new friends close behind. Jake went into the kitchen and washed his hands then sat next to Ben.

Five hours later, as shadows overtook the clearing and darkness seemed imminent, Nick returned to the cabin. A sheen of sweat covered her brow and she was huffing.

Jake and Jennifer sat on the front porch watching Amanda playing with Maggie and the other wolf, who was aptly named Tornado. Tornado sniffed at Nick once then returned to Amanda's side.

"Yeah, well, you wouldn't smell that great either if you'd hiked ten miles in leather pants," said Nick, falling into the third chair on the porch.

"We have secure communications. The smart phone I gave you is keyed into that tower. It also has push to talk, so you don't have to dial numbers. Just select the person you want to talk to and push the button on the side."

Ben grilled steaks outside for dinner while Nick took a shower and dressed more appropriately for their location. Ben's eyes were glued to Nick every second she was near him. If the old man's attention weren't so pathetic it would be funny.

After dinner, Jake brought Masters' laptop to Nick and told her the problems Mike had found. Turning on the power, she chuckled then turned to Jake.

"So, that's the problem machine. No worries. I'll just copy the hard drive to my systems and let my apps do the heavy lifting. I'll leave the old hard drive intact, so if anything happens to the data, we can start over."

Jake nodded his head and looked at her. "I really appreciate this, Nick. You're risking a lot by helping us and I'll never forget it."

Nick gazed at him for a moment then shook her head. "No problem, Buddy. I wasn't doing anything this week anyway. Plus, you owe me one."

Nick busied herself with setting up her computers, a small laptop she had retrieved from her backpack, and a huge computer she removed from one of the large boxes. Within twenty minutes, she had the huge old oak desk he had bought at a garage sale many years ago facing the windows, filled edge-to-edge with computers.

Jake brought her a beer and she twisted off the cap, swallowing half the contents in one swallow. When he returned, she had connected Masters' laptop to a box sitting near the edge of the desk. After making a few connections to her own computer, the data from Master's laptop began transferring.

"We'll copy this stuff over and see what we can see," she said, and Jake couldn't tell if she was talking to him or herself. "What the hell have you gotten into, Jake?"

Jake explained the situation, along with what he assumed Masters' research had produced. Nick never glanced at him once, just sat looking at the computer screens nodding her head.

"I've heard that cloning and DNA research has advanced a long way. Sounds like he conquered all of the problems. Of course he made an indestructible animal in the process," she sighed heavily and continued looking at the screen. "Hey, but what's a little violence and murder among friends? Give me a few hours and we'll see if we can't answer some questions."

Nick flicked her eyes at him once, smiled broadly then returned to work. Her fingers glided over the keys so fast, it almost sounded like one solid tone.

Ben told Jake about the message left on his voicemail. Jake wrote down the number, but didn't call. After considering the ramifications, he didn't see the harm in talking with Kelly. Kelly obviously knew where they were, at least approximately. Picking up the encrypted phone, he dialed the number and Kelly answered after one ring.

"Hello, Storm." Kelly said.

"What do you want?"

"I'm doing you a favor, which is more than you deserve. If you're wondering how I found you, it was easy. That means that someone else could too. I haven't turned this over to whitehair yet, but I'll have to eventually and we'll be coming for you. I just figured that I should warn you."

"Why would you? What's the catch?"

"No catch. Just don't shoot me. I'll try and delay this as long as I can but I'd imagine that, at the outside, we'll be there in forty-eight hours."

Jake was not convinced of Kelly's sudden change of alliances but there was nothing he could do except plan for their arrival.

"Thanks."

"I know you're suspicious. Just know that I'm not running things. I don't trust this guy and I don't agree with his tactics. They plan on executing the woman and her kid along with the rest of you and I don't believe in killing anyone who isn't a threat."

Jake snorted once but let his distrust subside.

"Don't expect another phone call from me. I'm risking my ass already. Just get ready." Kelly hung up and Jake stood for a moment holding the phone.

"People, our time frame has just shortened. We need to figure this out as soon as possible and get the fuck out of here."

§

TWENTY-NINE

Hindeman stalked through the offices, passing agents, who diligently and wisely exited his path. Wringing his hands as he walked, he looked so angry that smoke might erupt from his ears any second. He couldn't believe they had not found Storm and the others. He was under no orders to terminate any of the fugitives but he had been given the green light to use his judgment. In his opinion, everyone involved with the Darwin Project at Genetisource, who wasn't already dead, had to disappear.

Hindeman entered the conference room, closely followed by one of his operatives carrying a thick folder. He was so entranced by his own thoughts he failed to notice the man standing behind him. When the agent spoke up, Hindeman jumped as if shocked by unseen wires.

"Sir, I think we may have something," the agent said, placing the file on the table.

Hindeman turned abruptly and bumped into one of the chairs sitting at the head of the table. For a moment, vertigo clouded his vision and he had to place a hand on the table to keep from falling to the floor. Turning to the agent, he pointed at one of the chairs nearest him.

"Have a seat, Conroy."

"Yes, Sir," he said, sitting in a chair across from Hindeman.

Conroy was five feet seven and weighed a little over two hundred pounds. His powerfully built body, and lack of any discernible neck, made him resemble a fireplug. His white shirt was stretched to its limit, making every ripple stand out beneath the thin fabric. His wavy black hair, neatly trimmed mustache, along with his vibrant demeanor belied the finely honed soldier he was. After a short military career in the Army Rangers, he was recruited specifically for this black ops team. Conroy was a specialist in close quarters combat and strategic reconnaissance, making him the ideal agent. Hindeman also thought he was beautiful man, and once they contained this situation, he wanted get to know him.

"What have you got for me, young man?"

"I was going over Storm's service file and found out some interesting things. Navy Cross, several medals for conduct above and beyond the call of duty and for valor. His team specialized in the impossible and, until 2000, he never lost anyone. Then things changed. He was wounded gravely and nearly died. After retiring from the Navy, he joined the CIA. He owns a place in Florida where he lived while stationed there. From the photographs we have, it looks fairly remote with no close neighbors. It also backs up to the everglades on two sides. It looks like a good place to hide, if he were so inclined. I thought dispatching a team to check the place out was a good idea."

"Do it. It sounds a bit far to travel with the broad and a kid," Hindeman said, glancing at the young man's bulging pectoral muscles. "But you never know. Have you found anything else?"

"Nothing, so far, Sir. Kelly is checking his CIA records but has found nothing to indicate any other locations where Storm may go to ground."

Hindeman thought about the situation for a moment then nodded his head. "Send Baker and Gruber to Florida. I want no outside involvement in this. Make sure they have the location and latest satellite recon from that area. Have them check it out and report back to me. Tell them not to get cute and go after him alone, even if he's there."

"Yes, Sir. Right away." Conroy stood and walked out of the room.

Hindeman looked through the photographs again and nodded his head. *Gotcha*, he thought as he stood and left the conference room. Checking Kelly's office, he found it empty. He walked around looking for him but found him nowhere in the office.

"Has anyone seen Kelly today?"

Several people shook their heads and he walked back to Kelly's office. Sitting behind the desk, he went through several stacks of reports sitting on the blotter but found nothing new. Where the hell was he?

His deep distrust made him suspect Kelly of complicity with Storm. A voice in his head kept telling him that Kelly was not what he appeared to be but he was stuck with the man and his small contingent of agents from the NSA. Kelly was a part of the task force, in spite of his best efforts to get him removed. He would deal with Kelly later.

Returning to Kelly's office he tried calling his cell phone. It went directly to voicemail, furthering his idea that the man was fucking around. Kelly represented the political side of the government Hindeman thought was the worst part.

Hindeman left Kelly's office and returned to the conference room where he continued reading reports filed by his agents. There was somewhere else they weren't looking. Somewhere safe Storm could get to in just a couple of days. They hadn't found it yet, but he knew they would soon. It was just a matter of time.

§

THIRTY

Thunder crashed outside the villa in Cabo San Lucas as lightning cascaded from the sky to the ocean. Masters' double lay awake, drenched in sweat, mulling over the nightmare that had disturbed his sleep. In his dreams, he saw blood cascading down the walls of his former prison inside the laboratory but he couldn't tell if it was his blood or someone else's. He also heard his daughter calling for him, a call that he could not answer. Awakening in a dark room with thunder crashing outside, he jerked as if shocked. Marcella lay beside him undisturbed, sleeping quietly.

Rolling out of bed he walked to the window. The feeling he was being hunted wound through his body like a snake and that feeling made him very angry.

Making his way through the darkened interior of the house to the bathroom, he turned on the light, emptied his bladder then inspected his gunshot wounds. They had healed completely during the last couple of days. Several scars marked his chest but were fading rapidly. Touching the area where the bones had knitted, he found hard lumps just beneath the skin. Calcifications were normal but these were much larger than he would have expected. In just one day they had doubled in size, indicating continued bone growth.

When he looked at his face, he saw similar lumps there as well. He'd had no injuries to his face, so why was the bone repairing there? The healing process was supposed to cease once the repairs were made. Why was it continuing? Turning off the light, he left the bathroom and went to the kitchen.

Heat rose inside his body again, indicating he needed nourishment. Taking a plate of roast beef from the refrigerator, he made a sandwich using the roast beef and several onions, along with a large portion of jalapeños. Taking two bottles of Corona, he walked outside to the porch to eat.

He stared out at the cliffs as he ate, rocking slowly in the chair. Howling winds blasted palms and whipped small dust devils around the yard. Yesterday, the weather had been sunny and warm but in the early morning hours of Tuesday, Mother Nature turned her forbidding hand toward the beach town.

Devouring the sandwich, he swallowed beer from first one bottle then the other, in great gulps. If only the beer could quell the fire burning inside his body. Smiling, he thought about returning to his family. Were they looking forward to reuniting with him? Or would they fear him as they had feared his creator. His creator had not seen the value of having such a wonderful gift but he would not make that mistake. He would make certain they knew he loved them and if they didn't return his affection, he would correct them until they did. They would hate him, at least for a while, but he would convince them it was for their own good. *All it took was a firm hand and everything would be right as rain,* he thought chuckling.

Finishing his meal, the creature took the plates inside and left them in the sink, tossing the empty beer bottles in the trash. Returning to the bedroom, he found Marcella awake. Rolling toward him like a cat she purred, smiling up at him. How he had loved that smile when he first saw her, now he felt her mocking him. His head hurt and he placed his hands on either side of his skull, trying to squeeze away the pain. Turning away, he went back to the bathroom and turned on the light.

Looking in the mirror he recognized the anger in his eyes. He knew what he had to do. It was time to correct her. Marcella had made a mistake when she disrespected him and he wouldn't stand for it. As he turned, he saw Marcella standing in the doorway. She gasped when she saw his face.

"What happened to your face?" she asked, backing up a step, placing her hand over her mouth. Glancing in the mirror again, he noticed the skin on his face rippling as more calcium built on to the bones underneath.

"Nothing is wrong with my face," he said angrily.

Marcella backed away another step and the look in her eyes resembled that of an animal trapped in a cage.

"Am I not handsome enough anymore to deserve your company?" Masters double growled. "Am I ugly?"

"No, that's not it... You just look so..."

"So what? Do I repulse you? Is that it?"

"No," she cried, tears coursing down her cheeks. "Jonathan, what's wrong?"

"How long did you think it would take me to find out?"

"Find out what? Jonathan, you're talking crazy," she said backing away another step. "What have I done to you that is so bad?"

He hated her accent and the sound of her voice; he couldn't stand the way she looked at him. How had he ever thought that this woman could be good enough for him to bed? Yes, she was beautiful, but there were lots of beautiful women. He advanced on her and she turned and ran. Still naked, her fear of him outweighed her modesty.

The creature chased her through the house and through the kitchen where he saw the back door swing shut. He ran to the back door, kicking it open. As he stepped through the doorway, he caught a flash of light on metal and felt a blade plunge into the left side of his chest. The blow rocked him for a second, giving Marcella time to turn and run across the courtyard around the side of the house. Grabbing the hilt of the butcher knife he had used earlier on the roast beef, he pulled the blade out of his chest. The hole it left made sucking noises as he breathed and he could feel the lung collapse. Seconds later, his lung reinflated and he resumed his chase. Marcella had made it to her car, but naked, had forgotten the keys inside the house. Seeing him turn the corner, she ran for the trail that descended the cliff to the beach. He was much faster than the young woman and overtook her as she entered the trail leading to the beach. Gripping her dark shoulder length hair, he pulled her backward.

Bruised from the fall, Marcella tried to get to her feet, but Masters' double grabbed her again. Throwing her over his shoulder, he carried her toward the edge of the cliff. Beating at his back with her fists, she screamed as loud as she could as he hauled her to the edge. The howling wind prevented anyone outside the immediate vicinity from hearing her cries. Marcella's howling penetrated his brain like daggers as the tissue beneath his skin re-fused and thickened, creating pressure inside his skull.

Swinging her naked body around to face him, he took her by both arms suspending her two feet above the sandy yard. Marcella kicked him, squirming in his grasp. Holding her right arm tightly to prevent her escape, he twisted her left until he felt the bone snap in her shoulder; continuing until he pulled it free of her body, like pulling the drumstick from a turkey.

Marcella howled as blood jetted from her ruined shoulder. Her eyes widened as she watched him toss her ruined arm, the white bone jutting from the torn shoulder glinting starkly in the cold moonlight, over his shoulder into the bushes. Still holding her by her right arm, he swung her out over the edge. She bleated at him like a scared lamb, but her cries quickly weakened from blood loss.

"Shush. You really shouldn't have stabbed me, lovely," the creature said, his voice flat and absent of emotion. "I would have made your death quick and painless had you just stayed in bed. We might have even had more time for sex. But now, I have to teach you a lesson."

Dangling her as far as he could over the cliff without falling himself, she realized that he intended to throw her over the edge. Turning her over, he gripped her by the ankle so her head angled downward. Blood sprayed him and the sandy ground. Her screams weakened as she began to lose consciousness. Slinging her outward using her ankle as an anchor, he propelled Marcella toward the rocks a hundred feet below, her body cartwheeling off the rocky cliff landing on the jagged rocks below.

Masters' double stood for a moment, looking down at her body, lying on the flat boulder surrounded by the crashing surf below. It was a sad scene but necessary if he was to return to his family.

When he returned to the house, he showered, rinsing Marcella's blood from his body. Dressed and clean, he left the house and walked across the yard to Marcella's car. Using her keys, he started the engine and drove to the airport. He purchased a ticket on the shuttle to Mexico City and formed his plans to take care of his business there; then he would devote all his time to getting his family back.

§

THIRTY-ONE

The day before Masters' double dropped Marcella over the cliff, Cedric's plane landed at the Los Cabos airport. When he landed, he had no idea that he was just miles from his quarry. Had he known, he might have ignored Jake's warnings and tried to take the double out. Taking a taxi from the airport, he went to his hotel and checked in, dropping his bags in his room.

Police involvement was out of the question. In many countries, the police were often worse than the criminals and couldn't be trusted. In many areas in Mexico, this was the case. They could take offense to his searching for the double and he would be out. He had to keep his head low and find the double on his own.

After changing into shorts and a tank top in his room, Cedric headed for the beach. He showed Masters' photograph to vendors and patrons but received no solid information. Several of the beach vendors thought he looked familiar and one woman wearing a string bikini so small he could practically tell her real hair color, said that a man who looked like Masters had picked her girlfriend up at a cantina the night before. She had no idea where they went but they must still be partying, because her girl-friend hadn't returned.

Cedric returned to his room around mid-afternoon and took a nap. At 6:30 he awoke to the sound of someone banging on the wall. After draining a bottle of water, he showered, put on his party clothes and ventured out to the club where the woman had claimed she'd seen Masters.

Cedric found the club in a rundown neighborhood not far from the beach. Owned by an American, the place was popular with tourists. It was crowded with twenty and thirty-year-olds from the states. Pushing his bulk through the dense crowd of tourists, Cedric reached the bar and ordered a Corona. Rock and roll music blared from a stage built at the far end of the long room. When he showed the photo to the bartender, the blonde, obviously from the States, told Cedric she remembered Masters from the night before.

"I've seen him in here before a lot, although before last night it had been about a year. The guy must think he is a real lady killer because he walked out of here with two women on his arm."

"Did you know the two young women?"

"No, but one might have been a local; at least she looked local. She spoke fluent Spanish and not the kind that they teach you in school," the blonde smiled at Cedric like he would understand, being from America.

She had no idea Cedric spoke six languages fluently, including Spanish, and not the way they taught you in school.

"She was very friendly with Carlos, one of the other bartenders. This guy," she said pointing at the photo, "sat at the bar talking to her, then her friend joined them. After a few drinks, they left. There was something about the guy though, he was intense."

Cedric considered this then thought of something else but before he could ask, she distracted him.

"Oh, one more thing, Cutie," the bartender said gripping his arm. "He must be close, because he walked here. I was out front smoking a cigarette when he walked up from the beach. He had a local VIP card because he didn't have to wait outside."

"Did you see which direction he came from, besides the beach?"

"No, but I'll bet he shows up tonight. He seems like he's always on the hunt. Hang out and maybe you'll run into him," she said. No such luck, Cedric thought turning away from the bar. Every time he glanced at the blonde bartender, she was watching him. When the clock struck ten, the thumping of the kick drum from the stage turned him into a pumpkin. Ducking out the door, he sought shelter from the bad rock and roll and the blonde, in the refuge of his hotel.

Cedric watched the ocean waves from the balcony. Wind blew through the palm fronds and the humidity was spiking. Calling the concierge, he asked about a map of the area. When the man brought the map, Cedric inquired where he might purchase beach property. The concierge referred him to two local real-estate agents.

Dark clouds obscured the moon, drenching the entire landscape in shadows. Sitting on the bed, he looked over the map, circling areas where Masters' double had been seen. Homes lined the area near the beach. He had to admit, he agreed with Blondie. The creature, if that was truly who she had seen, was within walking distance of the club.

Stripping down to his shorts, he spread out on top of the bed. After an hour, he awakened and closed the door to the balcony then fell back to sleep.

Near dawn, he stopped trying to sleep. After a shower, he dressed casually, and went outside on the balcony, ordering breakfast from room service. The storm had passed, but low hanging clouds still blocked the early morning sun. When he finished breakfast he called the bell desk and ordered a taxi.

When the taxi arrived, he told the driver to take him to the club where he had spent most the last evening. The cab apparently only had a high gear because the driver nearly broke the sound barrier along the narrow streets. When the cabbie reached the club, he slammed on the brakes swinging the cab violently into the parking lot on screeching tires. Cedric paid the driver, and walked toward the beach from the club.

Hundreds of sun worshipers crowded the sand and after only ten minutes of talking with a few of them, he found two girls who remembered the man in the picture very well.

"That guy was on the beach yesterday," said the shorter woman. She was curvy and large breasted, wearing a thong that would have made a normal man blush, but Cedric led a worldly life and merely smiled. He simply admired her behind his sunglasses. "We were considering trying to hook up with him, but she was a little worried the guy was too old."

The taller girl looked a little young to be in Cabo by herself or even with friends, but Cedric was no expert. She was dressed in a striped thong but wasn't pouring out the sides like her friend.

"Did you see where he went?"

"He talked with a couple of girls on the beach, bought them a couple of drinks and one of them headed off with him. They walked that way," she pointed south. "Toward the cliffs. I think he lives up there."

Cedric thanked the two women and headed back to the taxi stand. As he neared the car, he heard sirens and paused long enough to see two police cars race up the hill. He told the cab driver to follow those cars, his intuition telling him he had found Masters' double.

Cedric spent the day looking around and finally found a trail winding into the cliff face at the end of the beach. The trail disappeared around a bend but he saw it reappear about fifty feet up, then make another turn and disappear for good near the top of the cliff.

Cedric couldn't believe his luck. He only needed to stake the beach out and the double would find him. Cedric returned to his hotel and called Jake to update him on the progress.

An hour later, he rented a chair and umbrella and tanned on the beach, forty yards from the staircase. Keeping his eyes trained on the staircase was complicated because the beach was so crowded.

As the sun fell toward the ocean, Cedric glanced at the staircase and saw the creature stepping onto the sand. Cedric nearly dropped his drink. It took all of his self-control to keep from attacking. But he remembered what the thing had done to his friend and Mike was as competent a warrior as Cedric. Few could take a SEAL in hand-to-hand combat but Jake told him the thing had killed Mike with one hand after Mike emptied his MP-5 into him. It seemed impossible, but Jake wouldn't have lied about it.

Cedric watched the two young women he had spoken to earlier as they walked toward the clone. They smiled, and then he heard someone call out *Jonathan*, diverting the double's attention from the young women. A gorgeous young Latin woman sprinted across the sand toward Masters' double, her shoes dangling from one hand and jumped into his arms. Cedric wanted to warn her, to scream that the man was a monster, a killer, but he just watched as they walked past him up the stairs and out of sight.

Cedric had trouble sleeping that night, knowing the young woman was with the creature. Eventually, exhaustion overtook him and he nodded out for a short time. Thunder and lightning kept waking him throughout the night. When he awoke the next morning, he decided to check out the house where the staircase ended.

Exiting the hotel, rain still threatened from the west. Getting into a taxi, he told the driver what he was looking for and the young driver nodded and headed for the beach road. The taxi driver pulled to the side of the road just past the beach parking area. Several police cars with their lights and sirens devastating the early morning silence passed by, climbing into the neighborhood sitting atop the promontory bluff. Half way up the hill, the cops turned off the road.

Cedric told the driver to let him off at the dirt road where the police had entered and followed the cops. Emerging into a clearing he saw several cars and a search and rescue van parked next to a small, nicely built bungalow. Cedric glanced across at the house and saw stains near the door that could have been blood. Several uniformed officers stood across the yard, looking over the cliff. None of the cops seemed to notice him standing in their crime scene, so Cedric had a look around.

Walking around the house he saw a blood trail leading from the side door of the house and followed it to the cliff. Near the cliff's edge, it looked like an animal had been slaughtered. Partially congealed blood covered the plants and tree near where the men stood. Some of the blood still dripped from the leaves. Approaching the edge, he saw there was no railing.

Looking over the edge, he saw the body of a one-armed woman floating in the rising tide below. There was a boat near the corpse, trying to fish the body out of the water before it was pulled out to sea. Cedric could see even from this distance that the woman was the same one the creature had met on the beach the day before.

Cedric watched them for a moment, then he heard one of the officers yell at his colleagues. They all ran to where he stood and looked under a bush and saw a thin discolored arm that had once been tan and waving at Masters' double from across the beach.

Making his way down the trail to the beach, Cedric tried to control the anger seething within him. He wanted to torture this thing, not for information but just for fun. Reaching the sandy beach, he made his way to the parking area and flagged a taxi. Cedric told the driver to go to his hotel.

Once he was inside his room, Cedric called Jake. The phone rang twice then an unfamiliar voice spoke from the other end of the line.

"Hello."

"Who is this?" Cedric asked.

"Nick. You must be Cedric, how have you been?"

"Fine. Tell Jake I've found the double's trail."

§

THIRTY-TWO

Jake and Ben were walking the fence lines around the property, installing extra cameras and repairing motion sensors when Cedric called. Jake wanted as much advance warning as he could get. In the last hour, the wind had picked up. Ben said they were due a storm tonight that could drop a foot of snow. Jake prayed for it to happen; it might give them more of an edge against the mercenaries that would soon attack.

Jake ran to the cabin when Nick called him. Entering the den, he picked up the house phone.

"What have you got, Cedric?"

"That thing left the body of a dead girl here in Cabo. The cops are all walking around trying not to puke. The damage Masters' double did to her body was severe."

"Was he there when they arrived?"

"No. They only found the path of damage he left in his wake."

Jake thought for a moment then asked Nick if she could get airline passenger information. She grinned and her hands flew over the keys.

"Cedric, we're trying to find out if he flew out. Can you call us back in about twenty minutes?"

"Sure. I'll go check out of my hotel and head for the airport."

Cedric hung up and Jake stood behind Nick with the phone still in his hand. She continued working, using a travel agency, whose computer network she had set up last year. Utilizing a backdoor she had programmed into their server, she hacked into their database. She keyed in Masters' name and an itinerary came up immediately.

"Apparently he flew to Mexico City this morning at 7:00 a.m. local time. He should be landing right about now."

"Check flights out of Mexico City for Los Angeles and see if he is on one."

"All ready ahead of you. He is flying out tonight for Los Angeles, landing at 6:00 tomorrow morning and is scheduled on a flight… Holy shit, Jake. He is on the 7:00 a.m. to Vegas. How does he know where we are?"

Jake said nothing, just stood smacking his palm with the phone receiver for a second, then checked his watch.

"Listen," Jake said, handing Nick the phone, "get Cedric routed back here as soon as you can. Direct would be best, if not, through LA. We need him. When he calls back, tell him what we found and give him his flight information."

Jake left the room, leaving Nick awaiting Cedric's call.

§

THIRTY-THREE

Nick booked Cedric on two flights that would have him landing at McCarran International Airport by 7:30 that night. Completing that task, she returned to work on the data that she had copied from Masters' laptop.

The security protecting Masters' files had provided a worthy task for Nick. After twenty-four hours of straight work with only a short nap, she had broken the last of the protection schemes an hour ago and was now cleaning up portions of the data that had been damaged during the process.

Five minutes later, Cedric called back and she relayed his flight information to him. He would fly American airlines to Los Angeles then switch to United and fly to Las Vegas. When she hung up, Nick saw that the application she had written to clean up Masters' files had completed its task.

When Jake had first given her the laptop, she copied the files from the laptop hard drive to her system to utilize the increased computer power to decrypt the files. Now that the files were decrypted and cleaned, she opened the first of the folders marked "notes" but it was actually a diary. What she read caused her to leap from her chair.

Running out of the den, she hurried outside. Jake stood high on a ladder, securing power and phone cables leading to the house to a tall pole, making them harder to cut.

Jennifer Masters stood on the porch, dressed in a leather coat with an alpaca lining, watching her daughter rolling on the ground with the wolf puppies Ben had brought to the cabin. The larger adult wolves played enthusiastically with Amanda, even though they could have easily eaten her for dinner. But when the puppies got into the game they kept watch silently as their off-spring climbed all over Amanda.

"Jake, can I see you inside for a minute?" Nick said, looking up at him from underneath his ladder. Jake looked down at her, nodded, then took his gloves off and stepped down the ladder.

"What's up?" Jake asked, as he came up the steps on to the porch.

"Just come inside and take a look."

Nick led him into the den and closed the doors behind them. Nick opened up the dated file and Jake looked closely at the screen, his eyes getting wider as he read.

"Oh, my God. He experimented on his own wife and kid?"

"Apparently he wasn't aware it had affected either of them. Jennifer apparently wasn't, but it certainly could explain Amanda's oddities. She has the same genes he did. He could get the cancer and so could she. He altered her genetic structure while Jennifer was carrying her. What other effects could that therapy have caused?"

Jake nodded. "Open up a more recent file."

Nick opened a file dated a week ago, the day before they found the body in the dumpster at Genetisource. Nick read:

2/09/2009: The subject is making threats against the entire staff. After attacking me last night and leaving some very nasty wounds, it calmed down and went to sleep. Every time it gets out of control, it seems to drain it; yet each time, its complacent periods are getting shorter. I am not certain we can keep this a secret much longer. I received a call from General Harmon today and he wants a progress report. I cannot bring myself to disclose the fact that I used my own DNA to perfect the process; if it is perfect at all. The tissue growth was amazing and growing the subject to adulthood in 13 mos., is success beyond all we had hoped for.

But there is something wrong with the subject I cannot explain. We have tested its brain and have found no abnormalities that would explain these rages.

His healing capabilities are extraordinary. Yesterday, I cut his arm, severing the artery but within seconds the massive blood spray became a trickle then stopped all together as I watched the skin knit before my eyes. I wouldn't have believed it, had I not seen it. I wonder how he would react to a nerve agent or biotoxin? It appears his body reacts, then adapts to whatever injures it.

Maybe we will get a chance to test something of that sort on the subject, once I have disclosed its existence to Harmon.

"Who is Harmon?" Nick asked.

"Joint Chiefs maybe? No doubt a DOD special projects guy. Maybe he'll be identified in one of the other files," Jake said shaking his head.

That was the end of the file but there were more of them with dates ending the day of the fire. Jake said he would take time to read later but he had to finish getting ready for the NSA and Masters' double.

Nick nodded her head and continued reading, as Jake went out to finish his chores.

§

THIRTY-FOUR

Jake walked the fence line surrounding the cabin, searching for damaged areas that could be exploited for entry to the property. As he walked, he thought about what Masters had done when Amanda was still in Jennifer's womb; how he had drugged his wife and injected her with a DNA cocktail in an effort to change the physiology of his own child. Jake thought the man was fucked up but this was beyond the realm of the bizarre. Even to save her from cancer, why would he try an untested concoction on his wife and child?

Masters obviously hadn't known the effect his experiments had on Amanda. How had she hidden her gifts? Had he really been that ingenious, yet so self-absorbed that he hadn't noticed his own daughter's special abilities? Obviously, once he figured she was normal, he had no use for her.

Jake saw an area of damaged fence and stopped to repair it. It appeared to have been pushed inward by an animal. The opening it left was just big enough for a raccoon and he chuckled. *Put an obstacle in an animal's way, and they will figure out a way around it,* he thought. Pushing the fence back into place, he drove a stake through one of the links and into the ground. Snow began to fall as he finished the last of the fence repairs and headed for the house.

Cedric would land at McCarran International Airport around seven, Jake would have to leave after he took a shower and changed clothes.

If both Masters' double and the NSA team arrived at the same time, his small band of rebels would have no chance at successfully fighting them off. All Jake could hope for was the attack team would find Masters' clone before he arrived, making an assault unneeded, but he knew that was just a dream. Kelly's handlers wanted all of them dead, making their odds of defending the cabin poor at best.

Walking inside, Jake smelled something wonderful cooking in the kitchen. He heard Nick's rapid fire typing in the den and decided to leave her alone for now. They could leave Masters' diary until later.

In the kitchen, he saw Jennifer removing a large pan from the oven. She basted the chicken resting in the roasting pan, then returned it to the oven and closed the door.

"How are you doing?" Jake asked, walking into the kitchen.

Jennifer jumped when he spoke, putting her hand to her breast, then shot him a nasty look.

"Damn, why do you have to sneak up on people like that?"

Jake was taken by surprise when she yelled at him. He smiled apologetically, shrugged his shoulders and leaned against the doorjamb.

"I'm sorry. I thought you knew I was standing here. I'm just a naturally quiet person."

"I should hang a bell around your neck," she said smiling. "My mom used to say getting scared like that took ten years off your life; if so I'm in trouble with the life I've led."

After pouring a cup of coffee, Jake went upstairs to take a shower while Jennifer finished preparing side dishes to accompany the children. The smells from the mixture of foods cooking was heavenly. Jake realized he had erroneously assumed that Masters provided a cook for his wife and child.

When dinner was served, Nick came out of the den and filled her plate, taking her food and returning to the den. When he finished, Jake grabbed his coat and told them he was going to the airport.

The snowfall had increased. Two inches of powder covered the dirt road leading to the cabin, with more building in drifts near the trees. Starting the Suburban, he warmed it up while scraping ice off the windows. When the windows were clear, he climbed behind the wheel and steered down the dirt road.

Once he had descended to the highway, the going became a little easier, although the snow was falling rapidly and beginning to stick to the asphalt. Jake could see by the external temperature gauge on the instrument cluster that it was already below freezing and the road was getting slick with ice.

Once he dropped below the Mt. Charleston Hotel, the snow changed to light rain, then stopped altogether. The glow from the lights of Las Vegas reflected off the low clouds giving them their own ambient light. Twenty minutes later, he pulled into the passenger pickup queue outside baggage claim. He was a few minutes late, but found Cedric exiting the building. Pulling to the curb, Jake honked the horn and Cedric jumped into the passenger seat, tossing his bag into the back.

Jake drove out of the airport and used the bypass to get back to Interstate 15. Within minutes he was driving seventy miles per hour through the heart of Las Vegas. Cedric pulled a coat from the backseat. He was dressed in a large flowered shirt and a pair of tan chinos. Jake almost burst out laughing.

"So, how was Mexico?"

"Humid, but with lots of terrific scenery. I wish I'd had more time to sample the local cuisine."

Cedric smiled, then sobered and turned to Jake.

"Jake, he pulled that girl apart. I've never seen anything like it. No wonder you and Mike couldn't take him."

Jake nodded grimly and waded through the traffic jam caused by nighttime construction on the Spaghetti Bowl, the freeway interchange where highway 95 crossed Interstate 15. Trudging slowly up the onramp he managed to miss a Toyota Prius that cut him off. Jake honked his horn and the Prius driver shot him the finger. Traffic moved freely again when they entered Highway 95. Jake quickly crossed into the far left lane, leaving the Prius in his wake.

"There was nothing I could do, Cedric. He had Mike and I tried to shoot him, but he just kept coming."

"If bullets don't work on this thing, what are we going to do about it?"

"I don't know, man," Jake said, shaking his head grimly. "I just don't know."

§

THIRTY-FIVE

As Jake was picking Cedric up at McCarran International Airport, Kelly was taking the discovery of Jake's cabin outside of Vegas to Hindeman. Walking slowly down the hallway, he headed for his adversary's office with a copy of the deed for the cabin in his hand.

Hindeman was gathered around a phone with four other agents, talking with the team they had dispatched to South Florida. They had watched the house continually for the past day, but saw no movement. Kelly walked into the conference room and closed the door behind him.

"I think I know where our boy has gone to ground," Kelly said as he sat down at the head of the table.

Hindeman could not contain his disdain for Kelly as he stared at him.

"What makes you so sure, *this* time?"

"It makes sense. Storm loves the ironic and this is about as ironic as you can get."

"What're you babbling about?"

"Storm is holed up in a place in southern Nevada, just north of Las Vegas. The irony is that the place is actually owned by the Company."

"What the hell? How do you know this?"

"I found some old records for cases he worked on with the Agency and went through them. Even though they own it, the title actually says an Agency shell corporation owns the place. The Agency doesn't even know it exists. Hell, I didn't know until just a few minutes ago," Kelly lied, tossing a copy of the deed across the table.

Hindeman looked at the document and slid it back to him. "This says the place is owned by the Great Southern Rock Company."

"GSRC is a CIA front. If you don't want to check it out, then send a team with me and I'll have a look. Jake never declared it and no one thought to ask."

Kelly saw glee emerge in Hindeman's eyes as he picked up the phone.

"Get a team ready to fly within the hour. We'll assemble in Las Vegas and hit the cabin tonight."

Kelly left the room and went back to his office. *I hope you're ready, Jake,* he thought.

§

THIRTY-SIX

Nick read Masters' diary files with growing apprehension. Most of the files were short and, in most cases, so technical that anyone who wasn't an expert in genetic engineering couldn't make sense of them. When Nick opened those, she printed them out, placing them in a pile for further consideration.

Nick's head began to hurt, so she took a break and stood, stretching her long body. The falling snow and howling wind that buffeted the cabin made her shiver in spite of the warmth inside the cabin. She wore a pair of spandex shorts and a tee shirt that advertised a Southern California Indian casino. She longed for her warm house by the beach with the ocean waves crashing on the beach.

Turning toward the hallway, Nick saw Jennifer Masters watching her. She was dressed in tight jogging sweats and an even tighter black sweatshirt with Penn State emblazoned across the front in large white letters. Jennifer looked stunning even when dressing down. Nick was jealous for no reason. She had been self-conscious all her life about her weight and some of the old resentment of the pretty girls still remained.

"So, what have you found in the files?" Jennifer asked leaning against the doorjamb. Nick walked back around the side of the desk and sat down.

"Don't you know how to knock?" Nick said, annoyed at the interruption. Opening another file she found more equations and other ideas related to the genetic design of the creature that looked like Masters.

"Oh, sorry. I wasn't aware that I was supposed to," Jennifer said, and Nick thought her tone was mocking. "Isn't it a bit chilly to be wearing shorts?"

Nick glanced sideways at her again. "These are my work clothes and it's rather warm in here. Is there a problem with the way I dress?"

"No, not at all," she smiled and Nick immediately felt stupid for her adversarial response.

Returning her concentration to the files on the computer screen, Nick felt eyes on her back and looked up to see Jennifer still standing near the archway.

"In answer to your other question, not much more than musings," Nick said. "The detailed stuff is more biology than I can understand."

"Care to let me have a try? I have a degree in biology. And he *was* my husband."

Nick stared at Jennifer, who had walked up behind her.

"Do you know anything about your husband's research?"

"Not really," Jennifer said, placing her hands on the edge of the desk. "But when we met, I was working for a competing laboratory. I told him but he seemed not to care. I'm not sure he even heard or realized I worked in the same field."

Nick felt she had a point, but wondered whether she would actually be able to figure out what her husband had created. She supposed anything was possible.

"Pull up a chair and let's see how much you can figure out."

Nick began opening the files containing the research material. Jennifer made notes on the yellow pad where Nick had been jotting her own for the past three hours. Jennifer copied down some of the formulas then whistled through her teeth.

"What?" Nick asked, not believing she had already come up with some defining information.

"This thing reads like a mad man's cocktail for disaster. I would imagine Jonathan felt a little like the guy who discovered nuclear fusion when he developed this. Taking the nucleotides and bombarding them with this type of radiation could cause cellular decay, or stimulate them to the point where growth was unstable."

Nick couldn't believe, nor did she really understand, what the woman was talking about. She had taken chemistry and biology in high school, but never beyond.

"You can tell that just from those two files?"

"Well, if you have more, we can make notes and put our heads together and maybe figure out how to deal with my husband's Frankenstein."

Nick opened another file then glanced at Jennifer. "Would you like a drink?"

Jennifer nodded concentrating on the computer screen, making more notes. Nick left her chair and went to the wet bar that was built into one wall of the den. She found a six-pack of Beck's beer and a mostly empty bottle of tequila. Opening two beers she brought them to the desk. Jennifer used the mouse to scroll through the open documents on the computer screen, finding nothing of interest.

"Just like I thought. The first experiments were failures. Man, he must have been livid when these things went south on him. I'm amazed that he didn't burn down the lab then."

"Your husband was prone to violent outbursts?"

"Let's just say, you didn't want to be around when he lost his temper."

"I would never let a man hit me," Nick said with disapproval.

Jennifer glanced at Nick and shook her head.

"Sometimes you can't stop it. The only thing you can do is leave, and when he has the kind of money Jonathan had, you had better know how to hide."

Jennifer left her at the desk and went to the kitchen. Nick continued opening files and saw more descriptions of what she assumed was the growth of the clone from a zygote to a fully-grown human being. It was interesting that Masters patted himself on the back for their successes but blamed any failures on the other researchers.

Jennifer returned with two bowls of chocolate covered berries and set one in front of her. Taking one of the berries in her long fingers, she waited for the chocolate to stop dripping then bit off the end, savoring the sweetness of the natural berry with the milk chocolate coating only adding to its flavor. Wiping her fingers, she opened the next file in the directory. It contained what looked like a medical record.

"What's this?" Nick asked. Hearing the growl of a diesel engine outside, she picked up her Baretta and peeked through the blinds into the front yard. Placing the gun back on the table she sat back in her chair as they heard the car door open and slam shut.

"Everything okay?" Jennifer asked from behind the computer screen.

"Yeah. The boys are back from the airport."

Cedric opened the front door with Jake close behind, snow whipping around them as they entered. Cedric carried his bags down the hall toward the kitchen and Jake came in to the den.

Jennifer looked closely at something on the monitor and Nick saw shock register on her face.

"What's wrong?" Nick asked, as Jake came into the den.

"Jonathan. According to the medical records contained in this file, he had the same disease that killed his father. It's a type of genetically passed blood cancer. He was terminal. He was dying."

§

THIRTY-SEVEN

"What do you mean he was dying?" Jake said in amazement as he walked over to the desk. He couldn't believe what Jennifer had said and, considering the look on her face, she couldn't believe what she was reading.

"It's all right here. About eighteen months ago, according to the date on the file, he took a trip to Cabo and fell ill. They ran some tests and found his white count elevated so they referred him to a hospital in Mexico City. While there, they ran more tests and diagnosed him with the disease."

"He seemed fine," Jake said, surprised by this revelation.

"Apparently they were treating him with a type of chemotherapy, hormone injections and vitamins. It wasn't working, according to the data in this file, but the hormones made him feel stronger. According to the last entry in this file, they recommended a bone marrow transplant, but the odds were low."

"Why didn't he go for that?" Nick asked, moving around Jennifer and sitting in her own chair.

"That one is easy. Jonathan had a very rare blood type. The likelihood of a match was, at best, remote."

Jake thought for a moment. The news that Masters had an incurable disease answered a lot of questions. He was dying so he created the clone to act as his donor, or, if that wouldn't work, his surrogate. Something had gone wrong because the doctor hadn't gone public and was still on the treatments he had originally been prescribed. Maybe he intended to use the genetic material from the clone to enhance his own makeup.

"Apparently, he had experimented on himself with the genetic material harvested from the clone. According to the diary entries for this time frame, he performed the experiments late at night and waited for their effect to metamorphose. According to this, he had only managed to slow the advance of the disease."

"My God, the man was suicidal," Nick exclaimed, causing Jennifer to glance at her.

"No, he wanted to live forever," Jennifer said matter-of-factly. "There were only two ways he could do that. One was to fix his own genetic makeup to make himself invulnerable to disease, or to make a copy of himself that others would believe was him."

"Well, I can tell you he succeeded in making a creature that seems to be invulnerable. Have you found any indications that the thing he created has a weakness?"

Nick and Jennifer both shook their collective heads and Jake sighed heavily.

"I'm sorry I got you guys into this," Jake said.

"There was nothing you could do about it, Jake," Jennifer said, smiling weakly. "If you hadn't gotten us out of the house when you did, I am afraid that his monster might have killed us both."

"There is no *might have* about it," Cedric said entering the den with a plate full of chicken in his hand. "I saw what that thing did to that woman in Cabo, and believe me when I say, he can take any of us. We have to find a way of dealing with him."

Jake nodded and stared out the window. They only had a few more hours at the most. The clone was coming for them. How had it known where they were? He had a feeling that Amanda held the answers to that. Jake thought that she was a beacon to the clone, sending out signals that led it to her, like a human GPS.

Jake was about to suggest something, when someone knocked on the front door. Grabbing a shotgun from the rack near the doorway, he loaded a round and aimed it at the front door.

"Let me in; it's Ben." The voice said from the other side.

Jake opened the door and the old man stepped inside, followed by two snow-covered wolves. "I thought you might need a hand with this. I brought these guys to keep watch. They'll protect this place and everyone inside. We were all restless, so I figured we could come and offer our help."

The two wolves looked at each other, shook the snow off their coats and padded quietly down the hall to the room shared by Amanda and Jennifer. Ben grinned and dropped his coat over a chair.

"I can shoot, and considering the way you guys look, you could use an extra hand."

"I can't let you get involved in this, Ben." Jake said, looking gravely at the old man.

"My decision, Jake. I ain't leavin' without my wolves and they won't go, so I guess you're stuck with me."

Jake snorted then grinned at the old man. "I think this is the first time I have ever seen anyone swim toward a sinking ship. Glad to have you."

Jake turned to Cedric and patted the man on the shoulder as he finished the last of the cold chicken off the platter from dinner.

"Put on some coffee and we'll try to come up with a plan."

Ben headed for the kitchen with Cedric. Jake stared at Nick and Jennifer, his palms up as if pleading for a good idea.

§

THIRTY-EIGHT

asters' double boarded a Boeing 767 in Mexico City, bound for Los Angeles. Before leaving the hospital, he changed out of his bloody clothes in a physician's locker room, stealing a pair of chino pants and sunglasses, a white button down oxford shirt and Reebok cross trainers. He wore the sunglasses in spite of the darkness. He also wore a hat that he had stolen from a street vendor near the hospital. Several rooms within the hospital were ablaze. He burned Masters' medical records. Now no one would ever know his creator had been terminally ill.

As he took his seat in first class, a flight attendant asked what he would like to drink.

"Water," he croaked. Over the past few hours the lumps in his face had worsened. Even with the glasses, he looked as if he had been in a bar fight. He knew that if he took the glasses off, the passengers on the airplane would probably have trampled each other getting away from him. The cellular growth was also causing problems with his voice; the replicated tissue was interfering with the operation of his vocal chords.

The young flight attendant delivered a bottle of water, which he gulped down, then asked for another. Blonde, tanned and gorgeous, the flight attendant reminded him of Jennifer. He was hungry and hoped they would serve a meal during the flight. His muscles ached from the need for nourishment.

Thinking about the hospital and the wreck he had left in his wake made him giggle. A man sitting across the aisle from him glanced suspiciously at him then returned to reading the in-flight magazine. Masters' double sat mute. He didn't want any-thing to delay his flight.

When the attendant arrived with his second bottle of wa-ter, he asked if they would serve a meal. She said they would not.

"I'm very hungry and haven't had food since breakfast," he said, his gravelly voice causing the man to look up again from his magazine.

"I'll see what I can dig up for you once we're in the air."

The creature thanked her and tried to sip at the bottle of water instead of gulping it as he had the last.

Masters' double thought about the doctor and nurse he murdered at the hospital. They had denied him his medical re-cords so he was forced to show them the error of arguing with him. He used the young female nurse as a hostage, making the doctor get his files from his cabinet then delete them from a com-puter on his desk. When all the computer records were erased, Masters' double made the doctor watch as he ripped the young nurse's head off her shoulders like pulling a stopper from a bottle. Shock kept the doctor from screaming just long enough for him to grab a lamp off of the desk and smash the man's face. He killed the doctor the same way he had the nurse, placing the heads on the blood-soaked desk. Searching through the desk, he found a bottle of brandy in one of the drawers. Dousing the corpses and his files then pouring a trail to the wall, he emptied the bottle. Using a cigarette lighter he found in the doctor's pocket, he lit the file in his hand and tossed the burning mass on top of the two bodies. In no time, the inferno overtook the office and he fled.

Now he was free of the damaging information contained in the files and the doctor who had treated him. In a few more hours, he would deal with the man who had taken Jennifer and Amanda. Only then would things get back to normal. *No, better than normal*, he thought.

His angry thoughts turned to his worsening condition. He had been mulling over compounds that might stop or even reverse the cellular growth but since he wasn't sure of its cause, he didn't know how to stop it. He wished he hadn't destroyed his old building but that was something that couldn't be changed. He was worried he would not have time to fix the problem before it was too late.

The creature felt the plane back away from the gate and taxi toward the runway. He was on his way back to the States.

Hang on my loves; Daddy will be there soon, he thought as the plane's wheels left the earth and began a steep climb out of Mexico City.

§

PART THREE

The Final Battle

THIRTY-NINE

L ight rain fell on the tarmac at Joint Base Lewis-McChord, a combined Army/Air Force Base, south of Seattle. Hindeman barked orders at his troops like a deranged general. Kelly stood just inside the hanger doors watching the meltdown as he smoked a cigarette, his head throbbing. He watched with mild amusement as the ghostly psychopath came unwound.

Hindeman had appropriated a second gulfstream jet operated by the ATF to handle the transport of men and support equipment to Vegas. They loaded large crates into the cargo hold of the second plane while Hindeman paced the floor, glaring at everyone he came close to.

Kelly smiled, happy inside that he didn't answer to the dictatorial fuck. Tossing his cigarette to the floor, he stepped on the butt. Several large "No Smoking" signs adorned the walls but what could they do to him?

When the crates were secured, Hindeman stomped to the front of the aircraft where the pilot was engaged in a heated conversation with a mechanic. One of the navigational computers had failed and, after attempting to reprogram it, they came to the conclusion that one of the boards in the avionics computers had malfunctioned and would need replacing. Hindeman heard the tail-end of the conversation and yelled so loud Kelly heard him clearly, in spite of the noise from the tow vehicles.

"I don't care what's wrong with it. Can't we fly without it?" Hindeman screamed, causing several of his men to turn in his direction.

"This plane won't leave the ground until its flight ready. I don't care about your mission. In the air, I'm in charge," the pilot answered as if placating a stubborn child.

Kelly loved it. For the first time since meeting the spooky bastard, his skin tone was something other than gray. Hindeman's face turned purple with rage as he screamed at the pilot's back as the man walked away. Kelly sat on a counter and watched as one of the tow carts hooked on to the jet and pushed it back inside the hanger, out of the rain.

Hindeman wrung his hands, turned away from the pilot and trudged back inside the hanger. Passing behind the tow vehicle, he glared disgustedly as the plane's nose passed through the open doors.

Kelly checked his watch. It was past midnight. Storm had fate on his side. The crew said the plane was operational upon arrival earlier in the day. The longer they were delayed, the more likely they would have to assault the cabin in the daylight. Storm, even badly outnumbered, was a fierce fighter and would be prepared. In the daylight, Hindeman wouldn't have surprise on his side. A group of mechanics opened hatches near the nose of the jet and began dismantling the flight computer.

Kelly stood near the tail section of the aircraft and listened to Hindeman yelling at his men. When Hindeman turned his back, Kelly saw several men glare at him as if they would have gladly turned the ghostly man into a real ghost if given the chance. Mostly, Hindeman's men ignored him and did their jobs but a few seemed to resent his outbursts.

Kelly thought Hindeman wasn't just egotistical, but psychopathic. Kelly wondered if he could use their feelings about their leader to his advantage if he staged a coup. He hoped they would stop short of killing the woman and kid and even Storm and the others. As much as he disliked the man, Storm was a patriot and a hero and deserved their respect. Executing them to keep the project a secret seemed a bit rash to Kelly. Something about killing them also seemed to get Hindeman off, especially the kid.

Shielding his lighter from the wind blowing outside the hanger, Kelly walked back to the hanger doors, lit another cigarette and leaned against the wall. Wind blew rain inside, drenching the concrete floor three feet inside the doors. One of the mechanics, descending the stairs from a storage room on the upper floor of the hanger, saw him smoking and started to say something, but Kelly glared at him and his jaws snapped shut.

Kelly hoped Storm had enough time to prepare for them but, in any case, his chances were slim. Hindeman's team consisted of thirteen well-trained mercenaries from every branch of the military while Storm had only two or three. Even under the best circumstances, they needed outside help and favor to succeed. Storm had another problem coming as well. Masters' abomination would be there soon.

Kelly had searched the airline databases before leaving the office and was now tracking its flights with his smartphone. Further checking confirmed that the person using Masters' identification had booked a ticket to Las Vegas. Kelly first assumed that Masters had survived the blaze that destroyed Genetisource but the preliminary results of DNA tests on bone fragments found inside the remains of the lab were identified as the doctor's. So this was something Masters had cooked up in his lab.

Without knowing all the details, Kelly couldn't answer those questions. Hindeman tasked him with searching for the person traveling under Masters' identification *after* the results of the DNA tests had returned, placing the doctor inside the building during the fire. Kelly wasn't as dense as Hindeman believed and he assembled an impossible conclusion. Masters had cloned himself, using government money, and now that clone was on his way to Las Vegas. After digging a little, he found a medical record confirming Masters' terminal disease. Kelly had pieced the rest of the story together. But why was the clone after Storm and Masters' kid?

Though Kelly wasn't prone to flights of imagination, it was the only scenario that made sense. He also heard the report from the agents who had confronted Masters' double, after he killed Monroe, on the night of the fire. They shot Monroe's assailant four times but the bullets hadn't slowed him. Of course, he could have been wearing Kevlar but where would a middle-aged scientist get body armor?

Kelly was pondering doctors in body armor when Hindeman surprised him from behind.

"We're delayed at least two hours. They have to replace parts of the main avionics system."

Kelly nodded, barely able to conceal his glee. Taking a draw off of his cigarette, he covered his smile with the palm of his hand.

"Well, aren't you going to say anything?"

"So we're delayed a couple of hours. It's a short flight to Vegas. You'll still get to take them by early morning," *but not under the cover of darkness you chicken shit bastard*, Kelly thought, trying to stifle the laughter building in his chest.

"Great. Another idiot who doesn't see the value of ending this operation before first light."

"Hindeman, you're a moron. And you might want to curb that attitude. I'm not one of your mercs and I don't work for you. Get cute with me again and you might find yourself in a world of trouble."

Hindeman gazed at Kelly for a minute in stunned disbelief then snapped his fingers.

"One word from me, Kelly and my men would take you out, just like that."

Kelly glared at Hindeman and waved the hand holding the cigarette butt. "Maybe, but I assure you, you'll be dead before they get me. But then you don't like doing your own killing, do you? I'll remember not to turn my back to you. You're a coward, but cowards are dangerous too. Stay away from me."

Hindeman regarded Kelly closely and, for a moment, Kelly thought he saw fear cross his grey face. Then it was gone.

"You can leave any time you like, Kelly. We don't need you."

"I have no intention of going anywhere but Las Vegas."

Hindeman turned away. Kelly watched him then turned back toward the door. Accidents happened and if he played it right, Hindeman could have one and no one would care.

Almost three hours after they were supposed to leave, the Gulfstream jets finally took off into the steel gray skies.

§

CHAPTER FORTY

W hile Nick and Jennifer continued reading the files, Jake and Cedric cleaned and lubricated the assault rifles he brought from the storage unit in Seattle. It seemed a lifetime ago. When they finished with the rifles, Jake stripped and cleaned both the Browning and the Glock, reloading the magazines and chambered rounds.

Nick called out to them from the den. When he and Cedric entered the room, she pointed at a box near the corner.

"Take a look in there. I anticipated the snow and brought something that might help."

Jake and Cedric lifted the box off the floor. Using a knife, Jake sliced the tape and opened the top. Reaching inside, he removed an insulated white snowsuit. Cedric pulled a second snowsuit from the box as Jake looked over at Nick. Nick's face, illuminated by the light from the LCD computer screen, looked ethereal. All she needed was a pair of wings to complete the image.

"I made sure to get one in gargantuan size for the big guy over here," Nick said, smiling at Jake. "They're tactical snowsuits. There are pockets for two handguns and enough room to carry several magazines."

"What made you think of this?"

"I knew this was bad; I could tell it from your voice. I figured every advantage we could get would help."

Taking the snowsuits, they returned to the kitchen and placed extra magazines in the pockets. Once they were outfitted, Ben entered to pour himself a cup of coffee.

"Ben, do you have extra cans of gasoline?" Jake asked.

"Yep. I have three full cans in the shed, why?"

"Get them and any usable glass jars. We don't have any-thing that goes bang but we can still make a few party favors for our guests."

When Ben and Cedric returned with the gas cans, Jake was sitting at the kitchen table with a saucer full of buckshot and powder in front of him.

"What the hell is he doing?" Ben asked Cedric.

"Ever seen a homemade landmine?"

Pouring equal amounts of the buckshot and powder into two plastic bowls, using powder and detonator cores from the shotgun shells, he created a detonator and plugged it into the bowls. Taking the makeshift mines, he connected the detonators to the motion sensors at the base of the backdoor. If someone attempted to get in the back door - Boom!

"What the fuck are you planning?" Ben asked, watching Jake place the IED near the back door. "How much damage will those things do?"

"If it comes to this, they'll have gotten past our outer perimeter so this is just to piss them off. It also might slow them down if we're going out the other exit. It's a great alarm system too. Even under the loudest of conditions, an explosion will let you know they're coming."

Pouring each of the ten jars Ben and Cedric found half full with gasoline, he turned each into a Molotov Cocktail. Once they were ready, he rigged them to one of the extra burn phones they were no longer using. After he placed each bomb into a plastic freezer bag, he donned his snowsuit. Jake took the jars and went out into the blizzard. Half an hour later he returned, covered in snow, wearing a smile on his face.

He removed the snowsuit as the first gray touched the eastern sky. Jake walked through the house securing windows and checking all their internal defenses. When he entered Amanda's room, he found her asleep with the two wolves lying next to her bed. One of the wolves raised its head, growled once then returned its head to its paws.

Jake left the door to Amanda's room open, just in case someone gained access through her window, and returned to the den. Nick and Jennifer were still reading the files in the computer.

"Find anything?"

"The plane will land at LAX in about forty minutes. We think we may have found a chink in this thing's armor. Jennifer will tell you. I have to go to the ladies' room," Nick said as she slipped past him into the front room.

Jake walked to the side of the desk and looked over her shoulder. She was using the mouse to bounce back and forth between files and making notes on a legal pad. She was so engrossed that she jumped when she realized he was standing there.

"Please stop doing that."

"What do you have for me?" Jake said, ignoring her pleas.

"It's nothing more than a theory at the moment and I want to confirm a couple of things before I tell you."

With a wave of her hand, she shooed him away. Jake checked his watch and saw that it was 5:45 in the morning. *She had better be quick*, he thought, *or it would be too late to help.*

§

FORTY-ONE

Nick provided Jake with a laptop and set it up so he could watch the images transmitted from wireless cameras installed along the perimeter of the property. Daylight began to brighten the snowy skyline when Jennifer walked into the kitchen.

The wind had decreased so that the snowflakes were coming straight down rather than sideways, but the snow was mounting up quickly. Almost a foot had fallen overnight and if it didn't slow soon, their means of escape would be cut off.

Jake spent some of his vacations renovating and upgrading the accommodations in the cabin. They often had problems with burglars breaking into homes left vacant during the early part of spring and summer. Once the season got rolling, there was enough traffic to keep crime to a minimum but before the tourists and locals came to their summer residences, traffic was fairly light and the area remote enough to entice even the most inexperienced thief. He built the fence when he first bought the cabin, mainly to keep out cougars and other large wildlife. He'd added motion detectors and a few cameras when a woman from just down the hill was raped and nearly killed by someone visiting the neighborhood. The perpetrator was never caught.

"Ready to have a chat?" Jennifer asked.

Jake nodded. "It's about time. I was beginning to think you hadn't found anything."

"There may not be; I'm not a hundred percent sure the solution will work."

Jake followed her down the hallway and into the room adjacent to the den where Ben, Nick and Cedric sat waiting. Amanda was still asleep, so they spoke as quietly as they could.

"Where is Masters' clone?" Jake asked.

"Last time I checked, Nick said, "his flight had landed in LA and the flight to Las Vegas had just taken off. That was about ten minutes ago."

Jake calculated the flight time from LAX to Vegas and figured that they had about half an hour until he landed at McCarran and about another hour from the airport to the cabin, unless the roads were really bad. It didn't leave much time for planning.

"First, let me say that despite his faults, Jonathan was a fucking genius. So were the researchers he hired to assist him. He realized that he needed a host for his creation, but who would volunteer for that duty?" Jennifer said, pacing back and forth in the small kitchen.

She continued to talk, answering her own question. "One of his researchers, Mario Alonga, had some experience in engineering as well as bioengineering. He designed an incubation chamber that worked very much like a womb, but with several advantages. They could alter the DNA of the subject within the chamber from conception to birth without harming the mother, since, in reality, there wasn't one to harm.

"They harvested eggs from one of the females on the team, that person was not named in any of the files, but I am assuming that it was Marie Jenkins, since she was Jonathan's type. They created a DNA strand from several of the scientists then Jonathan found out he was sick again."

"Again?" Jake asked, surprised.

"Yes, he was sick with cancer when he injected me with one of the compounds while I was pregnant. The cancer was his motivation. By the time he was diagnosed the second time, his cancer was too advanced to fight with chemotherapy and radiation. He tried the compounds on himself but they didn't help. Jonathan altered the DNA strand making his own DNA the dominant strain. Once their creation began to develop, they placed it into the incubation tank. As it grew, they induced new healing patterns and other alterations by bombarding it with special types of radiation, causing an internal defense mechanism to kick into gear. They studied the result and made changes, adding DNA from several different species as well as cocktails they created from scratch, effectively creating something stronger than any human. And, it could heal itself from most wounds."

"Okay, so we know how they made it but how does that help us?" Cedric asked, a note of impatience in his voice.

"Okay, before you can defeat something, you have to study it to find its weakness, right?" Jennifer said, and Cedric nodded. "Then, listen. When a woman gets pregnant, the baby is a part of her for nine months. Everything that travels through the mother, nourishment, drugs, whatever, travels through to the baby. Not perfect systems, since any problems the mother has also affect the child but, nonetheless, effective. If a mother eats and drinks healthy, then the odds are better than average, she'll have a healthy baby. If not, then you can have all kinds of abnormalities."

Jake was concerned about the credit Jennifer was giving her husband. The gleam in her eyes reminded him way too much of the way Masters looked nearly every time Jake had seen him.

Jennifer placed a sheet of paper on the coffee table and they all leaned forward. There were two drawings on the sheet side by side.

"You see the one on the left is a gene strand from a normal human being. It represents the genetic structure of a person before outside forces change it. The one on the right is from our subject."

Jake saw some subtle differences but they looked very much alike. Then he noticed the complexities of the second strand. There were more links in the second than there were in the first. He voiced this and Jennifer nodded.

"Right you are. This thing was conceived in a test tube from two normal... well, somewhat normal, people. Then they mutated it like a virus, giving it impossible regenerative powers, brain capacity twice that of a normal human and looks just like Jonathan. He even manipulated the eye color to match his own. By all rights, the clone should have picked up the brown eye color that was dominant in Marie's genetic make-up, but Jonathan wanted an exact duplicate. So he merely manipulated the code to get rid of the brown and make them light blue."

"But how the hell did they grow a human being into a forty-year-old adult male in less than two years?" Jake asked, frustrated with the length of time it was taking to get to the bottom of this.

"It was actually a by-product of making the subject invulnerable to outside forces. Diseases have no effect on it because of the new genetic material introduced during its creation. They designed the creation to advance to adulthood at twenty times the speed of normal growth. Jonathan further sped up the production cycle with nutrients and radiation treatments. But doing that caused a chain reaction I believe is now out of control." Jennifer waited for them to ask questions and when none came, she continued.

"The one thing Jonathan hadn't planned on was the fact that eventually they would have to let the subject out of the incubation chamber. Jonathan was always shortsighted when it came to human interaction. Once they brought the subject into the world, birthed it if you will, it was a fully-grown adult with no concept of human feelings or attitudes.

"Jonathan stimulated it only with his own demented ideas. The clone's only interaction was with those inside the lab. Lack of outside stimulation and human experiences gradually drove it insane. It wasn't allowed sexual stimulation which is a major part of human development. It listened to the researchers talk about their lives and envied them. It longed for a normal life and resented their keeping him locked up. Over the past six months, it reached adult size and began building strength. It began rebelling, threatening the researchers. They didn't pay attention to it and eventually they paid."

"The problem with all of the mutations was they hadn't thought about what effect it had on the subject's brain development. We develop a conscience through our environment. If you take the religious stand, the subject was created in a lab, so it has no soul. From a psychological point of view, the subject has no conscience. It had nothing but the men and women on the project, especially Jonathan, to learn from and, considering his record, Jonathan was a lousy representation of how to act. It only knew its prison; therefore, it developed no sense of humanity.

"Add to that its ability to heal, the knowledge of which made him feel invulnerable and superior to them all. That eventually led to Wilma Braeden's death. He beat her to death that night during an experiment. Later, when Jonathan tried to feed him and apparently drug him, he did the same to Jonathan. Then he destroyed the prison they had kept him in."

"But how the fuck do we stop it?" Jake said, finally losing his temper a little.

"I spent a long time reviewing Jonathan's notes and found only one way that may work. Bullets will only slow it down and, by now, they may not even do that. Like I said, it's still mutating. By the time it shows up here, it may be able to eat gold and shit coins. But I think if you remove the control center, you will remove its ability to regenerate. Of course it's only a theory."

Jake thought for a moment then shook his head.

"What you're saying is that if we separate brain from heart, it might kill it?"

"Yes, and I would remove the head from the vicinity of the body just to make sure it doesn't attempt to reattach itself."

Jake thought about this and then went into the den. Taking one of the swords he collected off the wall, he returned to the front room and unsheathed the weapon.

"Think something like this would work?"

"You would have to swing it with incredible force, and it would have to be very sharp to cut through the muscle and bone completely with one swing, but yes, I think it would do the trick."

Cedric looked at Jake and began shaking his head.

"Jake, that means one of us is going to have to risk getting close enough to use that thing. You saw what it did to Mike. Whoever does that has to risk getting close enough for it to grab and kill them."

Jake nodded his head and watched as the light traveled up and down the blade. Using a stone hanging from the sheath, he began sharpening it.

"That's why your job is to lead everyone out of here when it arrives."

They all stared at Jake as he ran the stone down the edge of the sword. Cedric started to protest again when Jake heard movement behind him. He turned and saw Amanda standing there in her pajamas, a wolf at each elbow.

"It's coming, Mommy. Daddy's monster is coming."

§

FORTY-TWO

Half an hour after Amanda appeared in the living room and made her bold statement, they finished preparing for the coming battle. Turning the den into an operations center, Nick tied into the feed from each of the wireless cameras. They now displayed on two monitors in front of her. Jake explained she would be their eyes and ears, communicating everything she saw to him and Cedric. Gathering everyone in the living room, he went over his plan. They were all dressed in white snowsuits.

"We have to wait until it shows up to get everyone out of here. I know that sounds like we're cutting it close but I think we all know that this thing is tuned in somehow. It's drawn to Jennifer and Amanda. Once it's inside the cabin and I engage it, Cedric, you have to get everyone out of here to a safe place."

"So, you intend to face it alone?" Cedric said, skeptically.

"We don't have a choice. Someone has to evacuate them from the house after he is inside. There's no other way. Once he's inside, he won't leave here in one piece, I assure you. Remember that this thing is capable of doing a lot of damage. You have to protect them. One of us has to stay behind. I have the training with blades and you don't."

Cedric's expression was grim as he thought through the situation, trying to come up with a better plan. He struggled with the idea that he was being relegated to the sidelines while Jake faced this horror alone. Tears fell down Jennifer's face and Amanda was wide eyed with fear as they realized that this was probably the only chance they had to survive.

"Everyone stays in this room except for Cedric and me. You all have your earpieces so we can communicate throughout this ordeal. No matter what you hear from inside the cabin, you cannot come back. That's an order, Cedric. It's the first one I've given you since the Navy but if you ever thought of disobeying me, now isn't the time.

"Once I engage the creature, I want everyone as far away from here as you can get. Use the trees for cover. Remember that we have another enemy coming. We will have to deal with them and that may be a harder task. It isn't going to be easy to get past them either, but you have to do your best. If you fail, they'll kill all of you."

Jake went into the den with Nick as she sat before the monitors. Even in the dim light of the displays, she was beautiful. Jake stared at her for a moment, wanting to lock this vision inside his mind.

"Okay, we have camera views up on the north side of the perimeter. No sign of movement," Nick said as she surveyed the monitors.

"Outstanding. Let's perform a communications check; then we wait."

Jake began by asking each of the team to reply to him. Each one did so in unison. Once they were sure that everyone's COM link was working, he left Nick to watch the monitors for activity. He prepared his weapons.

Tucking his Glock inside a pocket of his snowsuit, securing it with a Velcro strap and taking one of the MP-5 assault weapons, he flipped a selector switch. This converted it to fully automatic and slung the strap over his shoulder. Taking the samurai sword he would use to take the creature's head, he secured the weapon across his back with a sash along with two Velcro straps on the side of his suit.

All in the group, save Cedric, watched in fascination as he prepared to do battle against a foe that seemed unbeatable. Jake hoped that Jennifer was correct in her assumptions about taking the head of this monster, because if she was wrong, they wouldn't get another chance.

Jake stared at all of them as they stood, awaiting the arrival of their quarry. Amanda's eyes were getting wider by the second as she felt the emotions within the room getting more strained. The little girl was wrapped in her mother's arms and seemed so small compared to the rest of the world. Jake knew that he couldn't let these people down.

Jake was still looking at Amanda when a wind gust hit the front door, making it creak. Up until now there had been no wind since the very early hours and he was surprised by the gust. Amanda stared into his eyes and spoke.

"I sorry," said Amanda, tears slowly rolling down her cheeks.

"What's wrong, honey?" Jake asked.

"I tried to stop him but I couldn't. He's here."

§

FORTY-THREE

When the double's flight landed at McCarran
International Airport, he was among the first
passengers into the jet way. Walking through the terminal, he
attracted the attention of nearly everyone he passed. He found
nearly every car rental line packed with impatient travelers. He
didn't have the time to wait. Bypassing the counter, he made
haste for the nearest exit.

Leaving baggage claim, he walked out to the pickup line.
Looking down the line of cars picking up passengers and taxis
waiting for fares, the clone saw what he needed immediately
parked at the curb, just thirty feet away. Smiling through his pain,
he walked straight to the huge black Ford Excursion. In spite of
the Homeland Security ban on parking and leaving your vehicle
too close to the airport, it appeared whoever owned this vehicle
had gone inside. An airport cop was walking toward the vehicle
so the double ran to the driver's door and jerked it open. The
Excursion's diesel engine was running so he climbed behind the
wheel and pulled away from the curb.

Entering the I-215 connector, he drove fast, traveling
through the tunnel under the runways, taking the onramp to Interstate 15. There was a constant low buzzing noise in his head
that guided his actions, leading him to his wife and daughter like
radar. His eyes hurt and his vision was hampered by the outcrop-
pings of new bone hooding the sockets. His rage at the man
who had taken his wife and child fueled him and pushed him on-
ward.

Entering I-15 northbound, he pressed hard on the accelerator and pushed the big SUV up to eighty. A low grey ceiling of

clouds brightened at the horizon as the night gave way to day. It was still early enough that no traffic snarls impeded his progress in spite of the rain.

Pain wracked his brain, causing his eyes to tear up. Pinching the bridge of his nose between his thumb and forefinger, he breathed deeply, trying to relax through the pain. The progression of rapidly building tissue on his face and body had quickened in the past few hours. At LAX, he had purchased $40 worth of food from a McDonalds inside the terminal and wolfed it down while walking from the international terminal to the domestic terminal. His body had processed the nutrients and was now feeding on itself, causing rapid tissue building and reduction. He was weaker than just a few hours ago.

Voices, like standing in the center of a crowded room, echoed inside his head impeding his focus, causing him to swerve the SUV. The blast of a horn to his right made him jerk the wheel to the left to correct his path of travel. Glancing to his right to identify the offended party, he saw his daughter sitting in the seat next to him. He blinked his eyes, but she remained.

"How did you get here? Where's your mother?"

Amanda said nothing, just stared at him. Completely entranced by this vision of his daughter, his attention once again diverted from the road and his driving. She wasn't afraid of him; her impassive expression made her seem insolent. She mumbled something he couldn't understand, increasing his ire.

"Speak clearly," he yelled, expecting her to flinch but her passive expression remained.

"You are not my father, even though you think you are. You have to end this now," Amanda said.

"I'm coming to get you little one. You and your mother. When I get there and deal with that man, we'll have a chat about your actions. Did that bitch of a mother teach you to speak to your elders this way? Where are your manners?"

Amanda's expression remained passive. Glaring at her, he had to swerve to miss another car.

"No. You must not come for us. You must take yourself someplace and finish this."

The creature waved a hand at her as he heard the sound of the tires hitting the reflectors between the lanes and corrected the SUV's course. Staring at the road, he chose the off-ramp leading to the northbound expressway. As he rocketed on to the highway, he strained to keep the vehicle from careening into the concrete guardrail.

Merging with westbound traffic, he steered sharply to the outside lane and pressed the accelerator to the floor. The big diesel responded immediately and he rolled first westward, then turned to the north, spraying fishtails of rainwater in his wake.

Masters' double glanced over at the passenger seat but Amanda had disappeared. Deciding the vision had been a figment of his imagination, he pressed even harder on the pedal. He had to get his family back.

When he arrived at the Mount Charleston turn off, he failed to see it in time to slow down and slammed on the SUV's brakes, sliding to a stop two hundred yards beyond. Turning left from where he was, he drove through a center median and turned onto the southbound lanes, causing several cars to slide to a stop to avoid hitting him. When he reached the turnoff, he twisted the wheel to the right and bounced on to the westbound road leading up the canyon.

Sharp pain attacked the base of his brain, causing him to swerve again. Blood trickled from his nose and ears as the pain intensified. Straightening the car, his stomach growled. The bleeding stopped as the vessels healed. He was so hungry he could have eaten his own arm but he thought he would need it in the coming battle and was afraid it might not grow back.

Stopping for food was not an option when he was this close. Ignoring his stomach, he tried to get more speed from the big Ford.

Strengthening his resolve, he pressed on. As his speed neared one hundred miles per hour, he held the shuddering vehicle in place with all his strength and the single-minded determination of an addict's pursuit of a fix. As he climbed and the rain changed to snow, he was forced to slow down. The two-lane highway became slippery with ice and mounting slush. He knew if he lost control at such a high rate of speed, even his ability to heal could not protect him. But he was not afraid because he also knew he would survive. The only worry he had was that he would be further delayed in his pursuit of Jennifer and Amanda.

§

FORTY-FOUR

At about the same time Masters' double was stealing the Excursion from the airport, the planes carrying Hindeman, Kelly and the rest of the assault team landed at Nellis Air Force Base, northeast of Las Vegas. When the planes taxied to the main operations building and stopped, Hindeman opened the hatch, descending the built-in stairs to the tarmac. His team unloaded the crates of weapons and armor from the cargo holds, carrying them inside the operations center.

Appropriating a briefing room, Hindeman went over the tactical plan for the assault on the cabin. Kelly grabbed a snow-suit and struggled his way into it, then sat at the rear of the room. One of the agents displayed satellite imagery of the cabin and the area surrounding it. Hindeman went over the details as if he was an expert, but Kelly ignored him. Glancing at the satellite images, he noticed something Hindeman had missed but several of the mercenaries noticed it as well. The cabin was located in a wide-open area with an excellent field of view. A small team of experts could defend the cabin against an attack squad for quite a while, if they knew what they were doing. Jake Storm knew what he was doing.

Inserting his handgun in a waterproof pocket on the front of the suit, he secured the flap with a Velcro closure. Accepting an assault weapon from one of the soldiers, he slung it over his shoulder after checking the magazine.

"You do know how to use one of those, right?" Hindeman mocked him. Turning, Kelly glared at him and smiled.

"Care to see a demonstration?"

Hindeman was obviously not pleased with his reply and turned toward three light armored Humvees awaiting them outside. The diesel engines had enough power to pull a semi as they rolled through the early morning rain like three of the four horsemen of the apocalypse. Leaving the base, they proceeded through the gate and westbound on Craig Road, passing bars and strip clubs that catered to the airbase with names like The Flight Deck, Runway 3 Right and SNAFU, speeding toward State Highway 95.

Kelly rode in the second vehicle, happy for the separation from Hindeman. The small caravan drove down Cheyenne Boulevard to the entrance to the expressway. After five minutes, they took the freeway entrance ramp and headed toward the mist-enshrouded mountains ahead.

I hope you're ready Storm, Kelly thought when they turned onto the mountain road.

§

FORTY-FIVE

"He's here." Amanda repeated, the words chilling the blood inside Jake's body, his head snapping around in her direction. Nick yelled from her post inside the den that a black excursion had stopped in front of the gate. Maggie and Tornado, the two wolves, growled low in their chests baring their teeth at the front door.

"Okay, is everyone ready? Wait for my signal, then run like hell," Jake said into his microphone.

Inside the den, Jake and Nick watched the monitors as the others awaited their chance to escape. The Excursion backed up then lurched forward, slamming into the gate. The gate buckled in several places, but held. Extricating itself, the SUV backed farther up, almost out of the frame then the front and rear wheels threw fishtails of snow behind the vehicle as it struggled for traction, slamming into the gate again. This time, they saw the chain snap into several lengths and the gates collapsed inward, the Excursion driving over the steel poles and into the perimeter.

As it disappeared from view of the cameras, a loud explosion sounded in the distance. Over the screaming wind, they all heard a howl that made both wolves leap to attention. Posting himself inside the front door, he awaited the arrival of his enemy. His battle instincts took over and he felt adrenalin tighten his muscles. Raising the assault weapon in front of him, he trained it on the solid oak front door. Howling wind rattled the door and made him jumpy as hell.

"Jesus, he pushed right through the gate. I don't think that explosion slowed him down, Jake."

"Okay, sensors have gone off at the north end of the access road."

"Everyone get ready," Jake spoke calmly to them, but adrenalin flooded into his body and he knew he was ready for the battle.

"Jake, the sensor near the shed just tripped."

"What the fuck?" Jake said turning toward Nick. "How the fuck did he get around the house?"

"He's flanking us, Jake," Cedric and Ben both said at the same time then the world around them exploded.

Jake's homemade Improvised Explosive Devices, placed by the back door had been tripped. The explosion ripped a hole, the size of small car, in the side of the house where the kitchen sink and range had once stood. The refrigerator was tossed across the kitchen into the opposite wall outside the bedroom where Amanda had slept. Leaving the others, Jake ran for the back door, climbing over debris, he saw the monster lying in a snowdrift just outside the back door.

Rolling to its knees, the creature roared at Jake, who triggered the MP-5, sending thirty rounds tearing into its face from seven feet away. The bullets exploded through its head, spraying the snow behind the creature with brain tissue, blood and chunks of bone. Jake noticed the thing no longer looked much like Masters. Its face resembled the Elephant Man more than the doctor, even before he shot it.

Rolling backward in the snow, the thing screamed and Jake reached for the sword strapped to his back. As quickly as the attack had begun, it was complete. Jake heard a strange ululating noise coming from deep inside the pile of flesh and bones.

Stepping around the center island, he saw the creature working its way to its feet. Jake was amazed the thing was still able to move. He had hoped the initial volley would buy them some time. But it hadn't. As Jake got within striking range with the sword, he saw the double's face and felt his gorge rise. He watched in horror as worms of tissue moved and rippled over ruined facial bones and flesh. One of its eyes, exploded by a round from the MP-5, reinflated with an audible pop.

Jake grasped the handle of the drawn sword with both hands and prepared to strike the subject. On his initial swing, the clone raised its arm to ward off the blow and the blade sunk in but stopped at the middle of the bone. Jerking on the sword, Jake pulled it out. The monster made it to its feet before Jake could swing again. Jake retreated inside the house as it charged him, wailing like a Banshee.

Jake yelled for Cedric to get everyone out of the house as he scrambled over the debris in the kitchen. With the deftness born out of years of practice, Jake stopped in the hallway, side-stepped the careening animal and swung the blade as it passed, striking it across the back of the neck. The blade sliced the skin, without causing any real damage. The clone had lost some of the catlike prowess Jake had seen inside Masters' home a few days ago. Whatever was taking place inside the creature, it had lost its grace.

Jake moved around the clone and backed toward the front door. In seconds, it scrambled to its feet and leapt toward him. Instead of charging like a wounded bull, this time it glided toward him casually. Maybe he had misjudged its lack of grace. It mumbled something, but Jake couldn't make out the words. Jake saw Ben standing behind the thing, just inside the hallway.

"Ben, get out of here."

Ben fired at the thing with a shotgun, blasting a hole through its middle. Stopping its advance on Jake, it turned on Ben as if it had been stung by a bee and quickly advanced on the old man. Ben backed away, firing once more before it grabbed him and threw him against the center island, his head colliding with the granite top and sliding into the rubble. Ben rolled on the floor and was still, his face covered in blood. Jake fired another volley at the monster turning it toward him.

Turning left, Jake moved into the dining room, right behind the den. As he readied for another attack, Jake heard another explosion in the distance and knew their second adversary had arrived. He wasn't sure how long they would be delayed, but it wouldn't be long enough. Jake watched the creature stumble into the dining room. It picked up the table, overturning the chairs around it, and threw it at Jake. Diving to the floor, Jake felt the wind from the table's wake pass too closely overhead, before the table slammed into the wall behind him. The table careened off the wall, narrowly missing Jake again and bouncing across the room into the hallway.

Jake scrambled to his feet, but the creature hauled him into the air by his suit. Tossing Jake at the opening formed by the short wall separating the den and the dining room, Jake bounced off the wall and hit the floor again. Trying to get his breath, it grabbed him again and threw him against the opposite wall.

Jake rolled to his feet trying to move as he recovered from the impact from hitting the wall. He moved into the hallway, heading for the front door. He was afraid he had underestimated the violence this creature could muster. He needed to escape and regroup or he would die.

The creature kicked the dining table aside and stepped through the opening Jake had slid through into the den. Stabbing pain in Jake's left forearm told him it was broken. He heard automatic gunfire in the distance and guessed that Cedric had greeted the assault teams on the road leading to the cabin.

Jake feared he didn't have the strength in one arm to swing the sword and cut through the creature's massive neck. Stopping at the entrance to the front room, it stared disbelievingly at Jake. It seemed amazed he was still standing. Blood ran into Jake's eyes threatening to rob him of his vision and he shook his head to clear them. Jake watched in horror as the creature turned toward the front door, moving quickly. Somehow it knew Jennifer and Amanda were no longer inside the cabin.

Jake saw his chance and took it. Moving behind the creature, he swung the sword with all his strength. The blade entered the left side of the thing's neck and passed through, continuing until it connected with its spinal column. Then it stopped. Jake tried to pull the blade free but it was stuck, having become wedged halfway through one of the vertebrae in its neck. The creature's knees folded and he collapsed forward, hitting the front door with his head. Jake placed his foot against the creature's back and tugged as hard as he could, but the bone held fast to the steel. Jake watched, horrified as the wound began to knit around the blade. Blood sprayed in every direction and the thing made a gurgling sound then used the wall and door frame to help him regain his feet. It tried to turn, with Jake still gripping the hilt of the sword.

Jake heard a feral scream from behind him and thought a cougar had gotten inside the cabin when they weren't looking. As the creature turned, he hit Jake across the side of the head with his left arm, launching Jake into the wall and causing him to release his hold on the sword. Jake saw Nick fly through the archway leading into the den and grab the sword.

Balancing in mid-air, Nick came down on the hilt with all her weight swinging toward the door. Her actions broke the blade off in the wound but also separated the vertebra it was stuck between, severing the creature's spinal cord. The resulting paralysis sent the thing to its knees again. Nick brought up another sword in her right hand and cut downward at its waist-high head. As the sword met the blade already buried in the thing's neck, it sliced through, freeing both the blade and its head. The creature's severed head arced through the air, bouncing across the floor like a basketball when it landed, coming to a stop in the wrecked living room.

Jake watched in amazement as the body of the thing twitched, blood from the severed carotid arteries spraying the walls, then lay still. Nick glared at it, dropping the sword. Keeping her eyes on it, she moved to where Jake lay in a heap against the wall. Grabbing a bag, she walked into the living room, picked up the head by the hair, and dropped it into the bag.

Sporadic gunfire crashed into the early morning stillness. Jake heard screams echoing through the canyon but also the faint sound of sirens. Jake struggled to his feet and limped toward the door, holding the MP-5 in his left hand. Nick covered the door with a shotgun as Jake kicked it open. No one waited across the threshold, so they moved out into the snow.

"Jake, are you guys still breathin'?" Jake heard Cedric's panting voice in is ear.

"Yeah, we're here."

"That fuckin' thing toast?" Cedric asked. Jake heard another short burst from an assault rifle.

"We got it. It's dead."

"We have one Humvee through the blockade and advancing toward the cabin. I'm hit, but it appears Jennifer is a pretty good shot," Cedric said, panting. "That Humvee ain't progressing too well because two of its tires are flat. And the undercarriage is severely damaged. We've taken out six of theirs, but more are coming your way."

Jake and Nick took cover to the right of the porch as they heard a diesel engine struggling to the top of the hill. They watched as an advance team moved into the yard, spreading across the entire area. Jake waited until they were close enough then fired the MP-5 at the ground near them, causing them to scatter. He thought he might have hit one of the men but his control wasn't very good with one hand. The effect, however, was exactly what he intended.

The Humvee stopped in the yard and the white-haired man yelled orders to his men from inside. Removing the Glock from the pocket on the front of his snowsuit, Jake fired one shot at the windshield, missing its occupants but causing Hindeman to abruptly shut his mouth.

Jake watched as the men inside the transport slid out through the left side doors, away from Jake and the gunfire.

"Boss, we got 'em in a crossfire," Cedric said. "This is like shooting ducks in a barrel."

"Hold your fire, Cedric. Let's see how this plays out."

"Ah, shit, man. They attacked us, remember?"

"Just hold your fire until I tell you."

Silence permeated the clearing as snow fell lightly into the foot of already fallen snow masses in the yard. Jake noticed there was no longer any wind. The snow fell straight down to the ground. He fell to his knees then lay down and slid across the snow to get a better position. He was allowing clearance for Nick to shoot if she needed to.

"Kelly, are you out there?" Jake yelled as loud as he could. He was pretty sure he had a few broken ribs as well as the arm and pain was now settling into his back.

"I'm here, Storm. Give yourself up. We can avoid a bloodbath here."

"Sorry, but that is totally unacceptable. You have one minute to get the fuck out of here and take that white-haired cocksucker with you."

Silence once again fell across the landscape then something incredible happened. Hindeman stood up and stepped into the open. He cursed his men and walked stiffly through the foot deep snow toward the cabin. He was holding a Colt automatic in his right hand, firing at Jake where he lay. Woodchips from the porch flew past his head as Jake aimed at Hindeman's head. He never got the chance to fire.

"Storm, you hand over that woman and child now and come out and fight like a man," Hindeman screamed, his voice cycling high with each word. "You all have to be dealt with right FUCKING NOW!"

Jake saw Kelly stand up and point an assault weapon at Hindeman but before he could pull the trigger, Jake heard screaming from the trees behind the assault team.

About twenty feet away, across the yard and behind the troops covered by the Humvee, Jennifer stood up holding Cedric's MP-5 in both hands. He could see Cedric trying to pull her down but she stood solid as she aimed the weapon at Hindeman.

"YOU WILL NOT TOUCH MY DAUGHTER YOU FUCKING MANIAC," Jennifer yelled, enunciating each word slowly and opened fire. Being unfamiliar with firing an automatic weapon, the first few rounds kicked up snow eddies around Hindeman, who tried to turn toward the assault. The next twenty cut him across the abdomen and chest. The man's body exploded in a rain of blood and his body launched twisting through the air, landing half on the front porch of the cabin. As quickly as it had begun, the barrage was over. Jennifer's hands unlocked and the weapon dropped to the snow.

Behind him, Jake heard Nick mumble something that sounded like "fuckin'A." He saw the men behind the Humvee turn toward Jennifer, who was standing in the open, and realized what was about to happen.

"NO," Jake said as he rolled off of the snow onto his feet and ran toward the Humvee.

"Everyone put down your weapons," Kelly yelled as he stepped out into the open, his rifle raised over his head. "They have us covered and all he needs to do is give the order and we're all dead. I think we can settle this peacefully."

One by one, the agents came out from behind the Humvee, their weapons raised over their heads. Some still watched Jennifer warily as she picked up Amanda and she and Cedric descended out of the trees. The two wolves marched in lockstep at their sides. Jake counted seven men, the number of agents minus Hindeman, that Cedric had seen. Cedric covered the group with the MP-5 that Jennifer had used on Hindeman.

"Okay, boys. You're going to ditch those weapons, one at a time, butt first," Jake said, aiming the Glock at Kelly's head. "Starting with you, Kelly."

Kelly did as he was told and the rest followed in unison. When they were disarmed, Jake stepped forward.

"What made you change your mind about me, Kelly?" Jake said, a grin spreading across his face.

"Oh, I still think you're an asshole. I just couldn't go along with executing innocent people for no reason. That wouldn't have been prudent."

"What about your career?"

"Fuck it," Kelly said, brushing the falling snow out of his hair. "I'm starting to hate this job anyway. Hell, you know they'll probably give me a medal just for shutting that asshole up."

Jake moved slowly toward Kelly, keeping the Glock trained on his head.

"So, what do we do now?" Jake asked Kelly, the latter staring at him in disbelief.

"Easy. You go away, forever. Leave Master's family with us. We'll see they're taken care of. Masters died during the initial attack that claimed Hindeman's life, so we have our fugitive doctor. This day is improving already."

Jake noticed those who were left in the team were nodding their heads in agreement. Not a lot of loyalty in this bunch.

"Why should I trust you?" Jake asked.

"Because I know one day I would wake up and you'd be sitting in my bedroom with a knife at my throat. I don't want to spend my days looking over my shoulder."

Jake smiled and nodded as his group surrounded the men. Jake heard a noise from the side of the cabin and turned expecting to see the headless corpse of Jonathan Masters walking out the door. Instead they saw Ben, leaning on the front porch railing, holding the shotgun he had attacked the clone with in his bloody hands.

Jake couldn't believe the old man had survived, but was glad just the same.

"Don't worry, I ain't dead, yet." Ben growled, grinning through the blood at Jake. Ben limped down the steps and joined Jake near the Humvee.

"Well, it's time we departed," Jake said, as Nick helped him across the yard. Kelly put his hands down and Jake let him. "You guys can put your hands down now. You look ridiculous."

"Jake, where are my video discs?"

"Inside the cabin." Jake answered, moving quickly away from the cabin he had loved so much.

Kelly started for the cabin door, but Nick yelled for him to stop.

"I wouldn't go in there. Something bad is about to happen."

Jake saw her remove the transmitter from the pocket of her snowsuit and flip five switches on the front. Kelly saw the transmitter and jumped off the porch, running through the snow, his men following closely behind. When they were a safe distance away Nick pressed the red button in the center of the transmitter.

The explosion quickly expanded, sending chunks of burning wood high into the wintry sky. Fire burned within what was left of the structure as burning chunks of wood, some as large as a breadbox, cascaded into the yard, bouncing off the Humvee and hissing in the drifts of snow.

Jake stared at Nick, who shrugged her shoulders and grinned. "Another of my gifts," she said, then leaned forward whispering, "I had to be sure. Decapitated, burned, if I had a wood chipper, I'd turn it into mulch."

Kelly watched as his valuable research went up in flames. He stepped over to Jake glaring at him.

"You just couldn't let me have it, could you?"

"No, we couldn't, Kelly. I didn't ask you to chase me here and I just lost a very valuable piece of property. I am not in a good mood."

"The CIA owns this property, Jake. It's not yours to lose."

"That's beside the point. If it weren't for me getting involved in this, you wouldn't have known this place existed. Now if you'll excuse us, we have pressing business elsewhere."

"Jake, what about the woman and the kid?"

"They go with us, for now. I'll put them on a plane myself, later."

Kelly frowned but nodded. Jake could hear the sounds of many sirens getting closer but they had some time before the emergency personnel arrived. Once they got here, Kelly would claim jurisdiction under Homeland Security and everyone would go away.

"Hey, thanks," Jake said grinning.

Kelly gave him the finger and Jake chuckled as his small group stumbled out of the yard and down the hill.

§

FORTY-SIX

The group hobbled down a narrow trail leading to the trailhead for the waterfalls where Cedric and Ben had parked the vehicles the night before. Jake's body hurt in so many places he could no longer differentiate one injury from another. Pain from his broken ribs and arm caused his breath to catch as they negotiated the steep trail. Several times, both he and Ben had to stop and rest. After partially recovering, Ben and Nick helped Cedric limp down the trail.

Jennifer continually mumbled the same words over and over as they walked down the slope. "I had to do it. There was no choice." Cedric spoke quietly to her and so did Nick, gradually quieting her, although the shocked look didn't leave her face.

Maggie and Tornado padded silently beside Amanda and Jennifer with Cedric, Nick and Ben behind the pack, going slower than the rest.

Nick stood guard while they loaded Cedric into the Suburban, watching for signs of attackers. The two wolves hopped into the back with Cedric and lay down on either side of the big man. Reaching out, he scratched the ears on one of the wolves while Jennifer and Amanda settled into the rear seat and Ben climbed into the driver's seat.

Jake climbed into the front passenger seat in the Escalade and Nick climbed behind the wheel. Silently she started the engine, reversed from under the trees and drove down the narrow lane to the main road, Ben following close behind.

Several police cars and fire trucks passed them as they wound down the freshly plowed two-lane highway. Jake saw blue sky through his window, while light snow pelted the windshield.

Changing his mind about the hospital, Cedric told them to keep going and they could take care of it later. The bullet had gone through the muscle, so there was very little doctors could do anyway.

Before leaving the mountain, they dropped Ben at his house. He said he wanted to clean up but promised to follow shortly. With one last lick for Amanda from Tornado and Maggie, Ben and the two wolves were gone and Jennifer took the wheel of the Suburban.

Nick and Jake remained silent all the way down the hill. Exiting the expressway on Cheyenne Boulevard, she pulled into a gas station. Everyone removed their snowsuits except Cedric. Cedric's would have to wait until they reached someplace they could recuperate.

Nick drove on through the city, pulling into the parking lot of a cheap hooker motel off Boulder Highway. Jake was a mess, so they agreed that Nick and Jennifer would rent two rooms. They wouldn't remain overnight but Nick asked for the rooms farthest away from the office for two days and requested no maid service. When she and Jennifer returned, they drove to the far side of the building and with Nick and Jake helping Cedric, they went inside.

Nick and Jennifer helped Cedric into one of the rooms and worked together to remove his snowsuit as Jake collapsed on the other bed. Nick returned to the Escalade and came back moments later with a medium-sized black sports bag. Jennifer and Amanda had gone to the connecting room and opened the door between them.

Opening the black bag, Nick removed a small brown zippered bag. She removed several cards from the bag.

"Jennifer, it is highly likely you are no longer in danger," Nick said. "They won't like it, but the NSA will accept that you knew nothing about your husband's work. They'll question you at length. Just keep to the same story and you'll be fine. Tell them your husband tried to kill you and that Jake saved your life but was killed at the cabin. You escaped before anyone showed up so you rented a hotel room at the Mirage.

"It's very important that Amanda doesn't display any of her special skills, and since Ben told me he would be bringing you a puppy from Tornado and Maggie's litter, you'll need to keep the puppy away from her while they're watching you."

"What will happen to you?" Jennifer asked, glancing at Jake.

"We have to disappear," Jake said with a finality that surprised even him. "Kelly will try to hide our escape but eventually they'll figure out we didn't die in the explosion so they'll keep looking for us. If we're careful, they'll never figure out what really happened."

Jennifer took this revelation surprisingly well. She merely nodded. Jake guessed she was still in shock at what she had done in defense of her daughter.

"I've called a cab to take you to the Mirage. I have an account set up there. Just buy any clothes you need and charge them to the room. In a few hours, Kelly will probably contact you and request a meeting. Let them debrief you, then go home and get on with your life."

They heard a horn sound outside and Nick led Jennifer and Amanda to the door.

Jennifer turned to Jake and smiled. "I can't gather the words to thank you enough for what you have done. You risked your lives for us and I won't forget it." She started to leave then turned back to Jake. "I was right, wasn't I? I had to kill him."

"Damn skippy. If you hadn't done it, he would have killed us all. Or at least had his men do it," Jake smiled at her. "Anyway, you saved me and Kelly from having to fight over who got to shoot him first. We were both going to fire, right before you did."

Jennifer smiled weakly and pulled the door open but her daughter wasn't quite ready to leave.

Amanda came over to Jake and hugged his neck, causing

pain to well from his arm and ribs and his eyes to water, but he hugged her back using his left arm. Her tears leaked into his for a moment then she broke the embrace, turned away and ran outside. It hurt to see Amanda go but they had a life to rebuild.

"Goodbye and good luck." Nick went outside with them and after a few moments, returned alone.

"Now, for the rest of us. I have taken the liberty of making a few alterations to each of us. Cedric, how fond are you of that beard?"

Cedric groaned and she grinned at him.

"You'll also have to grow back some hair on your head."

"Very funny."

Nick left to pick up some first aid supplies. Cedric had washed the wound as best he could in the bathtub, causing the bleeding to start fresh then wrapped it with a towel. The bullet had passed through his thigh with no damage to major blood vessels or the femur. It had bled a lot, leaving the bathroom a mess. When Nick returned, she carried several bags. One was from a Walgreen's drug store. She removed the first-aid supplies from the bag and placed them on the dresser.

Nick methodically cleaned Cedric's bullet wound, then sewed both holes. Cedric stomached the pain, thanks to the Vicodin she had picked up along with the other supplies. When Jake and Cedric raised an eyebrow, she just smiled and told them she had just refilled a prescription. The look on her face was one of pure sneaky delight, but Jake figured he didn't want to know how she had managed it. Nick taped Jake's ribs, set and splinted his left arm, promising to take him to a doctor once they were in California.

From another leather bag, Nick removed two large manila envelopes, tossing one on the bed in front of Jake and the other to Cedric. Jake opened his envelope and found identification, a birth certificate and a passport. The picture on the driver's license was him but not the way he looked at the moment. The man on the front had a neat beard with the slightest gray streak running through the middle. The license was issued in California, complete with the background and state seal. He was impressed. His new name was Nathan McCloud.

"This is incredible. How did you make this stuff so fast?"

"I always have stuff lying around for emergencies. I tapped into the computers in California and used my address. You and I will head there later tonight to pick up the rest of the stuff we need. There should be an American Express Card waiting for each of us in the mail. I tapped into their computers, created a history and generated a lost card claim."

"So this stuff has full backup?" Cedric asked.

"Absolutely. Nothing but the best for you," Nick said smiling at him. "Now here's the plan. Jake and I will head for LA and pick up the rest of my stuff. We'll rest at the house for a few days, then head for Miami. Cedric, it's up to you whether you join us there or not. There is a reservation waiting for you at the Delta ticket counter for a flight to Atlanta. Check into the Hilton near the airport. The desk has a package for you. You will appreciate the contents. Then, just go where you will. If you decide to join us in Florida, meet us in two weeks at Belforte house in Key West."

"Jesus, do you love this girl or what?" Cedric smiled weakly at Nick, then fished a cold pack out of the kit, squeezed it and placed it on his knee.

An hour later, Nick told them she was going to the store and left. Rising from the bed, Jake stumbled slowly into the bathroom. His face was bruised and swollen. His back and arm were giving him fits but he felt better than he had in days. He was leaving his old life behind and where he was headed, he had no clue. They would face whatever came along.

Turning from the mirror, he heard the door open. Whipping around in spite of the pain, he reached for his gun, realizing he'd left it on the nightstand. Cedric however, was pointing his gun at Nick who came through the door from outside, carrying a bucket of ice and several sacks with store names on them. She didn't react at all to Cedric pointing the gun at her.

Setting the ice bucket on the dresser that served double duty as bar and television stand, she tossed the other sacks on the empty bed. Without a word, she went back outside, returning a few minutes later carrying a set of crutches. When Jake eyed her inquisitively, she shrugged her shoulders.

"We needed clothes. I picked up a few things while I was out."

She leaned the crutches against the wall, near Cedric's bed.

"Cedric is going to need some money," Jake said, nodding toward his injured friend. "All the money I had was in the cabin when you blew it to hell."

"Already took care of it. Nick tossed a brand new Lord Buxton at Cedric. Blinking, Cedric opened the wallet and found his new identification and twenty one hundred dollar bills.

"I told you I deserved a bonus," Cedric said to Jake, holding the wallet open. "So what's this for?"

"Your trip to Atlanta. When you get to Atlanta, get your ear pierced."

"Why?"

"It'll help."

"I'll meet you in Miami in a couple of weeks and we can plan what's next," Cedric said, then his expression changed and he glanced to where Nick sat filling glasses with ice, and soda, "Hey, what about your computers? They'll find them unless the fire destroyed them, they'll know what Masters was up to and hire some other scientist to duplicate his work. It'll never be over."

"Now, Cedric, do you think I would be so stupid as to leave anything on my computers for prying eyes to see?"

Cedric shrugged his shoulders and looked at her questioningly.

"Everything on those the computers was erased before Masters showed. The only applications they'll find, if the fire doesn't destroy them completely, is a bunch of children's computer games. In fact, the only person who has that information is me." She removed a flash drive from her pocket and tossed it on to the bed. "The unfortunate thing is, I have no idea how much they already knew about Master's research. If they knew enough about what he did, then we may have to watch for another Genetisource to spring up."

Ben arrived an hour later with a present for them. The old man looked a little like a mummy, bandages covering wounds to his head and neck, along with one to his arm. Jake thanked him for helping them and Ben waved him off.

"Don't worry about it. You'd have done the same for me."

"How many times have you run from the government, chased by a sociopathic government agent and murderous indestructible clone?" Cedric asked, an amused expression on his face. "I mean, I doubt if you make this kind of thing a habit."

"I accept a thank you," Ben growled, glaring at Cedric who simply shook his head chuckling.

After lunch consisting of take-out fried chicken that Ben brought with him and sodas from the machine at the end of the building, Ben departed for Wyoming with Maggie and Tornado and the two puppies he had left in the Suburban. They were once again a threesome.

The present Ben brought to them, a small wolf puppy, piddled on the floor, causing Nick to break into peals of laughter.

Later, with Jake riding shotgun, Nick drove the Escalade through the desert toward the Los Angeles Basin and her home in Laguna Beach.

The wolf puppy lay in her lap, squirming as she scratched her behind the ears. Jake slept in the passenger seat, snoring quietly as she drove into the coming sunset. Exhausted, but too wired to even think of sleeping, she watched the sun descend behind the sand-covered western hills.

Just east of Barstow, Nick exited the freeway and drove

north into the desert. Within a half an hour, she found a likely place and stopped, leaving Jake sleeping in the car, the wolf pup lying in his lap. Taking the bag from the rear of the Escalade, along with a shovel she bought at a Home Depot in Las Vegas, she walked toward a rocky bluff rising out of the desert sand. Setting the bag on the sand, she began digging a hole.

Once or twice when she looked at the bag, she thought she saw it move, which caused her to dig faster. When the hole was about three feet deep, she tossed the bag inside and covered it with a few rocks she found then finished by raking the dirt she had taken from the hole. In the end, she covered the mound of dirt with more rocks so animals wouldn't be able to dig it out easily.

Returning to the Escalade, she drove back to the road then to Interstate 15. Safely back on the freeway, she picked up the wolf pup, setting the dog in her lap. The female wolf yawned once, trying to fight off sleep. Fingering the thick fur around the wolf's neck Nick chuckled.

"I hope we can give you a good home, little one."

Pressing her foot on the accelerator, they made their way southwest through the sand and cholla bushes, toward the setting sun.

§

EPILOGUE

Belforte House,
Key West, Florida, two months later

S unshine caressed the sunbathers as they made their way into the early morning heat. Already nearly eighty degrees, the humidity that oppressed the Keys for the past week had finally subsided. Jake sat on the beach, a cup of coffee in his hand, and watched the waves roll in from the Gulf Stream. Key West was an interesting place. The diversity of its inhabitants was well documented but Jake had never seen anything like this. On the beach, there were both same-sex and straight couples, walking, laughing and sunning. Most were very friendly and on a first name-basis with each other, sharply contrasting tourists from the locals.

Jake felt a warm hand on his shoulder and turned to see Nick standing behind him. Coming down the beach in a red speedo, its bright color standing out against his dark skin, was Cedric Jaynes. Cedric had grown out his hair, now sporting short dreadlocks and a diamond stud in his left ear. He also had a clean-shaven face, which was something Jake hadn't seen since they left the Navy.

Nick cut her hair to shoulder length and added blonde highlights. The changes made her even prettier. Somehow the new look made her seem much younger. They were traveling under the names Nathan and Nikki McCloud and were supposed to be married. She wasn't wanted by anyone, so she was able to keep her name. They were sleeping together before leaving California.

When they arrived in Miami, he risked a call to Martin Boroughs. Jake had pretended he was a new client and gave him his new name. Boroughs had placed his name on the board of CSS as treasurer, opening access to his bank account in the Cayman Islands.

Nick now had access to the accounts from her computer and opened an account at a local bank, closing her own accounts and transferring the funds to the new bank.

Boroughs sold Jake's compound in Miami within three days of putting it on the market. They were still unsure of where they wanted to reside permanently but they had lots of time. Cedric was looking for a place of his own and had already caught the interest of a couple of local women. He smiled most of the time now but that was one thing that hadn't changed from before. Cedric always seemed happy.

The wolf cub Ben had given them when they left Las Vegas had grown a lot in the past two months. Nick named her Corragio, the Italian word for courage. She couldn't resist it since she still barked at Cedric whenever he came around.

Nick sat down beside him and curled her long legs under her chin. Corragio lay down beside her, trying to ignore the birds that kept landing on the beach nearby. When she couldn't stand it any longer, Corragio leapt from the sand and ran off, chasing the gulls that paced the beach looking for handouts.

Nick smiled, but she sported a worried look he didn't like. When Cedric was nearer, Jake waved him over. Cedric saluted him casually.

"What's up, Honey? You look worried," Cedric asked Nick in a concerned tone as he sat down on her other side.

Nick shook her head and toed at the sand at her feet. Today she was dressed in a light blue bathing suit with the surfer print on it and a darker blue wrap around her long legs. Cedric eyed her cautiously.

"I did a little digging last night and then again this morning. It appears they bought Jennifer's explanation. Kelly backed it up and told them you and Cedric died defending them from her husband. They blamed him for the fire at Genetisource and the deaths of his researchers."

"Jennifer is rebuilding Genetisource, but working on cures rather than doing what her husband did. She e-mailed an article to me last night that told of your funeral at Arlington National Cemetery. Seeing the photo of your gravestone gave me shivers. That was such a close call, Jake."

Jake hugged her close for a moment then she shrugged him off and stared out at the incoming surf. Corragio, having scattered the seagulls, came back to where they sat, prancing with delight at her hunting prowess. Squatting in front of Nick, the wolf peered into her eyes, perking her ears, whining softly. Nick reached out and scratched her ears, causing the pup to roll in the sand.

"It's not just that," she paused, picking up a handful of white beach sand and letting it slowly trickle from her hand. "They apparently have enough information on the methods that Masters used to clone himself. They have contracted another research facility to study his files since Jennifer told them Genetisource would no longer work for Uncle Sam. It'll eventually start all over again."

Jake sighed heavily and placed an arm around her shoulders and Cedric placed his arm around her from the other side. Together the three of them watched the Gulf roll toward them and away.

"Will they ever give up?" She turned to him; no tears were in her eyes but the raspy sound of her voice meant they weren't far off.. "Will our lives ever see peace?"

Together, they sat watching the waves and the tourists, awaiting their future.

§

D.L. WHITEHEAD

AFTERWORD

First, let me say, thank you for buying and reading Darwin's Sword. I hope you enjoyed reading it as much as I enjoyed writing it. In the end that's why writers write; we want someone to enjoy the stories we tell.

I felt I should tell you that research programs exist in many universities around the world involving the use of stem cells to create living tissue. I have been asked many times if this book is a condemnation of these programs and I want to tell you emphatically, NO. In fact, I couldn't be more in favor of this research and anyone who would argue against it for religious reasons, or any reasons for that matter, is beyond me. I don't wish to offend anyone, but scientific research is the most important of human activities and must be supported.

For those of you who live in the locales that I used in Darwin's Sword who have located the discrepancies in the terrain and other timeframes, I can only say I'm guilty as charged in fictionalizing the locations depicted herein. I stand on the fact that it is fiction and I have taken liberties with the terrain and scenery. I apologize and beg your pardon.

I wrote Darwin's Sword to entertain. The concepts for this novel were cutting edge when I wrote the first draft in 1998. I think the questions and facts presented here are still relevant. The subject of cloning and stem cell research still fascinates me. I hope the current political environment doesn't interfere with that research, because I think it may hold the key to helping people who have catastrophic injuries. But, all in all, Darwin's Sword is about what too much knowledge mixed with too much ego when the only focus is one's own immortality. It also makes a hell of a good yarn.

Now that I have said my peace, I wish to thank several people. Many years ago, I interviewed three research scientists about the premises in this story. I observed the techniques they used, many of which are detailed in this story, although changed to match my storyline. I lost the notes containing their names years ago, but your input was invaluable. Thank you for your help making this novel more believable.

I would also like to thank Janice, Kathy and Lenore of LeRue Press for taking a chance on my first novel and on me. Thanks to Travis Szudajski for his artwork that made the cover of this novel and the artwork on my website amazing.

I want to thank my parents, Aubrey and Patsy White-head, for encouraging me to write even though my Mom never understood the stories or where they came from. My father passed away when I was eight years old, but I am certain that even then, he thought I had descended from an alien. My Mom left this mortal coil in 2010 and was one of my best friends as well as my mother. In any case, they encouraged my creativity and my imagination. I really appreciate it.

I would like to thank my brothers as well. They were much older than I, and thanks to them leaving me to my own devices, forced me to learn to play by myself. It encouraged me to develop a strong imagination that I used to create many games that worked when one was solo. They have also encouraged me as an adult to pursue my writing. What I write isn't their bag, but they have both pledged their support.

I also want to thank my wife Beth. She is always my first reader and she helps me find the areas where my stories need work. She is also my first editor. I also must say that she hates scary stories, so it often isn't much fun for her. She reads a lot during the day, then cusses me when she can't sleep at night. Thanks Honey.

Last but not least, I want to thank you, my readers. You make my novels possible. Your input gives me ways to improve what I do. Please go to my website at www.dlwhitehead.com to comment on all my stories. I invite you to follow me on Facebook at www.facebook.com/d.l.whitehead.88.

Take care and keep reading.

D.L. Whitehead

Look for more books from
D.L. Whitehead including:

Midas

White Death

And you never know what else…

Follow D.L. on his blog at:
http://www.dlwhitehead.com/

On yahoo.com at:
http://contributor.yahoo.com/
user/1462335/dl_whitehead.html

On Facebook at:

 www.facebook.com/d.l.whitehead.88

On Twitter at:

 @dwhitehead88

www.lrpnv.com